The Broken Trail

Sweet River Redemption Series

The Broken Trail

The Broken Trail

Sweet River Redemption Series

By

Christa MacDonald

MBI

The Broken Trail
Published by Mountain Brook Ink
White Salmon, WA U.S.A.

Scripture quotations are taken from the King James Version of the Bible. Public domain.
ISBN 978-1-943959-11-2

The Team: Miralee Ferrell, Nikki Wright, Cindy Jackson, Rachel Lulich, Kim Huther

Cover Design: Indie Cover Design, Lynnette Bonner Designer

Mountain Brook Ink is an inspirational publisher offering fiction you can believe in.
Printed in the United States of America

First Edition 2016

DEDICATION

This book is dedicated to the teachers in the trenches: the ones who stay late so their students have a place to do their homework, who buy their own school supplies, and who adapt to whatever new regulations come along because they're committed to their calling. God bless you and your work.

ACKNOWLEDGMENTS

I'd like to thank my sister, Karen Tucker, whose tireless dedication to her students inspired the character of Katherine Grant.

I cannot express enough thanks to Jodi Stoddard and Rachel Fausnaugh, who kindly read multiple versions of this book and provided me with invaluable feedback as well as encouragement when I was ready to quit.

I'd also like to thank my editor, Rachel Lulich, for taking the muddled bits of the book and making sense of them.

And I'd like to thank Miralee Ferrell for taking a chance on this story and me.

CHAPTER ONE

KATHERINE GRANT GLANCED OUT AT THE pine trees whipping past on the far side of the highway and then out the passenger window at the wall of rock on the other side. "This is looking downright uncivilized, Henry," she said, half-expecting her 9-year-old red BMW to answer. She knew that Sweet River, Maine, was a remote hill-town, but it was starting to look more desolate than remote. The last sign of life had been 'Mike's Bait 'N' Ammo', and that was over an hour ago. She hit the call button on the steering wheel, the ring of the phone sounding only once over the car speakers before her assistant answered.

"You rang?"

"Heather, remind me again. Why am I doing this?"

"Because Helena, the Washington kingmaker, asked you to consider it, and *nobody* says no to Helena?"

"Nope. Try again."

"Because you take contracts in school districts where you can do the most good, not where you can get the most notoriety."

"Makes me sound noble, but I don't think that's it."

"Because you need a vacation, and a tiny Christian school in a resort town in the middle of the woods sounded restful?"

"That's the one, but I'm seriously concerned about how remote this is. I've lost cell service twice, and the last thing I passed was a roadside shack advertising bait and ammo." She paused then added, "Bait and ammo, Heather."

"Second thoughts are perfectly natural. It's been a while since you've worked this kind of contract. I can't remember the last time you did an on-site assessment that lasted for months."

"California. That district where the mayor tried to fire the superintendent and replace him with his wife."

"Forgot about that one. Well, you've got six months up there to handle this one, and there is no way it's as complex. The school only has two hundred students; a quarter of those are boarding, and the town itself only has two thousand permanent residents. This is nothing like you've done before."

And that had been the point. Katherine was a bit tired of the 'another day, another city' kind of life she had been leading where home was more a P.O. Box than anything else. She had a beach house on Cape Cod near her mom, but she'd been renting it out for so long she really couldn't call it hers anymore. The place where she was headed, this quaint little hill town next to mountains and the lake, called to her.

"Since I'm trapped in this car for at least another half hour, let's run over day one again."

"Okay. First up, you meet with Stephanie Campbell, director."

"And she's been head for three years."

"Yup, and the dropping enrollment and issues with the state over the vocational program for foster kids in the last two years have all been on her watch, so today you set up an intro. Monday's the day where you have meetings with the department heads, the board, and the returning teachers."

"Got it."

"I took a look at the staff like you asked, and the heads are all her appointees. She cleaned house the first year she was in."

"Okay, that could be interesting or it could be nothing. What's up after the meeting with Stephanie?"

"You get to check out your rental house. Katherine, the pictures are just … *I* wanna live in this house."

"You have your own."

"My house is a disaster zone covered in the kids' toys and Michael's dirty socks. It's not a cute little Victorian cottage with a garden."

"True, but you can't have Nerf wars in the family room of a cute Victorian." Katherine would know, since she often participated in those wars with Heather's three boys. It wasn't uncommon for chairs to be upended, rugs to go flying, or the occasional small body to launch itself at her in a sneak attack.

"I suppose I would miss the children," Heather sighed, a bit theatrically. "After your meeting, I didn't schedule anything. You can take the rest of the day to settle in. Then you have the weekend to check out the town. I've been doing research, and it's like Norman Rockwell-land."

"Really? This place is in the middle of nowhere."

"It's because of that resort and the lake. The town attracts a ton of tourists, so they have all these shops and restaurants. Well, three restaurants and a bar called, you will never guess, 'The Smooth Moose.'"

"Punny," Katherine said with a chuckle, liking the idea that at least some of the residents might have a sense of humor.

"I have got to come visit." Heather sounded excited, but Katherine knew just like every year, it was unlikely Heather would spend her vacation time on a getaway for herself. Despite the extra week Katherine had added with her last bonus, Heather still saved every day of her paid-time-off to spend with her family. "I'm calling your spare bedroom for a long weekend. As your assistant and best friend, I have dibs."

"You got it."

"Great. Now that you're feeling calm," Heather began cautiously, "I'll also remind you that they have a church in town. It seems to be a living church, very active in the community, and they support the school." Katherine withheld her groan, but Heather didn't miss much, and her silence spoke volumes.

"Katherine, you're the one who said you wanted out of your

rut, that you weren't happy and wanted to find a way to connect with people again. A church is a good way to do that. Maybe while you're there you can reconnect with God, too. You want to find a place that feels like home, right?" That last bit was Heather's frequent refrain.

For Katherine, home had been a small town, her loving parents, and her two little sisters. They'd lived in her family's two-century-old house on the coast with the sprawling lawn and the stables. Sundays had been her favorite, since her dad never went in to work, and they'd walk together as a family to church. She'd belonged there, sitting in the same pew her great-grandmother had sat in. But that home was gone, torn away from her years ago.

"Give it a chance." In the background, Katherine could hear the telltale sounds of escalating tensions among small children. "Ugh, there they go. I've got to settle that or there'll be bloodshed. Or at least bruises. Call me if you get lost or if you want to brag about how nice that house is."

"Will do. Love you, Heather."

"Love you, too." Click.

Katherine refocused on the drive, managing to not get lost even when two of the turns had absolutely no signage. GPS was no help since it didn't work this far north. Years of finding her way around new cities had given her a ninja-like sense of direction. Eventually, the winding secondary road she was on opened up to what appeared to be a town. The first indicator was the gas station, Ernie's, with an attached convenience store looking a bit limited. After that, a series of little houses seemed to come out of the tree line on either side; one-story affairs with long front yards and broken-down garages.

The road then narrowed a bit, and the houses got nicer and closer to the road. Then she hit the real downtown; both sides of the street lined with shops and restaurants. The architecture was 'Old-fashioned Main Street'—tall buildings all in a row with storefronts below and apartments above. The apartments and shops all had their flower-boxes tricked out, spilling over with delicate vines and late-season flowers. This was more what she'd been hoping for.

She passed a large wooden structure with nineteenth-century windows and a nicely landscaped yard. It was the town hall, painted a sunny yellow with a sign out front advertising an all-town picnic and a farmer's market/craft fair on Saturday. The church was next door. It was a classic Second Great Awakening New England church, displaying white clapboards with a tall spire. Across the street was a long oval of lawn with park benches ringing it: the town green.

Following the directions Heather had provided, Katherine parked behind the fire station in the municipal lot and walked across the street to the school campus. It was set back from the road, but the large brick building that housed the classrooms and offices was visible from the street. The sign on the post next to the walkway read 'Sweet River Christian Academy.'

Katherine took a deep breath and headed inside. The building was old and beautiful. It was brick, covered with ivy and large windows. Inside it was all wood, brass accents, and that smell...she didn't know if it was what they used to clean it or simply the wood itself, but all old wood buildings smelled like that: paper and pencils, soap and lemons, chalk dust and carbon. She found the office, and happily there was someone working, which meant she didn't need to search for the director.

"Hello, I think you might be expecting me?"

The woman behind the long counter looked up from a stack of papers. "Oh, of course! You must be Dr. Grant." She came around the counter with a bright smile. To her credit, she only let her eyes flick to the long scar down Katherine's right cheek for a moment. Most people stared. After ten years it had faded to a thin white line, but it was hard to miss. "I recognize you from the Capitol Report. You were on with that senator from Maryland, am I right?"

Katherine nodded. The cable news shows called her in from time to time as an education-policy expert. She remembered that show with Senator Baxter. He was trying to push through an overreaching national standard that was badly designed and would inevitably be underfunded.

"You were talking about that new bill. What did you say that was so funny? Oh, I remember, 'This bill is all show and no go.'" She chuckled. "I got such a kick out of that."

"I'm glad you did." The woman held her hand out, and Katherine shook it.

"Elaine Winters. I'm the office administrator."

"Is Stephanie Campbell in? I have a two o'clock with her today."

Elaine's expression changed to both troubled and frustrated. "During the summer, it's tough to keep tabs on where the director is or when she'll be in, but hold on and I'll try her cell." Elaine went back to the long counter and grabbed a phone, punching in a number with one long fingernail painted what looked like watermelon pink.

She hung up the phone. "Got her voicemail. But I know she and her husband were out on the lake earlier. They own a bunch of the rentals down there, and every Friday afternoon they sort of patrol their properties to be sure their renters are out on time. I doubt she'll be here by two. I doubt she'd make it here by four, to tell you the truth."

"Ah, must have been a misunderstanding." Katherine didn't believe that for one moment, but Elaine was already looking uncomfortable. No point in making it worse. She'd been concerned that Campbell would be a challenge. "Actually, it gives me the excuse to move into my own rental house a little early."

"Oh, well, go get settled in! We'll see you Monday, when the staff starts to trickle in. I've set aside an office for you." Elaine led her to a little office across from the admin counter. It wouldn't be quiet, but it would be right in the action, which was good.

The office was small but serviceable, with a relatively large desk, task chair, and two straight-backed wooden chairs in front of it. It was furnished to grill students, probably used to be a guidance counselor's office, but Katherine didn't mind. She wasn't fussy.

"This is perfect. Thank you so much."

Elaine beamed, and Katherine wondered if she either was a naturally cheerful person, or if she didn't get a lot of praise. It was a nugget of info to store away until she understood the culture of the office a bit better.

"I'm so glad it will work for you. Now, I'll get back to my mailings, and you can get settled into your house. I'll see you Monday." She slipped back behind her counter and got back to work, sending a cheery wave in Katherine's direction.

Katherine headed out to her car and drove the half mile to the row of houses where her little rental stood. She was pleased to see that the house was as charming as the pictures promised. It was painted the perfect shade of yellow, with dusty blue shutters and a white picket fence. One side of the yard was a nice patch of grass, and the other side had a true English, cottage-style garden. She felt a flutter of pure happiness in her chest. It had been years since she'd spent more than a week in a place so lovely.

Katherine parked and headed up the walk, catching sight of lavender lining the brick pathway leading to the front door. She smiled and took a deep breath of the gentle flowery scent. The garden was still blooming its heart out. Petunias spilled out of the two planters on either side of the porch, and the window boxes were stuffed full of pink and purple verbena against vivid green, trailing ivy.

The email from the board of trustees had instructed her that the key would be left under the flowerpot to the right of the door. Katherine found the flowerpot easily enough, but the key wasn't there. Taking a step back, she examined the other pots as well. She peeked into the window boxes but found nothing there either. In the end, she decided to try the side door. New Englanders rarely used their front doors, which were 'formal doors' versus 'everyday doors'. Typically, neighbors or family members would go to the side door, but when Katherine reached it and looked, there was not a pot in sight, no key, and no hidey-hole for one either.

Sitting on a step, she set her purse down and called Heather to figure out why the key hadn't been left and how to get ahold of someone who might have it. Heather didn't pick up, so she left a quick voicemail. She was pondering what to do next when she heard, "Yes. Thank you. I'll be waiting." A woman was standing at the bottom of the steps, talking on her cell phone and giving Katherine the once-over, her eyes narrowed with a look of suspicion. The woman disconnected the call. "What do you think you're doing?" her voice was sharp an angry.

"I'm sorry?" Katherine stood up, brushing off the back of her skirt.

"I asked what you think you're doing." The woman dropped her cell phone into her bag and stood with her arms crossed in front of her, while staring up at Katherine as if challenging her right to breath the same air. She had long blond hair, blow-dried perfectly straight with bangs swept to the side, and she was dressed stylishly, with leggings tucked into tall boots and a flowy peasant blouse belted at the waist. It was the sort of outfit that Katherine longed to be able to wear, but only a lithe sort of woman could pull it off. Katherine's sturdy curves could never do it justice.

"I probably look like I'm 'casing the joint'." Katherine added awkward air quotes, but the woman didn't so much as smirk.

"I'm Dr. Katherine Grant." She climbed down the stairs and held her hand out. "I'm working with the Sweet River Christian Academy. I just arrived in town, as a matter of fact." The friendliness was not working on this woman, since she ignored Katherine's outstretched hand. "I'm beginning to think there's been some sort of mistake. This is the house that was rented for me, but there's no key in sight."

The woman's mouth fell open. "Well, of course there's no key. You're not living here. This is *my* house."

"I'm so sorry!" Katherine looked back at the house and then at the woman. "I must have the wrong address then. I was given 53 School Street."

"This is 53 School, but this house is not available. I rented it a week ago, and my lease is for the year."

"How odd; this is the house that the school owns, and they said they had it reserved for me. I've got the email right here." She held out her phone.

"That's not my problem." The woman's tone was caustic and Katherine felt her temper flare. She had started off feeling foolish and nervous, but those feelings were quickly morphing into irritation and offense. Despite this obviously being a misunderstanding, and Katherine having the paperwork to prove that it was her rental, this woman wasn't listening or being very nice about it. Katherine was about to use her 'principal' voice to set her straight when a police cruiser pulled up behind them and an officer stepped out. Katherine turned to the woman. "You called the cops on me?"

"You were breaking into my house."

"I most certainly was not!" Irritation and offense was now a memory, as downright anger flared to life right as the officer approached and stood between them. He coolly assessed the situation behind his aviator sunglasses, taking in the other woman's aggressive unhappiness, as well as Katherine's defensive posture and Henry, full of Katherine's belongings, parked beside the house.

"Erin, I believe you called in the report of a burglary in progress?" His tone was professional, but Katherine could tell that he thought this was amusing; there was a slight quirk to his lips. His voice was deep, with a slight accent that hinted of New York rather than Maine. "Is this your burglar?" He nodded at Katherine, his big hat making the gesture larger.

"I am not a burglar! I can show you the email that says the school rented this house to me. It has this address. In fact, I can call my assistant and verify that the booking was made."

"It doesn't matter what your 'assistant' says; I've already

moved in," Erin told her, looking back at the officer for support. He didn't say a word. "Mindy already rented it to me. I have it for the year. I've even paid first, last, and security. I have no idea what this woman..." she paused to give Katherine a dismissive look before turning back to the officer, "...has in her email, but I'm all moved in. Suddenly *she* appears, trying all the doors, attempting to break in."

"Were you attempting to break in?" The officer's shades turned back to her again.

"Not at all."

"Really. What do you call it then?" Her tone was sarcastic "Were you just feeling through all the potted plants for nothing? You tried both doors. I expected to see you jimmy a window next."

Katherine tried to take a breath and not fly off the handle, but she was tired from the drive, worried about her missed appointment, and now disappointed to be losing a house she'd looked forward to.

"This is unbelievable." She spun to face the officer, who no longer appeared amused. "Do you see my car full of stuff, Officer?" She pointed at it. "Do you see this email confirmation?" She waved her phone at him, and he leaned back with a frown. "Of course I wasn't breaking in." She rolled her eyes. "It's ridiculous to even suggest it. Obviously any rational person can see that this is a misunderstanding. It's hardly something we need a cop for." She gestured toward the officer, giving Erin a scathing look.

"Hey, this is Captain MacAlister, the chief of detectives for this county," Erin told her, as if that meant something. "And I don't know you from Adam."

"Erin, thank you, but I think I can handle this." The officer's tone was brusque. He pivoted to Katherine. "Ma'am, you need to leave the property. Immediately."

Katherine felt disapproval roll off him like a wave. She tried to respond, but he interrupted.

"You need to leave and sort out your misunderstanding

somewhere else."

"Ya think?" she asked sarcastically, unable to stop herself from snapping back at him. With her feelings still stinging, she tried to march off to her car but was stopped short. An unhappy Captain MacAlister stepped in front of her and stood about an inch away. His face was so close she could see the slight bit of stubble on his chin and catch a slight hint of a woodsy sort of scent.

"A bit of advice, ma'am." His tone was curt.

She felt a rush of apprehension, but she didn't look away.

"You were technically trespassing, and I'm letting that go since it seems it was a misunderstanding, but don't complicate matters by being disrespectful." He looked from the out-of-state license plate on Henry back to her. "It doesn't matter who you are or where you're from; in this town even the tourists are expected to behave themselves."

Katherine took the hit and said nothing, since every single possible reply that flew through her head was probably going to land her in jail.

"Are we clear?" His voice was practically a growl.

"Completely." Her answer was quiet, but firm. He stared at her as if he didn't believe her, and she felt her cheeks get hot. She kept her mouth shut since she felt her emotional state deteriorating. There was a strong chance she'd end up saying something utterly stupid—or worse, get weepy. After a stretch of time that stopped just short of awkward, he stepped back and to the side so that she could scoot past him to her car.

"Dr. Grant?" she heard her name called and turned to see an older man in a game warden uniform jogging up to her from across the street. He had white hair and beard, but he moved as if he were twenty-five. "Looks like I'm a bit late." He smiled when he caught up to her. "Greg Watson called and asked me to meet you at the school. He was calling you, but only got your voicemail."

Katherine sighed. Greg was the head of the board of trustees, and although she'd given him her cell a half-dozen times, he still called the office, which got him Heather, not her. "He must have called my office rather than my cell. Are you a trustee as well?"

He nodded. "Greg called me in because I'm closest. He wanted me to tell you that there's been a mix-up with your housing. You're not staying here after all." He looked up at the house and Erin. "Which it looks like you figured out. Mindy Houghton's on the board and takes care of housing. I guess she forgot we were holding it for you and rented it to Erin instead. Found you a new spot today. You're actually out at Mac's rental, of all places." He looked between her and the officer who had recently told her off. Katherine felt her stomach freefall to her toes.

"And I suppose this is Mac?" She pointed a thumb over at Captain MacAlister.

"Well, yeah. It's a kicker that he's here." The man had a sly sort of smile on his face.

Mac stood there, still as stone. "Imagine that."

"Yes, imagine that." She tried not to freak out about the rather scary and definitely-not-friendly cop being her new landlord. "I'm sorry, sir, who did you say you were?"

"Peter Coleman." He held out his hand. He had a sort of gentleness about him despite being at last half a foot taller than her, and broad as well. He looked like a typical weather-beaten outdoorsman, but his eyes were kind and he had an easy smile. "Call me Pete."

"Thank you, Pete. I appreciate your help and your timing. I'm sort of in need of a rescue."

"Oh, well, sure." And again he looked back and forth between Katherine and Mac with confusion that turned quickly into understanding. "Greg said you were coming up here from Cape Cod. That's a haul. I bet you're real tired."

She rolled her eyes heavenward. "You have no idea."

"That your car?" he asked, nodding back to Henry. "I've got my Jeep right down the way. I'll jump in and you can follow me, okay? I live on the other side of the cabin. I'm a half-mile off, but that's practically next door up here." Katherine couldn't help but give him a genuine smile. Pete was one of those instantly likeable people.

"Thank you, Pete."

"Not at all, Dr. Grant."

"Oh, no need to call me Dr. Grant. It's Katherine."

"You got a nickname?"

"I've had them all, feel free to choose which you like."

"Well, how about Katie?"

"Sure. My mom calls me that."

"Katie it is." Pete moved towards his parked Jeep.

"Ma'am," Captain MacAlister called after her. She turned toward him and didn't miss that his expression was stuck at cold and unforgiving. But it didn't matter anymore. She had a new friend in Pete; she didn't care if the almighty Captain Mac didn't like her. "Your purse." He nodded to the porch where she had left it. She mumbled a thank-you and fetched the purse, catching once more the sweet smell of the lavender lining the walk. A pang of disappointment hit her, but she brushed it off. Maybe this cabin would be even better. As she pulled away, she could see Erin smiling up at the Captain and tried not to feel angry. Instead, she followed Pete up the mountain and into the woods.

CHAPTER TWO

THE DRIVE OUT TO THE NEW house was longer than she had expected, but it was beautiful. They left the downtown area, skirted the lake, and drove further up the mountain. The forest closed in around them, with the sun breaking through here and there. The road got tiny, with fewer and fewer driveways and side roads, until they came to a turn marked with a wooden sign that read 'Meadowview Road' nailed to the trunk of a pine tree.

They came to a stop in front of a cabin-like structure, which she was fervently hoping was not the rental. It was set back from the road; a small, cedar-shingled building with a peaked roof, short deck, and small windows. She could feel a frown forming as she looked it over. "Pete, is this it?"

"Sure is. Come on in; I've got the key."

The cabin looked old, but not in a cool vintage way; more in a way that she wouldn't have been surprised if it suddenly lost the will to remain upright and tumbled down at her feet. The little lot it sat on was compacted dirt, pine needles, and tree roots. All around the house sat tall pines, oaks, and a few birches. With the trees surrounding it there wasn't a lot of sunlight getting through; it was like someone had carved a notch into the forest and stuck the cabin there. She could forget about window boxes, forget about cute little English cottage gardens. There wasn't even grass in the back or side yards; only more dirt and roots.

A short set of steps at the front of the cabin led to an uncovered porch and the door, a large wooden one with a window in it. Pete muscled it open, and the fears raised by the state of the exterior were confirmed by the interior. Pine boards stained dark brown ran from floor to ceiling, making the dark house appear darker. Pete turned on the overhead light, the fluorescent bulbs casting an orange glow over the space and failing to add an iota of warmth or cheer.

The cabin was basically one big room with a little back hallway, which she presumed led to a bathroom and bedroom. To her immediate left there was a table with three chairs set up against the wall as a sort of dining area. That led into the kitchen. The cabinets were stained the same color as the wood on the floors and walls, which did nothing to alleviate the oppressiveness of the room. The appliances looked pre-Industrial Age, and Katherine quickly noticed that there were a few things conspicuously missing—no dishwasher, no microwave. Not a deal-breaker, but not a good sign either.

The rest of the space was taken up by a living room of sorts. Along the back wall was a good-sized stone fireplace and hearth, flanked by windows on either side looking out into the tree-filled backyard. Facing the fireplace was a large, ugly couch. The print was harvest gold, brown, and something that probably was once green, but had faded to a sort of gray. 'Hideous' was not an overstatement. She'd seen better on the side of the road waiting for a garbage truck or an impoverished college student to take. Prying her eyes off the couch, she peeked down the hallway to see what was there. Two doors stood open, revealing a storage room and a bathroom. The door at the end of the passage led out to the back deck.

"Where's the bedroom?" Pete pointed up above the hall entrance. She looked up to a sort of shelf space created over the storage room. She could see a short loft with a bed—or perhaps just a mattress—in it. Granted, the roof was peaked and the loft itself was open, but it was still little more than a shelf. "Is that loft big enough to stand up in?" she asked, trying to shake off her disappointment. After all, it was what it was.

"Uh…" Pete began reluctantly. "Afraid not, but I've stayed here before, and the bed's nice. I mean, it's on the floor, but it's big and comfortable. There are little shelves on the other side for your stuff."

"I don't see a TV." She looked around and noticed that not only was there no TV, but there was no phone either, and nothing that looked like a desk, or a modem where the internet might be found.

"Well…to tell you the truth, there's no cable out this far, and you can't get a satellite signal, so Mac never put one in." There was a note of apology in his tone.

"Please tell me there's internet out here," she almost whispered, closing her eyes for a moment.

"Sorry, no." Pete sounded genuinely sorry. "Back here you pretty much get electric and water. That's it."

"No phone?"

"No, but take out your cell and see if you get a signal. One of the carriers paid the town an arm and a leg for permission to build a tower. You should get something." She pulled out her phone and checked. Relief washed over her. It wasn't great, but it was enough.

"Got it."

"Oh, good!" Pete seemed to be a look-on-the-bright-side sort of person. Katherine was trying hard to do that, but this was too much.

"I don't want to seem ungrateful, but this cabin isn't really ideal. I need internet access to do this job. Maybe a place in town will open up soon? Is that likely?"

"There's nothing available in town. We tried there first."

"Oh, of course." Katherine looked around the room, taking it all in. The kitchen was big, if not modern, and the range looked in good shape. Maybe she could change some lights out, make it brighter. It was time to give in and find a way to make this place work. "This is okay. I can make this work. I really don't have that much stuff." She poked around a bit more. "Closets?" Her question was more hopeful than anything else.

Pete looked at the floor for a moment, probably wishing he were somewhere else. "Not as such."

"But, where do I put my clothes?"

"The storage room off the back here, that's where you can store your gear. It only has shelves, but I bet I could rig up a closet pole for you. There's a little space in the loft for slippers and the like, too." Her eyes lifted to the tiny loft as he said this, imagining what mornings were going to be like up there, and feeling fairly certain that she was going to whack her head multiple times on the low ceiling.

"Okay. Good to know."

"Let me show you how to run the washer and where the clothesline is."

"Clothesline?"

"Yeah, you got a washing machine here, but no dryer. You'll need to hang your clothes out." He said this as if all normal people dried their clothes outside.

"You're kidding me." And she lost hold of her inner Pollyanna. It was one thing to have 'pioneer woman' as an option, and another to have it thrust upon you.

"Here's what we're gonna do." Pete's tone was the calm one he likely reserved for feral animals. "We're gonna move you in. Then I'm going to the store, and I'll get some stuff to make this place a little more livable. You can use that back room as a closet if I hang a pole. I can get you an indoor drying rack for your clothes and a few power strips so you have a place for your phone and computer. We'll make it work."

"Okay." She took a breath and tried again to see things in a positive light.

He gave her a smile and began to help her bring in her things. He told her all about the town while they worked, finally getting around to its resident policeman. "It looked like the two of you were squaring off in town. Normally folks don't challenge Mac. I'm guessing you've got a bit of a temper, though." There was a twinkle of merriment in his eyes.

"You know, Pete, normally I'm perfectly reserved; actually, some people think I'm cold."

"What?"

"My brother-in-law, David, calls me the ice princess. Of course he was a jerk the first time I met him, and I may have held a wee bit of a grudge. I might've earned that nickname." David and her little sister Amy married at twenty-one. Most guys that young were often full of themselves. He had said some mean things about the scar on her cheek, and at that time it had been a good deal uglier. Katherine had cut him down to size and spent the next few years either freezing him out or mocking him. They got along better now, but the nickname stuck.

"Your buddy, Captain What's-his-face, was not very nice to me. I'm afraid that sort of person brings out the worst in me. I don't like bullies."

"He's prickly, that's for sure, but it's the nature of the position rather than the nature of the man. You must have caught him on an off day. He's usually the one protecting people from bullies."

"I'll take your word for it." Her tone was glum as she unpacked a box of framed photos, heading to the mantel over the fireplace. Then she remembered that Mac was the owner of the cabin, and that she'd be living here for the next six months and would have no choice but to interact with him. "He's really my new landlord?"

"Yeah, but don't worry about it. He's nicer than he seems. Besides, most of the time he has me do his repairs and upkeep here. He's a pretty busy guy."

"But aren't you a pretty busy guy? Game warden is a tough job, isn't it? Don't you rescue hikers and stuff like that?"

"Sure, we do search and rescue, but the majority of my job is enforcing the state's hunting laws. We've got a real problem lately with poachers. A couple of large employers in the county went out of business, and that means people are hurting. When that happens they make a buck where they can. I understand why most of them do it, but it's still illegal, still cheating when you get right down to it, and it endangers everyone's use of the land when they don't follow the rules."

"There's some crushing poverty up here, isn't there?"

"Yeah, but it's the gentler kind. What you see in cities…" He shook his head.

"Well, I suppose you're right. It's not thousands of people stuck in tiny apartments in a city slowly decaying, with rampant crime. But it's still poverty, and I wonder about the rates of domestic violence. That's crime you don't always see."

Pete paused in the act of stacking another box. He turned to her and gave her an assessing stare. "Did you grow up with that kind of poverty?"

"No." She shook her head as she arranged her family photos on the mantel. "My mom's an artist and my dad was a district attorney. I was raised on the family estate in Rhode Island, where we had a private stretch of beach and a stable of horses. My life was lightyears away from poverty."

"I've read your bio; your entire career has been about helping kids educate themselves up the ladder. I wondered where that drive came from."

"My dad used to talk to us about noblesse oblige—the idea that if God blessed you with wealth and power then you were obligated to use it to help others. I started off teaching first grade, and later I shifted my focus, concentrated on the kids who needed someone in their corner." She went back to the box and pulled out more photos of her nieces and nephews.

"Well, the foster kids who come for the vocational program definitely need someone in their corner. Is that why you were willing to take it on?" He gave her a side glance. "I know what the job pays."

She sighed. "I kind of needed a break. Taking a few months off from the rat race isn't going to do me any damage." She looked around at the cabin. "This place might, though."

"Now, don't say that. We'll get it livable. You'll be all right up here, Katie. It's nice and quiet; just the cabin, my house, and Mac's place on this road. His house is down the driveway next to you." He gestured to the side yard with his head. "Both his property and mine back up on Martin's Meadow. I've got a few acres, but Mac has a huge place and a little ranch, although he doesn't call it that. He's got a cow, a couple of goats, and two horses. They're named something stupid..." Pete seemed to be working on remembering. "Misery and Agony." He laughed. "That's it; their owner raced them for a while until he got into some kind of trouble. He ended up dumping them, and Mac adopted them."

"But it's pretty much a forest up here. Where does he ride them?"

"All around us are trails. I'll get you a map in case you want to explore. Your front door is only a mile from great hiking."

"Uh, to be honest, hiking isn't my thing."

Pete looked shocked. "You're in an outdoor paradise. Maine is like a wonderland for all things outdoors." He paused like he was deciding if she was nuts or simply dim. "We'll convert you." He sounded confident.

"Hmmm... I don't see that happening, but I'll give it a go."

Pete went out again and brought in the remainder of her boxes. "I think I've got it from here, Pete." She stood and took another box. "And thank you, seriously, for the encouragement. Today's been a bit of a rollercoaster."

"Oh well..." He waved off her praise. "The people up here are good people, overall. If you come to church on Sunday you'll meet most of them. Calvary Bible is right in town. It's got solid preaching, great coffee, good choir. Small, though – we'd love to have you."

"I think I need to settle in first, but maybe after that."

"I'd be happy to give you a ride if you need one. Come winter you probably will." He looked out the window at her car. "That's a nice little BMW. I once had a girlfriend with a Cabrio. What's yours?"

"Henry's an M3." Then she grimaced. "I know it's stupid to name a car, but he's my buddy. I'm on the road a lot, and if the job is within driving distance, Henry comes with me."

"You probably want to think about leasing a 4x4 up here."

"No, he's great in the snow," she insisted.

"Well...I guess if you're used to rear-wheel drive in the snow you should be fine. But put bags of sand in the back."

"Okay," she was quick to answer, although she had no intentions of piling sand bags in her trunk. She was used to snow. Pete gave her a sharp look.

"You're only saying that to shut me up, aren't you? Oh, no, don't deny it," he chuckled as she sputtered a half-hearted denial. "I've got three grown daughters, so I know when I'm being tuned out."

"Do they live in town?"

"No, unfortunately. Ally and Beth are in Portland, climbing the corporate ladder. Lori moved out to Bangor and opened up a little shop there, sells fancy housewares. It's called 'A Little Something.' Hey, speaking of shops, if you got time tomorrow, I'll give you a tour of town. We should do it before you start on Monday so you can get a feel for the community."

"I'd love it."

"Great. I'll come by tomorrow."

"Thanks, Pete." And he left her alone to get back to the business of unpacking.

CHAPTER THREE

MAC HEARD THE SCREEN DOOR TO the station squeak open and bang shut. A minute later, Pete ducked his head in the office door. "You in?"

"No. I'm a mirage."

"Well now, glad to hear you're still in a great mood." Pete's voice held more than a hint of disapproval.

Mac looked up from the pile of paperwork on his desk. "What's up?"

"I was going to ask you that." Pete gave him a sharp look, and Mac's brain surfed through what possible reasons he might have for giving him the stink-eye. "You were a bit harsh with Dr. Grant, the school's new consultant," he explained.

"The new what?"

"Don't you know who that woman was that you nearly arrested today? Dr. Katherine Grant?"

Mac knew exactly who she was, but he didn't want to talk about her. And he hadn't almost arrested her. Not that he hadn't been tempted. "It's been a long day already, Pete. I've had a troop of Boy Scouts in and out of here today with four hundred questions, I've had Dave White calling to let me know if I don't take care of his trespassers he'll – that's gonna end up your problem by the way – and Mrs. Gunther had another close miss. She drove off the road this time, nearly mowed down a biker, so now I gotta go have 'the conversation' with her son. Again. He's got to do more than simply hide her keys."

"Dave called us about the trespassers. I meant to tell you that you didn't need to worry. We put up game cameras to see if we can get a picture of who it is. He's got neighbors on either side he's feuding with so it could be vandalism. I'll let you know as soon as we have a suspect, and if it's something we need your help on." Pete took a seat in front of Mac's desk as if he were going to stay a while. Normally Pete was good company, but Mac was feeling anti-social.

"Thanks. I'll follow up with him again and remind him not to go confronting anyone, especially not with his .22." Mac watched Pete smirk. "So what else do you need?"

"Well, I wanted to tell you how your tenant is settling in. She's nice, despite having a bit of a temper. Of course, if someone called the cops on me for trying to get into a house I was told was mine…I might be a bit angry, too. Come to think of it, Erin should have known who Dr. Grant was since her kids go to the school. All the parents got a notice."

Mac sighed, "Erin had a lot to say, Pete, and I have to admit I didn't listen to all of it."

"Yeah, well, that's not surprising. Don't know why she still bothers flirting with you for all you ignore it." Mac silently willed him to shut up and just leave it there. "Nice woman, Erin."

"Give it a rest, Pete." Erin was a friend, and that's all she'd ever be. They didn't have a single spark between them. She was certainly pretty, and she had three great kids, but it wasn't meant to be. They'd settled all that years ago. Of course, being single, everyone in town assumed he was dating any eligible woman that he stood next to for longer than three minutes.

"Sure. I'll give it a rest." Pete hid a smile by running his hand over his beard. "Katie wasn't exactly pleased with the cabin. It's fine for hunters and hikers, but it's not really meant to be lived in long-term."

"I told Greg I'd get a wood stove for it."

"It's not just the heat, Mac. Katie's gonna be working, and there's no desk, no internet, and it's kinda--"

"Mrs. Connors and her crew were there three days ago, cleaning the place," Mac interrupted. "And they stocked the cabinets, which is more than she'd get if she was staying at a hotel. It has everything she needs, and it's hardly 'roughing it'. I lived there for the better part of a year while building my house. It's not that bad. If she's too much of a princess for the cabin, that's not my problem." He looked back down at the pile of paperwork on his desk.

"What's your deal with her, anyway? I told you she's nice."

Mac winced, knowing he was being harsh, but not sure how to stop. Katherine Grant was a stone in his shoe he did not need. "She's a stuck-up brat, Pete. You got all the sweetness and smiles and missed out on the sarcasm and attitude."

"Oh! My opinion can't be trusted because she was sweet to me?" He laughed. "Well, she was, but she also let me know she didn't think much of the cabin."

Mac didn't doubt it. He hardly expected a woman who drove a BMW and probably had a house to match to be satisfied with the cabin's 'rustic charms'.

"Did you know she's never hung clothes outside? I had to walk her through where to find the clothesline. Oh..." he broke off, fishing through his pockets and producing a list. "That reminds me. I'm going to pick up a few things she needs since she didn't come up here prepared to live in a cabin."

"What was she prepared for?"

"A walk-in closet, for one. She's got a ton of clothes, so I'll put in a closet rod in the storage area. Other than that, she's got a bunch of sewing stuff and at least one box of books. That's about it. I told her I'd try to find a little bookcase, figured you wouldn't mind. Also, a power strip, since there are no safe outlets to charge her computer and phone. You need anything?" Pete asked and Mac shook his head. "I should mention that she's not your biggest fan right now. Why don't you finish up here and go make nice?"

Mac sighed. "Like I said, Pete, it's been a really long day. I'll see her some time and smooth it over." He was thinking about the look she'd given him as he had warned her to check her attitude. She'd lowered her eyes until her lashes practically touched her cheeks. Those lashes were now burned into his brain. Something else he didn't need. "I guess I was a little rough on her."

"Yeah, well, I think it might be more than that, but we'll leave it there. It's best if you take care of it today, Mac; don't let that settle in. I get the sense that she's softer than she appears."

"Sheesh, Pete. Fine. I'll stop by."

"All right then." Pete said it as if Mac had talked *him* into it. He headed out, and the screen door banged shut behind him. Mac put the paperwork down and leaned back in his chair.

When he'd first pulled up to Erin's house, he had recognized Dr. Grant straight off from the cable news program that Pete had shown him when the school was trying to hire her. She looked even prettier in person than she had on TV. He'd known there was no way she was breaking in. He'd even found it kind of funny. But then she had stared up at him, and it had hit him, right in the gut – attraction. She had large hazel eyes and light brown hair, almost blond. She had it up in a bun, but pieces had escaped and were curled all around her face, and only made her more appealing. Her fair skin was a little flushed, and her lips almost pouted.

The pull he felt was undeniable, but it was also a mistake. Telling her off was like a knee-jerk response. So instead he had pushed her away. When he'd taken this job, he had made a promise to himself and to God. His life was going to change. He was going to be a better man. In New York he'd left behind his pursuit of prestige along with meaningless pleasure. Over time he'd gotten smart enough not to react to a woman who attracted him unless a relationship was possible. Otherwise it was torture. He'd been ignoring that kind of desire for so long now that it was almost automatic. Until today.

Katherine Grant had looked up at him with her combination of soft looks and hard edge, and had blown a hole right through his control. He'd responded bluntly, with absolutely no finesse, and now he was going to have to apologize. Something he was not looking forward to. She'd be spending a few months here, and then she'd be gone. He knew better than to give in to the allure and try to pursue a relationship, since it would be over before it even started. The best thing would be to avoid the woman if at all possible. Anything else would be asking for trouble that he didn't need.

CHAPTER FOUR

IT HAD TAKEN A FEW HOURS, but Katherine was finally unpacked. She had made a few unhappy discoveries along the way, like the fact that the cabin had a total of three outlets, none of them in the bathroom or the storage area that she had redubbed 'the closet', or the bed loft. That meant no drying her hair in front of the bathroom mirror, no light in the closet, and no reading in bed. But she figured she could get a battery-operated lamp for that, at least.

There were two outlets in the kitchen and one on the far end of the house by the fireplace. That one contained the plug of the cabin's only lamp – a free-standing specimen, circa 1960, with a little integrated tray table. It was old enough to be charming, and it reminded her of her grandmother's house, so she decided it could stay right where it was.

While stowing her clothes in the back of the storage room she found a treasure: Christmas lights. After unraveling the knot they were in and shaking off the dust bunnies, they looked like the rest of the cabin; old, but in decent shape. She headed for the hearth and plugged in the lights, smiling as they instantly lit, not a single dark bulb. She carefully arranged them around her pictures on the mantel. Then she took a second string and wound them around the empty andirons inside the fireplace. When she was done she stood back, admiring how the light glinted and sparkled off the picture frames.

Another pleasant surprise she had found in the cabin was that the ladies of the Calvary Bible Church had stocked her kitchen. She knew they supported the school but didn't think they'd go so far as outfitting a consultant with perfectly stocked cabinets. The ladies had left her a little note telling her what was where and giving her their contact info in case she needed anything. It was such a sweet gesture that Katherine got a little misty-eyed. After the day she'd had, their thoughtfulness was like receiving a big hug.

She used their groceries to make dinner - grilled cheese. It wasn't much, but she was exhausted and wanted something comforting. She sat at the dinette, which was as old as everything else. The table was heavy wood and coated with a thick layer of poly which had yellowed over the years and was cracking in a spot or two. The chairs with it had low backs and vinyl-covered cushions, brown like everything else, but otherwise pretty comfy.

As she ate her dinner she watched night fall, casting funky shadows into the corners of the cabin as the overhead light became brighter by comparison. Katherine got up and switched it off, leaving only the kitchen hood light, corner lamp, and Christmas lights on. This was better; not exactly cheerful, but an improvement. Tomorrow she could ask Pete if he would replace the overhead with track lighting, providing she paid for it. It would certainly be worth the money.

She started to redecorate the cabin in her head, imagining what she could do that would bring in a degree of cheer. As she thought it over, there came a loud, sharp knock on the door, and she almost jumped out of her skin. Hopping up, she went to the door and peeked through the window to see who it was and felt her stomach lurch. It was Captain MacAlister, King of the Mounties . . . or whatever he was.

If it hadn't been for the window in the door through which she could clearly see him and he could clearly see her, she would have simply waited for him to go away. Childish, but she wasn't feeling up to being a grown-up right then. Instead, she put curtains at the top of her to-do list and opened the door with what she hoped was a friendly smile. It faded when she saw his puzzled expression. He was looking past her at the stone hearth with the Christmas lights on it.

"What's that?" He pointed to the lights.

"Uh . . ."

"Are they Christmas lights?" he asked, as if they were live snakes.

"Well, yes, they were in the closet, and I needed more light in here, so I strung them up along the mantel. I think it makes the place a little less gloomy."

"But how are you going to use the fireplace if you've got those lights up?" he asked, stepping inside, still fixated on what she thought really wasn't a problem. He was frowning down at her, and she realized that he was waiting for an answer.

"It's August," she said as if it was obvious the fireplace wouldn't be used for three months at least.

"That fireplace is your only source of heat for now," he explained as if she was unaware that the thermometer went down as well as up. "And it might be August, but in a few weeks it will feel like November in the early morning."

"I saw baseboard heaters in the bathroom and kitchen."

"That's to keep the pipes from freezing. They'll never heat the house. The temperature plummets up here at night. You'll need that fireplace."

"Well, I'm going to order extra lights, so I only need these until they come," she said in frustration, and he shook his head.

"You don't have to order anything. Tell me what you need, and I can get Pete to put it in for you,"

"It's late, Captain; maybe we can deal with this tomorrow."

"You can call me Mac," he said, clearly not remembering that he hadn't bothered to introduce himself, or to be polite in the least.

He looked down at the table and the last piece of her grilled cheese. "That's not much of a dinner." He scowled at her as if her meager cooking was yet another personal failure worthy of his disdain.

That was about all her temper needed. Whatever hold she'd had on all the day's emotion broke. "Well, Mac, after a long day that began with driving forever, having my meeting blown off by the director I'm supposed to be working with, finding the house I thought I'd be living in already occupied, having the cops called on me, getting yelled at and nearly arrested for being in the wrong place, and then fighting serious disappointment over the state of this place, I'm a bit tired. I'm going to clean up, then crawl into that tiny little shelf up there and go to bed. Do you mind, *Mac*?"

He was silent for a moment, but she could see that he was trying to control his own temper far better than she had hers. His jaw was set, but instead of angry he looked intense, and there was something about that look that caught her attention. Her anger began to slip as she looked him over, finally taking him in. Captain MacAlister hadn't been a remarkable man when she first got a look at him. Under his big hat and behind his sunglasses he was all authority, but standing in her little cabin without either, he was more the man and less the job.

"So, this cabin that is being provided to you free of charge with a fully stocked kitchen falls short of your expectations?" Those words proved authority still seemed to be his default.

"Housing is part of my compensation, sir, so it's not 'free of charge'. I accepted this contract under the assumption that housing would be adequate. A cabin with no dryer and a shelf instead of a bedroom is not adequate. It's fine for a weekend, but I have to live here for a whole lot longer than that. Would you want a shelf for a bed on a permanent basis?"

"It's a loft, not a shelf." His face was still set in stone while he defended his property.

"I think the word 'shelf' is far more accurate. I can't even stand up in it, and it's not like I'm tall."

Mac's eyes took a quick sweep over her. "No, I guess you're not," There was a slight change to his tone, and his expression softened as if he was looking at her in a different light. She stared right back, noting that, while he was older than her, it probably wasn't by much. His thick black hair was slightly curly and shot through with gray, and the lines on his face were put there either by laughing or exposure. Considering the fact that she had yet to see him smile, she was guessing it wasn't the former. He was attractive, but not the hit-you-over-the-head-and-make-you-stupid kind of attractive.

His eyes, though, were remarkable. He had what she always thought was the good kind of hazel eyes - blue and green. When she was a kid she'd wished her hazel eyes were like that, but depending on what she wore, her eyes looked more like brown than anything else. Mac's were like the ocean at dusk, a mix of deep blue and bottle-green. They had a dark ring around the iris and thick black lashes framed by well-shaped eyebrows. She watched while those eyebrows rose.

Great! Just go on and stare at the man. Katherine kicked herself and then covered up with a huff of impatience. "Yes, well, it's like I said, fine for a weekend or a short stay, but I have to live here for months." She dropped her gaze to the floor, not knowing how to get out of this situation with her pride intact. His eyes might have been swoon-worthy, but she shouldn't actually be swooning.

"I guess coming from where you do it's a real step down."

"What? Rhode Island?" Katherine asked, her temper right back in the red zone. "Listen, I am not some pampered little princess who's pitching a nutty because I don't have granite counter tops, buddy. I've worked jobs where the only housing was a Bates Motel wannabe with the management to match, or a dump next to a strip joint with actual bullet holes in the wall. I go where the work requires, but this time I agreed to the job based on having a house and yard rather than the usual one-room kitchenette. They even sent me pictures of it. It's a house they own, so I have no idea why a week before I'm due here someone on the board rents it out from under me."

That seemed to have an impact. His brows drew together like he wondered that as well. "Just a misunderstanding. Erin can...overreact at times, but she's a reasonable person. I'll make sure she knows it wasn't your fault." His voice was softer now, as if her rant had calmed him.

"Thank you." Now that the wind was knocked out of her sails, she felt spent and a little ashamed for having been so sarcastic and nasty. She wished he'd leave.

He seemed to catch on to her mood and was quiet for a long moment before saying, "I'm sorry about earlier today. I guess I was a little harsh."

"No worries. It was just another blow in a day full of them."

"Then I'm sorry I added to your bad day." He headed toward the door but turned back around after putting his hand on the knob. "If you need anything, you can give Pete a call. He's usually around during the week, and he can get hold of me if it's something he can't handle."

"Okay," she said, with not a small amount of relief. She'd much rather work through Pete and avoid any further contact with Mac. Normally she was pretty good with people, if in a superficial kind of way, but with Mac...he seemed to bring out the very worst in her. She'd never lost her temper so quickly.

"Well, goodnight then," he said, and stood there as if waiting for something. She gave him a little wave, and he hesitated before finally turning and leaving. Katherine locked up after him. Mac was a puzzle, but not one she wanted to spend her time trying to solve. What she needed now was hot cocoa, a book, and then bed. In the kitchen she found chocolate syrup and smiled, thinking of the ladies of Calvary Bible. She heated the milk in a saucepan. The lack of a microwave would mean more dishes, which made the lack of a dishwasher hurt a little more.

"Stop sulking," she told herself, and got a mug out of the cabinet. Picking up the chocolate syrup, she struggled with the cap for a moment before it popped open, squirting all over the cabinets, wall, and counter. For a second, she was tempted to scream in frustration, but instead she broke out laughing. "This is not my day." She made her cocoa, cleaned up the mess, and read until she felt sleepy. Then she climbed up on the shelf, hoping tomorrow would go her way.

CHAPTER FIVE

KATHERINE WOKE UP TO THE SOUND of her phone happily singing to her from across the cabin, where she'd left it plugged into the outlet in the kitchen. She sat up and tried to disentangle herself from her blankets and shimmy down the ladder before the last ring. Right as she was picking it up, the call went to voicemail. "I hate this cabin." The cabin didn't reply.

While waiting for the caller to finish leaving her a message, she started the coffee. When she played the message, she heard Heather's cheery voice reminding her about the day's events.

"Don't forget the town has that market day. Looks like fun. And . . . it's a fundraiser—see what I did there? So you should really go. Says that it's being catered by one of the local restaurants, so the food should be good. Remote or not, they've got a four-star rating on Yelp." Katherine smiled into the phone, listening to Heather prattle on as she poured a cup of coffee.

Grabbing a book, she headed for the couch, intending to spend a quiet morning reading. She started to sit, but when the backs of her bare legs touched the material she immediately jumped back up with a squeal. Something stiff was all over the couch, and it wasn't only a stain. She ran her hands over it and drew back in disgust. Someone, at some point, in an incredibly misguided attempt to make it livable, had actually painted it. She didn't doubt that they had used fabric paint, and that they had tried really hard, but it was awful.

Katherine put her coffee down and headed to the wanna-be

closet to dig through her stuff until she found the set of organic—and rather scratchy—cotton sheets she'd twice meant to dump in Goodwill but never gotten around to. They were beige and hefty, perfect to cover the extremely nasty couch. She tossed the sheets over it and tucked them in, so that at least for today she had a place to sit. Tomorrow maybe she'd pull out her machine and actual try to sew them into a cover.

She sat on the couch and calculated the pluses and minuses of this job. Plus: the school was in a lovely town. Minus: it was the middle of nowhere. Plus: the head admin, Elaine, was friendly. Minus: her landlord Mac wasn't. Plus: Nature in all its glory was right outside the window. Minus, and it was a big one: the cabin. She'd much rather stay in walking distance to the school, but there was no point in getting upset about it.

A knock sounded on the door, and Katherine spotted Pete standing on the front steps. Ten points for the plus column: Pete. He was old enough that she didn't have to worry he'd get the wrong idea from her accepting his friendship. He seemed to be a wealth of information, he was on the board, and, most importantly, he was kind. That went a long way in her ledger.

For the next hour, Pete took Katherine on a tour of Sweet River, from one side to the other. As a game warden, the town was a small part of his territory, but it seemed like he knew every square inch of it. Sweet River wasn't small, but the year-round population was what gave it a small-town feel. The downtown area was quaint, like a lot of others in New England, but with the nearby state park and the lake with a large resort and two separate luxury lakeside subdivisions, it was far busier and a bit more upscale. It had shops covering everything from a traditional general store to designer outdoor gear.

After the tour, Pete took Katherine to what he said was the best restaurant in town, a diner called 'Maria's'. From the outside it looked like a store in a strip mall, but inside it was done up in chrome, '50s-style Formica, and red vinyl benches. Pete explained that the restaurant had been owned by the same family for thirty years and that 'Maria' had been a baby when it opened, but was now the owner and chef.

They took two stools at the long counter, and Katherine perused what proved to be an eclectic menu. It had a mix of traditional diner classics, home-style Italian, and a number of original creations. Unsurprisingly, all Pete's favorites were old-school classics: chicken pot pie, shepherd's pie, and New England boiled dinner. No way was she going with that last one: meat, potatoes, and veggies all boiled in one pot. Yuck.

After they ate, Katherine and Pete ordered coffee, and he insisted they each get a piece of pie. The coffee arrived in the standard heavy mug with a little pot of cream and a sugar dispenser. Pete smiled as he watched her empty two teaspoons full of sugar into her cup, along with a heavy dose of cream. "I know it's not exactly healthy, but I've never learned to drink it straight," she explained.

"I think you have to start young," Pete nodded at his own cup of black coffee. "When I was in the service you either drank it black or you went without, so I got pretty used to it."

"Army?"

"Yep. Ten years. Vietnam for most of 'em."

"Wow, Pete," Katherine said, hand frozen in mid-stir.

"I was a medic, I didn't do the shooting; I did the ducking," he said with a smile.

"I can't imagine all you must have gone through."

"Nothing more than any man does when he puts on a military uniform."

"That's so beyond anything I've ever experienced."

"Really?" he asked, his eyes searching her face and falling on the thin white scar along her cheek.

Katherine beat down the unease that surfaced. She didn't like being asked about it because it wasn't the kind of survival story anyone would want to tell, and it certainly had no happy ending.

Pete wasn't asking, though; it was more like he was simply giving her an opening to talk about it and letting her decide if she would. "There's a difference," she said carefully, "between enduring a trauma and living one daily."

"Yes, but it marks you just the same."

"You're not wrong," she said softly, but was saved saying anything further when a woman called his name and came over to them. She immediately launched into the discussion of a problem she was having with a herd of deer munching through her backyard, as if Pete was personally responsible for each intruder. She was reading him the riot act when she noticed Katherine and started apologizing for interrupting.

"No worries. This sounds important." Katherine hopped off her stool and motioned to the woman to sit. "I was planning on hitting that market, and the green's a short walk. Pete, I'll catch up with you later?" she asked and he nodded, although the expression on his face made it clear he wasn't done with their conversation.

Back outside, she headed off to the green and consciously slowed her steps, letting herself enjoy the sunshine, soaking it up like a leaf preparing for fall. She'd worn a jersey top with cap sleeves and a jean skirt that hit right above the knee, so she had enough bare skin to soak in some vitamin D, but not enough to shock anybody. Katherine had rules for her clothes; they had to make her look good as well as look her own age. Holding onto youth wasn't something she understood. There was so much pressure to appear perfect when she was in her teens and twenties that hitting thirty had been a relief.

When she reached the market, she was surprised by how many crafters and farmers had set up under the canopies selling produce, baskets, jewelry, and homemade goods. It was like the flea markets she'd been to in the south; sprawling and varied. Katherine stopped at the first booth and bought herself a large basket with a wide handle to tote around the fair so she could buy what she liked. Two hours of happy shopping later, she had three bars of homemade soap, a new pair of handmade dangly silver earrings—which she put right on—two jars of local honey, a bag of apples, a batch/cluster/bunch of basil, and a half-dozen tomatoes.

She checked out the antiques tent and found herself mulling over a rocking chair that would be perfect for the cabin. It was old, but more like vintage than antique - probably 1940s. It had a nice high back and seemed to be made of maple. She was trying to figure out how she'd tie it to the top of her car when she remembered that she hadn't driven here. *Rats*. Pete had his Jeep. They could probably wrestle it on to the top. She'd have to find him before she bought it.

The dealer wanted eighty for it, but she was pretty sure she could talk him down to fifty. Running her fingers over the smooth arm of the chair while still making up her mind, she jumped when a deep voice spoke behind her. "That's not gonna fit in your basket."

CHAPTER SIX

IT WAS CAPTAIN MACALISTER. OF COURSE it was, because that was just her luck. He was in uniform, but no sunglasses or hat so at least it was a more human version of him. She took a second to get over her surprise then smiled, "You don't think it will? Shucks. It's too bad, since it would be perfect for the cabin."

There was a hint of a smile on his face while he looked over the rocking chair. "You're right. I've got my truck. I can take it home for you." Without giving her a chance to answer, he leaned over to the man selling it and said, "She'll take it," and then handed him the eighty dollars. Katherine was sure that her chin must have been on the ground. Mac walked away, towards the parking lot, with her chair in one arm as if it weighed nothing.

"Hey!" she called as she caught up. "You didn't have to do that."

"No, I didn't," he said over his shoulder.

"Well, that's very nice of you. But I was pretty sure I could've talked him down on the price."

Mac laughed, and it was a nice sound, deep and resonant. "Kevin Murphy wasn't going to take a penny less on this chair. He's allergic to haggling. Besides, it's maple, in good shape, and if he's patient, and I know he is, he'd get three times the price online. It was a bargain." Katherine absorbed the new information that Mac appeared to be a savvy shopper, as she watched him place the chair in the bed of his pickup and climb up to secure it. Once he had it safe, he jumped down.

She was trying to think of a way to refuse this gesture without being the world's biggest jerk, but she failed. Then she tried to figure out why she was so keen to refuse it. Finally, she gave. "Thanks, Mac. I appreciate it."

"You're welcome, Kate."

She smiled almost involuntarily. No one had called her 'Kate' in years.

"Does that nickname meet with your approval?" There was something soft in his voice. "I remember you told Pete to pick one."

"No one ever picks that one so, yes, I approve."

For this she got a smile, a real one, and it looked good on him. He seemed kinder and even younger when he smiled. "Are you planning on staying for the barbecue? It's likely to start soon." Mac nodded over to the far end of the green where the caterers were set up.

Katherine thought it over, knowing that barbecue likely meant meat and a lot of it. "I know this will probably tag me as a latte-swilling, BMW-driving, book-reading leftie, but I don't eat much meat."

For a second he just stared at her.

"See, I knew it. I can see the censure right there." She pointed at his eyes

"I'm from New York, Kate. For five years I was a detective in Manhattan. Trust me; I will not judge you for being a vegetarian." His lips quirked. "Or for driving a BMW and reading books. Lattes, though?" And he pulled a face that made her laugh out loud.

"I suppose you drink your coffee black like Pete and eat your steak rare?"

"Is there any other way to eat steak?"

So Captain Mac did have a sense of humor. She liked that almost more than his smile. It meant he didn't take himself too seriously. "I'm not a real vegetarian, though. I don't eat cow, lamb, or pig, but I do eat fish and chicken."

"How'd that come about?"

"One of my sisters is a vegan and the other does Paleo, so I hear it from them all the time and became a 'vegetarian'" she added in finger quotes. "Mostly to shut them up. I tried to go the whole nine yards, but it made me miserable."

"I'm pretty sure the barbecue has beans and salads, so you should be good. How about you let me buy you dinner?"

Katherine's brain screeched to a halt. Up until now this had been a friendly landlord-tenant sort of thing. With that invitation it became something else. But this was only a town picnic, essentially. He was a town official of sorts and this could be him being nice. After doing the math, she nodded her yes.

"Great. I know the perfect place to sit."

She let him walk her back over to the other side of the green where rows of tables had been set up.

He sat her at a small picnic table, on a slight hill overlooking the action. "You wait here. I'll be right back with the food."

"But you don't know what I want."

"Trust me," he said with a wink, and off he went.

Not likely, she thought. Katherine didn't trust anyone beyond Heather, her mom, and her sisters. And sometimes not those last two.

Mac returned with two plates piled high with food and two water bottles hanging from a crooked finger on each hand.

"Goodness. I hope you got all that because you're starving," she said with a laugh.

He set down the plates and then sat across the table from her, handing her a water bottle. "A sampling of the best of the bunch: barbecue chicken, corn bread, beans, potato salad, and 'Spinach....Something-or-Other'. No idea what that is, but the girl serving it said it was 'the bomb'. And I got you water since you don't seem the soda type."

"Well-spotted."

"Do you mind if I say grace?" he asked and she shook her head no.

She was glad that he wanted to, since it meant he was likely a Christian, and asking to say grace meant he was confident in his beliefs. Good news for the people he policed.

Mac bowed his head, she followed suit, and in a low voice he said, "Bless us, o Lord, and these thy gifts which we are about to receive from thy bounty, through Christ, our Lord, Amen." *Nice*, she thought. *Old school.*

They dug into their dinners, and she found the spinach stuff was spanakopita. It was indeed 'the bomb'. Mac didn't try to engage her in conversation, probably because he was plowing through what looked like beef brisket with clear appreciation. Considering that she didn't see a wedding ring, and she doubted he would have invited her to dinner if he was married, she assumed he was single and probably had to cook for himself. Then again, maybe she was jumping to ginormous conclusions.

"Penny for your thoughts." He was giving her a searching look, and she realized that she had sort of been staring at him.

"I was wondering if you knew how to cook."

"Because I'm eating like a pig?" He looked a little guilty. "Yes and no. My repertoire ranges from hamburgers to tacos."

"You'd make a horrible vegan."

"Yes, I would." It was said with enough conviction that she knew she was dealing with a meat and potatoes man.

Mac leaned forward and wiped his mouth with a napkin. "Why'd you take a job like this one?"

"You mean a job this small?"

"Yeah, it's doesn't seem to be your thing."

Katherine wondered how he would know what her type of thing was. Had he looked into her? "I don't really know what you mean by that."

"Well...you drive a BMW, you're on TV, you've written books." He didn't smile as he said this and there was nothing in his tone that was friendly or joking. "The job only lasts a few months, so it's not a lifestyle change you're looking for."

She could feel her temper rise as he spoke.

"I guess I wonder why you're here."

"I'm here because I'm needed."

"Are you the Mary Poppins of troubled schools?" This he said with a slight smile, and said by someone else, somewhere else, she might have laughed, but she didn't appreciate hearing it from him. It was like he had already decided who she was and what she was worth, and neither was enough for him or his town.

"I could ask you the same thing. What are you doing here?" The attitude he'd warned her about yesterday had begun to return. "Big-city policeman trades it all to become sheriff of a tiny town? Escaping city life? Stress?"

Mac sat back from the table. "You know I'm not a sheriff, and I suspect my question got your back up, but I'm honestly wondering why someone like you would take a job like this."

The phrase 'someone like you' cut deep. Usually she had a pretty thick skin, but somehow, hearing those words from him hurt more. "Are you wondering in your professional capacity?"

"Of course not," he answered, his tone dismissive. "You're overreacting to what was an innocent question."

Katherine knew that he was right, but she was confused by her own reaction and vulnerable response, an emotion she worked hard to avoid. Realizing that this was going to go from awkward to confrontational, she got up from the table, picking up her basket and her plate. "Well, it's getting late so it's probably a good idea that I go. It was good to run into you, Mac. Thanks for dinner." And she stepped over the bench, walking away. She found a trashcan on the way, chucked her plate in, and headed for the dessert table. Suddenly she really needed a brownie, or a cookie, or maybe a whole cake.

Chancing a look over her shoulder, she saw Mac back at the table, fork in hand, slowly shaking his head. He might think that her stomping off was a fit of bad behavior, but he wasn't prepared for what would have happened if she had unleashed her temper on him. Her anger was like a mean dog at times, and if she let it off the chain it could tear someone up. She didn't want to do that to Mac, even if he did think she was some kind of over-educated carpetbagger.

She bought a large chocolate brownie with fudge frosting and tucked it among the rest of the goodies in her basket before scanning the area for a friendly face who might give her a lift home. She finally spotted Pete at a table filled with teenagers. "Hey, Pete," she said as she approached, and the kids all turned to her. She smiled while they assessed her and decided she wasn't worth their notice, as is the way of teenagers. "Is there a chance you could rescue me twice in as many days? I'm in need of a ride home."

"Well, sure, but I saw you with Mac. Figured he was giving you a ride."

"Yeah, well, that's not going to work out." Most of the kids were still ignoring her, but a petite and pretty blond girl on the end stared at her rather intently. Katherine gave her a smile that the girl didn't return. "Listen, I don't want to pull you away early, so I'll grab a seat and eat my brownie,"

"Ma'am, you can sit here," one of the boys said, getting up. "I'm getting an ice cream. Anybody else?" Another boy and two girls left with him. Pete, the blond girl, and a boy sitting opposite her were the only ones left.

"I'm sorry if I'm interrupting," Katherine said, sitting down across from Pete.

"No, the kids were keeping me company. Some of them you'll meet soon anyway. Jake and Brittany will both be at the Academy this year." He turned to the two kids left. "Dr. Grant is the consultant you probably heard about." The boy looked curious, but the girl immediately nodded, and Katherine wondered what sort of things they had already heard about her.

"I'm glad to meet you both. Is this your senior year?" she asked, guessing their age.

Jake spoke for the both of them. "Yah."

She could hear the local accent in that one syllable. "Do you have plans for after graduation yet?"

"Brit's thinking University of Maine at Orono. I should be able to go right to work with Stone & Field. I've been placed with them both years up here."

"Oh, you do the vocational program; that's great. Graduating with a job lined up is a good way to start off." And it was one of the main reasons she was determined to help the school succeed. The future they were helping Jake to reach for was a much brighter one than other kids exiting foster care would have. "Will you be moving here, too?"

"Yah, or nearby. Still working that stuff out." The look he gave the girl across the table from him made it obvious what they were working out. They were on two separate paths to adulthood but clearly wanted to stay together. That was going to be a serious challenge.

"Brittany!" she heard a woman half-shout from a relatively close distance. Marching up to them was none other than Erin, the house-usurper. "We're leaving . . . now," she said, and there was no mistaking her tone. Brittany gave Jake a longing glance and hopped up. With Erin's eyes now on the whole table, Katherine gave her a little smile and a finger wave. Erin's mouth tightened slightly, and she nodded her head once, more to Pete than anyone else.

"She still don't like you," Pete said after Brittany and Erin had gone.

"No kidding," Katherine said

"You're not on the 'Erin Sullivan approval list' either, huh?" Jake asked, looking amused.

"Slight misunderstanding," Katherine admitted. "Nothing, really."

"She'll come around . . . give her time," Pete said, but it was unclear if he was speaking to Katherine or Jake. At least now she knew the reason for Brittany giving her that odd look. No telling what Erin had told her daughter about her.

"So, Stone & Field." Katherine decided to change the subject. "Masonry?"

"Close," Jake said. "It's construction, mostly residential. I've been learning as many trades as I can. The owner wants a go-to kind of guy he can get out to a site and handle anything. I'm going to stick with electric and get my license, though, since that pays the most."

"Smart plan."

"Hope so. We'll see." Jake stood and grabbed his plate. "I'm headed out. I want to stock up on those brownies I spotted."

"Better run, then." Katherine pointed to her own. "I got one of the last ones." Jake did just that, getting up and jogging over to the dessert table. Pete turned to her as soon as Jake was gone.

"Okay, now that we're on our own, what did he do?"

"What did who do?"

"Mac."

"Oh, that was . . ." Was that? It wasn't all Mac's fault. Once again her temper had gotten the better of her. She wasn't a slow-to-anger kind of girl and, admittedly, she could hold a mean grudge.

"Mac being Mac, I suppose?" Pete asked, and Katherine knew that wasn't fair.

"Me being me. He has a knack for irritating me, Pete. No worries. It's not like we have to work together or anything."

"Huh. Anyway . . . you ready? The sun is almost down, and the mosquitoes are feeding." He swatted the side of his neck as if to emphasize his point. She stood up and gathered her things. He peeked into the basket. "You've got a ton of tomatoes in there."

"Dinner for tomorrow: tomato pie." She was excited to make one since she hadn't had the opportunity in a while. It was only good with summer tomatoes. It would also be huge, more than she'd need. "Hey, why don't you come over? I can pay you back for lunch today. The recipe I have is three generations old. You'll love it."

"Sounds . . . interesting." He made a face.

"It's delicious, and it beats the heck out of boiled meat and potatoes. These tomatoes are so fresh you can see they were picked today, and that means they will taste out-of-this-world good. I've got fresh basil as well, and onions. Seriously, it's going to be transcendent." She wasn't sure exactly why she was twisting Pete's arm, but she felt like it would be nicer to have company than not.

"Oh well, transcendent–then how can I say no?"

The ride home was quiet. Either they both were in a reflective mood or it was a food coma. As they neared the cabin she heard Pete say, "Now, what is that?" She looked up, and sitting on the porch beside the front door was a rocking chair. *Rats.* It was the chair from the market, the one she'd forgotten all about. A wave of guilt ran through her at the sight of it, and she remembered how nice Mac had been to buy it and what a jerk she'd ended up being in return.

"That, Pete, would be Mac's rocking chair, or rather, the one he bought for me before we had dinner, he ticked me off, and I stormed off."

"Well . . ." Pete didn't seem to have an answer for that. Katherine decided to simply let it alone.

"I really appreciate the ride home, and all of your help. I really do, but promise me that you'll tell me if I'm asking too much. I feel bad having you chauffeur me all over town and fix up the cabin on top of all your other responsibilities."

"I'm a semi-retired widower, Katherine. I think I can handle giving you a few rides and buying a power strip. It's nice to have someone to do things for. Keeps me young."

"You can't be that old. What are you, like sixty?"

"Sixty-four. But I need a diversion. If my Rebecca was still here, I would have driven her nuts by now."

"Was that your wife?" she kept her voice soft.

"Yes, lost her a year ago. She had MS. Struggled with it for years. She was pretty young to go like that, only fifty-seven. That's a disease that takes it out of you, though."

"I'm so sorry, Pete."

"The last year was bad, so I went to part-time with the wardens, and I've stayed that way, so now I have all these extra hours and nothing to do with them. My daughters aren't near enough to take up my time, although they call me five times a week to check up on me and ask what I'm eating. It's sweet, but annoying."

"Well then, I'm not going to feel guilty for monopolizing your time. I'll see you tomorrow." She said goodnight and headed into her house, tugging the rocking chair in behind her. Mac had left it on the porch with no note or anything, so maybe this was his non-verbal attempt at an apology, or maybe a non-verbal 'see ya later'. "Or maybe he didn't want it in his truck, you moron," she said aloud. Sometimes her ability to overthink things was truly stunning.

Katherine put her purchases from the market away and then dug out a quilt she'd brought with her that would look great draped over the rocking chair. Once she had it in place, she grabbed a book and settled in. Perfect. The cabin had begun to feel like home, and with each new person she met, Sweet River was growing on her.

CHAPTER SEVEN

ON MONDAY MORNING, KATHERINE TOOK AS long a shower as she dared with the cabin's limited hot water. She'd had a restless night up on the 'shelf'. The bed was comfortable; it was her head that was working against her. Sunday had been peaceful and, although she wasn't ready to brave church, she did read a few chapters in the Bible and attempted to have a quiet time. Her head wouldn't shut up, though; hard to hear God's voice with all that noise. Part of it was stress over the job . . . the beginning was always stressful. Once she started the actual work she'd be fine.

After enjoying the heat and steam as long as possible, she stood inside the closet in a towel and tried to pick out an outfit that would be perfect for her official first day. It was going to be eighty degrees, so she went with a sleeveless dress in navy blue, with a thin red belt at the waist. It was a 'fit and flare' sort of dress that flattered her figure and made her feel confident. The sandals she chose to go with it were perfect, and they'd give her an additional three inches. It was one of her tenets of fashion - height was a confidence-booster.

She took her hair dryer into the kitchen since there wasn't an outlet in the bathroom. Drying it always took an age because her hair was both long and thick. Her sisters frequently told her how lucky she was to have hair like that, but they weren't the ones standing with their arms over their head, trying to blow it dry for thirty minutes. About halfway through, she heard a weird noise and felt a shock of electricity hit her palm. She dropped the dryer with a shriek and jumped back.

She grabbed a pot holder and yanked the cord out of the outlet. The dryer was off, but she was afraid it might burst into flames. She didn't smell any smoke, but right above the outlet on the kitchen wall she saw a smudge of brown as if the charge had gone up into the wall. Scrambling for her cell she called for help. "Pete," she said when he answered, "this cabin tried to electrocute me. It fried my dryer, shocked my hand, and there's a scorch mark on the wall. I'm not sure if something behind there is on fire or what. Can you come help me? I don't want to call the fire department if this is no big deal, and I can't tell if it is."

"Help will be right there. Don't touch anything," he said, his voice calm and collected as if he answered calls from distressed women about possible fires every day. After Pete hung up, Katherine stood against the far wall and watched the outlet, waiting for smoke or flames to shoot out. It was only a few minutes until she heard someone running up her front steps, but it wasn't Pete banging on her door; it was Mac.

"Where's the fire?" he asked, panting slightly when she opened the door. Katherine was so thrown by his appearance that she failed to answer. He was in jeans and a white undershirt with his feet stuffed into a pair of old boots. His hair was wet like he'd barely finished a shower. He didn't look like Captain MacAlister. He looked like someone utterly different, and she stood in shock as a sudden rush of attraction swamped her.

"Fire?" she asked.

"You called Pete and said you had a fire."

"Oh! No, it's the outlet." She pointed to the wall. "I was drying my hair and it shocked me, then I heard a pop, and now there's this little scorch mark on the wall. I was worried there might be a fire in the wall or something."

Mac immediately looked relieved. He walked into the kitchen and set down the fire extinguisher she'd only now noticed he was carrying. After taking a look at the wall and the outlet, he turned back to her, an amused look on his face. "Not a scorch," he said, taking a paper towel, wetting it at the sink, and then wiping the wall over the outlet, erasing the smudge. "Chocolate," he said. Looks like you might have a heavy hand with the Hershey's syrup."

She huffed out a relieved breath; apparently she'd missed a spot when cleaning up from cocoa the other night. Now she looked like an idiot.

"Why were you drying your hair in the kitchen?" he asked, cocking his head and looking at her like she was a half-insane, half-errant toddler.

"Had to; there's no outlet in the bathroom," she explained.

"On the wall, right side of the mirror," he said calmly.

"What?"

"C'mere." He took her by the elbow, towing her into the bathroom. Standing next to her in the still-steamy room he pointed out the outlet—a modern-looking one—installed on the wall next to and slightly behind the large mirror.

"How did I miss that?"

"I'm guessing you couldn't see it in the fog," He waved a hand in the still-steamy room. His tone had a good deal of the disapproving policeman in it now, and despite the fact that he had clearly rushed out there to help her and that he'd found her another working outlet, her temper flared.

He continued as though nothing were amiss. "That's another thing; use the exhaust fan. There's no other way to get the steam out since there's no window in here, and the wood will rot." He pointed behind the door, where there was a switch for the fan she'd also missed.

"Well, thank you very much, Captain." She felt like a moron, and that alone added more ice to her tone than was reasonable. "I'll get back to drying my hair, and you can get back to...whatever it was you were doing. I'm very sorry to have taken up your time."

"I'm checking that outlet before I go." His tone made clear

there would be no arguing, not that she would. She turned her back on him and started drying her hair again, waiting for him to go away, knowing full well that she was being a brat, but unable to stop herself. She was nervous about her first day, and getting shocked hadn't helped. Being around Mac wasn't helping either.

A few minutes later she decided that her hair was as dry as it was going to get. She left it down and slid on a headband to keep it out of her face. After applying minimal makeup, she went into the kitchen to check on Mac. He leaned a hip on the counter, legs stretched out in front of him, feet crossed at the ankles as if he owned the place. Then again, he did, so she supposed he had a right to make himself comfortable.

He watched her walk in, and she didn't miss the frank appreciation in his expression.

Katherine was used to being considered attractive, minus her scar, but somehow it felt different seeing that expression on his face.

He ceased his perusal. "Pete's here. I fixed the outlet, so you're all set. He's out at his truck, getting the surge protector you asked him to pick up. He's going to install the closet pole you asked for as well."

"Great! Pete is now officially my favorite human on the planet," she said brightly.

Mac had no comment. He pushed off the counter to stand upright and head for the door.

It seemed like he was angry, although she had no idea why. *Oh, duh,* she thought. She was gushing over Pete bringing her a surge protector after Mac had rushed over to fight a fire for her, and she didn't even thank him. "Thank you, Captain MacAlister. I appreciate you coming by," she said with as much genuine feeling as she could muster.

Mac turned around and sighed. "It's Mac, Kate. Can we forget about the Captain MacAlister bit?"

She was being a jerk again, a big one, considering all he had done for her. "I'm sorry, Mac," she said, looking down at her toes. "I really do appreciate you coming out here and helping me."

For a moment he didn't answer, and when she finally looked up he said, "You're welcome, Kate," with a smile so slight she wondered if it wasn't her imagination, then he turned back to the door and left. She watched him get into his truck as Pete walked up the steps.

"All ready for your first day?" Pete's jovial tone greeted her when she opened the door. "It's almost eight now."

"What?" She bolted over to where she had her phone plugged in and saw that he was right; she'd completely lost track of time, "Pete can I give you my key and you can lock up when you're done?"

"Sure thing. I'll drop it off at the school later."

"Thank you!" she shouted to him as she walked out and jogged to her car.

Four hours later she was sitting at her desk, laptop out, finishing up her notes from the three back-to-back meetings she had completed; one with the full board, one with the new teachers, one with the returning teachers. There was trouble in Sweet River. Trouble with a capital T. She got up from her desk and opened the door of the office. "Elaine?"

Elaine came almost immediately, sliding into the office and pointedly shutting the door before sitting down.

Katherine felt her stomach sink. She'd scheduled two more

meetings today, one with Elaine to give her background on the recent changes at the school, and the last one of the day with Stephanie Campbell, the director with whom she still hadn't exchanged more than two words.

Katherine nodded to the shut door. "Can I assume I'm about to hear something I'm not going to like?"

"Nature of my job." Elaine's lips lifted momentarily, and then she launched into it. "I know you said you wanted background on the recent changes. I wanted to start by saying that Stephanie Campbell is a powerful and influential resident of this town. Her husband is a deacon at the church. Her sister is on the town council. Her mom runs the post office."

"Wow."

"Yep. You got the picture." Elaine sat back and crossed her legs. "When Stephanie was appointed director, she made some pretty big changes with staff, and she did that by hiring friends and family. The athletics director is her brother-in-law. The custodian was replaced by a cleaning company her husband's best friend owns. Mr. Franks, Miss Quinn, and Miss Fini are all children of her friends."

"How is that even possible? It's against the school's own guidelines."

"The board never interviews candidates themselves; they simply approve whomever she says is best for the job. The first two went by without much comment, but by the time they were approving the third and the fourth it was too late to argue."

"But they must have addressed it."

"Oh yes. Now all interviews have to be with both the director and the board. She also has to submit to them a list of candidates, and all open positions now have to be advertised in at least three outlets, and the ads have to run for a set number of weeks."

"So they fixed that, but we still have her hires."

"The teachers are fine, but that cleaning company is not. The offices are dirty, and under their contract they don't have to clean the dormitories other than emptying the dumpster once a week, so the boarding students and the two couples that act as dorm parents have been stuck doing their own cleaning for the last two years."

"What?" Katherine was stunned. No reputable school would do this. Clean their own rooms, sure. Bus their own tables in the cafeteria, of course, but clean their bathrooms, their common areas—no.

"I knew you wouldn't like that. I'm not sure the board even knows, and I never felt it was my place to point that out. The dorm parents are such sweet spirits, they never questioned it. They look on this work as their mission field, not a job, so they just dealt with it. The kids know it's not right, though. And it's hard for them to keep up with homework, extra-curricular duties, and their apprenticeships while also doing some pretty heavy cleaning. I mean, they have to do the dishes in the cafeteria on the weekends because there's no kitchen staff on Saturday and Sunday. The dorm parents cook, the kids clean."

"If they were compensated for it . . ."

"Right, my daughter cleaned her dorm's bathrooms in college as part of her student employment. That's one thing, but that's not what's happening here. They don't get any compensation at all. Stephanie explained . . ." Elaine's face grew troubled, and Katherine knew they were about to walk that line. "She said the students who are funded through the state's foster program weren't the same as the tuition students, and we needed to be sure everyone, especially them, understood that."

Katherine gasped. She couldn't help it. This was almost unbelievable. "Did anyone else hear this? Was this only said to you?"

"It was just to me. I don't know if she really meant it like that, and I didn't want to say anything because Stephanie is a very nice person. She does a lot of volunteer . . ."

"That is completely irrelevant," Katherine interrupted with a wave of her hand. She hadn't meant to interrupt, but she didn't want to hear any excuses for treating kids whose status was entirely out of their control as second-class citizens. She caught a look at Elaine's face and knew she needed to be more careful in how she reacted.

"Thank you for telling me this. My first recommendation, hopefully to be implemented before the students get here this weekend, will be to change the terms of that contract or hire a custodian for the dorms. We're going to need a weekend kitchen crew. We can't have students operating a kitchen, even to clean. The liability... If you could get together names of local folks who might be interested in the job, let me know."

Elaine nodded, but she looked worried.

"Please don't think you've done the wrong thing in telling me about this."

"I want to be sure that we're doing the correct thing for the school. I've worked here for twenty years. It's important to me that we do things right."

"And we'll make things right, I promise." Katherine didn't know if she really had the authority to make that promise, but she was definitely going to try.

When the meeting was over she asked Elaine to keep what they had said confidential and headed to the director's office. It wasn't located with the rest of administration. The director's office was its own suite on the far end of the building, in what looked like it was once a conservatory. Katherine knocked on the door and heard Stephanie call for her to enter.

When she'd set up the meeting, the director had insisted she was far too busy to go down to the admin office and asked for Katherine to meet in hers. It was a power play, but Katherine didn't mind. If Stephanie needed to feel in control, fine. Walking into the office, she couldn't help but admire the beauty. One wall was made up of the school-building's brick exterior, and the other three were short brick walls with huge, nineteenth-century windows topped by a copper roof. It was an impressive space. It was also wasted on an office. It should be a study hall or even a science classroom.

The director's desk stood at the far end, next to a small wood stove vented through the roof. The cement floor was covered by rich-looking carpets, and a seating area was arranged in the middle, with four chairs surrounding a round table. A section of the brick wall had a floor-to-ceiling book case, which was surprisingly empty. It had a few pictures, trophies, and school yearbooks, but little else.

"You have a great office." Katherine smiled as she said it, crossing the ten feet from the door to Stephanie's desk.

"It's adequate to my needs." Stephanie remained seated and did not offer Katherine a seat, but she took one in front of the large desk anyway. The director was a tall woman, probably five-ten at least, with gorgeous, long black hair beginning to gray. She wore little more than lipstick and mascara, but with her porcelain complexion, Katherine imagined she rarely had the need to wear much makeup. She was an attractive woman hitting middle age with grace.

Stephanie looked up from her computer, sat back a bit, and folded her hands on the desk in front of her. "I can imagine that you're here to assess me."

If Katherine had any doubts about Stephanie's feeling towards having an educational consultant called in to her school, they were put to rest with both her statement and the tone in which it was said. "I'm not here to assess anyone."

Stephanie raised an eyebrow at this.

Katherine tried to give her a reassuring smile. "I'm here to observe and then develop a strategy for addressing the concerns both the parents and the state have raised. The enrollment numbers are concerning, but the dropout rate amongst the vocational students was the real red flag that changes are needed."

"Six students dropping out shouldn't have raised any alarm with the state. These kids are at risk for dropping out. They're not regular kids. We shouldn't be criticized when they fail. We're one of the only schools that will even take them on." Stephanie had a good point, but the wrong end of it.

"Right, but that's the thing. They're here so they won't drop out, and they didn't with any kind of regularity until last year."

"That's not my fault."

Katherine tried not to be annoyed by Stephanie's attitude. "No one's saying it is. That's the reason I've been hired. I'm going to look at the program from every angle. We'll figure out what's working and what's not and come up with a plan. This first week is just for evaluation. I want to work with you, not against you. In situations where the state is looking so closely at how their money is being spent we need—"

"That's why we should end the vocational program and stick with the day students. We don't need the state breathing down our necks." Stephanie sat forward, a blush of color on her cheeks now. "I've about had it with the state questioning what we do. We're a religious institution; the way they treat us is terrible, and I can't help but wonder if it's because of our faith. They've done nothing but criticize and scold us for months now, because their foster kids can't hack a rigorous educational environment." She stabbed at the desk with a long, tapered finger, her face full of feeling. "Their failure to educate these children is not our problem. When we get them they're barely up to the work. Do you know how hard it is dealing with these kids? They're lazy, disrespectful, and foul-mouthed. These are not kids we would normally admit."

Katherine buried her knee-jerk reaction to Stephanie's frustrated words. This wasn't an easy program to run, to be sure, which is why every administrator needed to be careful not to build a resentful attitude towards the challenging students. Responding carefully, she said, "I think you probably know that's not really true."

Stephanie blinked and then sat back, maybe realizing she'd gone too far.

Katherine continued. "The state-supported students aren't

here because they're lazy or ignorant. They get into the program by showing how hard they work. From day one they have a heavier course-load than the day students because of their internships and apprenticeships. They've already proven they can work, so the school needs to support them."

"We do."

"By giving them additional tasks like cleaning their own dorm?"

"That's teaching them self-reliance and self-discipline. It's a simple fact that if you hand someone housing they don't respect it. If you make them take care of that housing, they will."

"They aren't being handed anything for free. Their housing is paid for."

"Not by them."

"No, because they don't have parents to do it." She felt her temper rising and knew she had to keep it in check, or she and Stephanie would end up in a shouting match. "The state is acting as their defacto parent."

"I'm sorry, but I do not believe it's the same. The state can't parent anyone. The state won't encourage them or hold them accountable. We have to. These students need a more rigorous and regimented schedule or they will fail."

"They *are* failing, Stephanie. You had six kids drop out last year when your program only holds fifty. That dropout rate is stunning."

"It's not a true dropout rate; they go back to public school."

"Perhaps, but it's still your school failing those students; not those students failing out of your school."

Stephanie had no answer. Her face was a stone wall.

Katherine knew she wasn't getting it, and unless a miracle occurred, Stephanie might end up being impossible to work with. "You and I clearly do not agree on this one particular point, so let's set it aside. I'm going to take a close look at everything the school offers, and if there's a good reason to terminate the vocational program, I'll recommend that. My goal is exactly what my contract says it is: to return this school to optimum enrollment and efficacy."

"Then I don't see a problem." Stephanie said it like she definitely saw a problem, but Katherine wasn't in the mood for another throw-down.

"I'll need to meet with your department heads next. If you don't mind, I'll start that tomorrow, and we'll meet again on Friday."

"My calendar is very tight."

"No problem. I'm sure you have it up to date on the server so I'll check it before I send you a meeting invite. Thanks for your time today, Stephanie." She stood and waited for Stephanie to do the same, or offer a handshake or . . . Instead, Stephanie sat like a rock, so Katherine gave her a nod and headed out. There was no doubt in her mind that there were rough waters ahead. So much for her simple assignment.

CHAPTER EIGHT

THE REST OF THE WEEK FLEW by with preparations for the return of the students. On Saturday, the boarding students began trickling in. They had all weekend to come since they would be living on campus and needed time to get settled in. Their dorm parents were ready with getting-to-know-you activities and campfire-style meetings at night that Katherine had the chance to sit in on. She'd always imagined summer camp would be like that, surrounded by kids the same age, toasting marshmallows, and singing songs. Her parents had thought summer camp a bit plebian, so she hadn't been allowed to go. They got her and her sisters memberships to the club instead, and they spent their summers swimming, playing tennis, and riding. Not terrible, but not this kind of freedom to get to know their peers, that's for sure.

Sunday came and Katherine got ready for church, since Pete had talked her into it as an easy way to meet parents and the members of church who supported the school. She spent an hour getting ready, trying to be sure her outfit looked appropriate. The last time she'd stepped foot in a church had been for a christening, and that was at least two years ago. Attending a church service was courting a panic attack. "Why did I agree to this?" she asked her reflection. The answer was already in her head, had been there all morning. She wanted to reconnect with God; she just wasn't so sure about his people. "Pete's God's people. You like Pete. He isn't a judgmental hypocrite out to hurt you. They won't be either. They don't even know you." Pep talk complete, she picked up her purse and waited for Pete to arrive.

It was a good thing he was driving today since she couldn't find her calm. She tried to sit still as they drove to church, but completely failed. Pete finally said, "You're so jumpy you're almost shaking the dang vehicle apart. What's up, Katie?"

"I have not been inside a church for anything other than a wedding, funeral, or christening in ten years." Pete turned to her, looking stunned. An uncomfortable silence fell, and Katherine sort of giggled. "Speechless, huh?"

"Well . . . There were a number of years I didn't go either. Thought I could be a Christian on my own and worship God in his temple."

Katherine gave him a puzzled look.

He clarified. "The woods. Sometimes in nature you can feel closer to God. Hear His voice a bit better."

"God stopped speaking to me a long time ago. It doesn't mean I don't still love Him. It doesn't mean I don't still pray. I just haven't heard His voice in a long time."

"Best cure for that is church."

She made a scoffing noise.

He smiled. "We don't have time to get into it since the parking lot is right here." He pulled his Jeep into a little dirt lot and parked under a large pine tree next to a minivan. Taking the key out of the ignition, he shifted in his seat to face her. "I know two things about you, Katherine Grant. The first is that you have a heart the size of the state of Maine. I've heard all about how you treat the staff and the kids."

She raised an eyebrow at this.

"Elaine," he explained. "The second thing is that you're hard as stone."

Katherine jerked back.

"As warm and funny as you can be, you've got a kind of sharpness to you, and it's pretty clear you're in the habit of pushing people away."

Katherine had no argument since he was completely correct.

"You're protecting yourself. We all do it, but you've made a career of it." She nodded, unable to say a word. "I'm not going to ask you to tell me about it today. When you're ready you can tell me what it is and why stepping inside a church makes it worse. Don't worry that I'm gonna run my mouth, either. I know something about deep cuts and what it takes to heal them." His eyes lingered on her scar for a second before he opened the door and climbed out.

She should be all kinds of freaked out by his perception. Pete wasn't buying any of her usual spin. He seemed to see right through the happy, successful, professional façade she showed the world. That should be troubling, but instead it felt freeing and . . . safe. She got out of the truck and stood with him on the sidewalk. "Okay, Pete, if you're done with the words of wisdom thing, let's get this over with," she said, looking up at the church.

He chuckled. "You're gonna love it."

The Calvary Bible Church was not what she was expecting. The building looked like every other New England church she'd been in, and the order of service was pretty familiar, but the people were far more humble or down-to-earth or . . . she didn't really know what exactly it was; they simply seemed real. Not fake or hypocritical. Erin was there and ignored her, as did Stephanie Campbell and her husband, but the others seemed to genuinely care that she had come. They went out of their way to introduce themselves, smiling like they meant it.

The service started with praise songs, and they were different than the ones she was used to. Most of the time praise songs were not her thing. They sounded like bad pop to her, since "baby" could be substituted for "Jesus", and it would be a love song. The words in that morning's songs were weightier. There were times she'd have to stop singing because she found her throat closing with emotion.

The hymns were classics; the same ones she'd sung for years at her old church. By the time they were singing the final hymn, she was feeling less self-conscious and sang it like she meant it. It was "For the Beauty of the Earth," one of her favorites. As they sang the final verse, someone standing two rows ahead of her turned around. It was Mac. He was dressed in civilian clothes; nice dress trousers with an Oxford-style button-down shirt and tie. Catching her eye, he gave her a smile before turning back around. She stuttered over the words and caught back up in time to sing 'Amen'. She could practically feel Pete smirking next to her.

Afterwards, she waited outside in the sunshine as Pete hung around to catch up with a few people he knew. She had pretty much hit the wall and needed time to recover from all the polite smiling and hand-shaking. At the edge of the sidewalk there was a little bench overlooking the town green, so she headed there. As she walked, she was stopped in her tracks by the sight of Mac playing a game of football with boys on the green. He was still in his Sunday best, his shirtsleeves rolled up and his tie flapping a bit as he ran.

She stood and watched while they played. The boys were third through seventh grade, if her professional estimation was right; the ages when they needed to run off excess energy. He was throwing the ball to each of them in turn, calling out plays and watching while they ran left or right. One boy missed the ball twice, and was clearly headed for a meltdown when Mac jogged over to him and leaned down to speak into his ear. A minute later, the boy was running backwards and Mac threw again, a perfect arc that landed right in the boy's hands. She could see his smile from across the street.

Mac must have felt Katherine's eyes on him, because he turned around, spotting her. She gave him a little finger wave, feeling her cheeks get hot for some reason. Instead of returning her wave and going about his business, he chucked the ball to one of the older kids and jogged up to meet her. *Rats.*

"Waiting for Pete?" he guessed when he had closed the last

few feet to stand near her.

"Yes. He's chatting with half the population of Sweet River so I'm just . . . hanging . . . here." *Stupid.* Why couldn't she have left it at yes? "Are you coaching?"

"No, simply tossing the ball around. The boys tend to hang around after church ends, and I've found it's better to distract them with something like football, since the alternative is me or one of the deputies chasing them and their skateboards off the library steps or the convenience store stoop . . ."

"Or the school's porch. I'm familiar with the exploits of unoccupied youth."

Mac laughed a little, and they lapsed into a mostly comfortable silence. Katherine was thinking of something to say to break it when he raised a hand to wave at someone across the street. A glint of silver caught her eye. Looking closer, she saw a bracelet on his wrist. It was so unusual that she had to have a closer look.

She reached forward and caught his wrist on the way down. "How beautiful!" She stepped closer to him, her head bent over his arm, turning his wrist so she could see the details. It was several braided black leather cords wrapped with a wide, smooth piece of gleaming silver twisted around them as a clasp. In the center of the silver was what looked like a Celtic cross. "Is this handmade?" she asked.

Looking up, she saw that Mac was staring down at her a little bemused, his eyes warm. It dawned on her that she had grabbed his arm and that was perhaps the tiniest bit presumptuous. Besides, she didn't want him to think she was hitting on him. She dropped it and purposely linked her hands behind her. "Sorry, that was a bit rude." She laughed a little. "I love silver jewelry, as you can probably tell." *I am a moron*, she thought.

He didn't seem to mind, though. He hadn't moved away and his eyes were still fixed on her, a small smile developing on his lips.

"You would not believe the sheer number of pieces I own. Yours is quite exceptional, though."

"It's Erin's, or rather, it's her work. Birthday present," he said simply.

"Oh." And Katherine began to put two and two together. They didn't appear to be a couple, but clearly Erin had marked her turf. That was not a bracelet you'd give to a man with whom you wanted to be friends. It was lovingly done. She took an unconscious step back. "Erin is incredibly talented. Does she do it for a living or only for friends?"

"If she had the time, I think she could make it a living, but she's got a lot on her plate."

"Well, you should encourage her, because if the rest of her work is that stunning she should be doing it full-time."

"She gets by okay as a personal trainer. She's a single mom so her full time is for her kids," Mac said, as if that was obvious.

Katherine wondered if he was the sort of man who believed motherhood was the highest calling women could aspire to, and that anything else was a letdown, second-best, or a waste. That would be disappointing, since, like plenty of other women, Katherine hadn't had the chance to be a mom and never would. "What's wrong with sharing some of her focus on her God-given talent and maybe securing a reliable income as well?" she argued. "Since she's clearly gifted, she just needs the infrastructure and support. There are organizations that band artists together to do exactly that. There are a number that cater to women particularly, and with their help she could set up a studio, get a small business loan to cover materials, secure a website, and even buy health insurance."

Mac was staring at her, and she couldn't figure out if it was in disapproval or not. "What?" she asked.

"Do you always do that?"

"Sorry?"

"You're arguing rather passionately for a cause that's not yours and a person you don't know. I gotta ask, why do you need to win every argument?"

Normally she liked a healthy debate with a person of lively intelligence. For all of Mac's stoic authority, he was just that — intelligent. But, she found that he hit too hard where she was too soft. "Well, that was fun, but I think I've had enough sparring with you, Captain." She started to walk away, backwards. "I'm going over to that little bench there and wait for Pete. You have a nice day." She turned on her heel and walked down to the bench and sat down, resolutely not looking at Mac as he walked back to the green and his game of football.

Remorse trickled in as her anger faded. Twice now she'd walked away from him like a brat. He might have said it in a jerky way, but he hadn't been wrong. She did want to win every argument. Chancing a quick look across the street, she spotted Mac playing with the kids again. What was it about the man that brought out the worst in her? Or maybe she brought out the worst in him, and it spiraled downward from there.

Deciding to take advantage of the quiet, she let her eyes close. She wanted her brain to fall silent and to listen for the still, small voice. The whole purpose in coming to church was to feel better, not worse. What she longed to feel was free. She wanted to feel like she did before her life went off the rails, before she'd shut out the world, before she'd thrown herself into her work and left behind everything else that mattered.

The minutes passed as she listened to the light sounds all around her, and she forgot about Captain MacAlister, forgot about the school, forgot about her worries. The heat of the sun and the gentle breeze lulled her into a kind of doze as she waited for the voice to speak to her. But exactly like at home when she sat on the beach at sunrise waiting for Him, God was silent.

CHAPTER NINE

"YOU'VE GOT TO READ THIS," HEATHER'S voice sounded over the speakerphone. Until a minute ago, they'd been running through the schedule for the first week of school. "It's the Sweet River Lowdown. It's a blog run by someone in town – anonymous. Take a look, I sent you the link."

Katherine heard the ping of an incoming email, opened it, and hit the link. It pulled up a blog that was pretty basic in nature, mostly text with a few pictures. However, instead of the usual stuff a town website would have, it was nothing but a gossip rag, a sort of rural version of *The New York Post*'s Page 6. It had a few pictures from the Saturday picnic, including one of her and Mac. They were sitting together at the picnic table. Katherine was looking out over the crowd, but Mac was looking at her. The text along with the picture was a bit distressing.

Sweet River Lowdown

The Firehouse Fundraiser was a huge success, with $7,000 raised for the new station. And if you weren't there we'll let you in on the hot news item. That would be the arrival of Dr. Katherine Grant, a consultant hired by Sweet River Christian Academy to fix what ails them. Dr. Grant hails from Bristol, RI, and is the daughter of the artist Lauren Gibson and former RI District Attorney Philip Weston Grant, who famously prosecuted Vinnie 'The Heat' Amoretti before retiring. Dr. Grant did her undergrad at NYU Steinhardt and her doctorate at Boston College. She has written several books on education and is a frequent guest on cable news programs.

And that's all very nice, but here's the good stuff. She's single, and apparently she has already caught the eye of the most eligible and difficult-to-land Captain MacAlister. Word is that Dr. Grant is renting a cabin from him, and from the looks of their cozy dinner at the picnic, things are progressing nicely. Way to be the early bird, Mac!

"Are you kidding me?" Katherine asked Heather.

"Nope. I've read through the archive, and it's full of stuff like this. In case you were wondering, 'Captain MacAlister'—who you didn't mention, by way—hasn't been linked with anyone in the past other than Erin Sullivan, but that was a while ago, and the item was making a bit of noise about the fact that he helped her buy a car."

"This place is . . ."

"Mayberry, agreed. But why did I not get the scoop from you on the good captain?"

She should have realized that Heather, with her research superpowers, would eventually figure out that there *was* a Mac. While he annoyed the stuffing out of her, Katherine was also starting to, sort of, find him attractive; maybe if he weren't so annoying, she'd want to spend time with him. Heather would make much of this since she hadn't found anyone attractive or annoying in probably a decade.

"There is no scoop. He's the owner of the cabin, and he was there at the town picnic. He bought me—well, bought the cabin a rocking chair I said I liked, and then we ate together. Pretty much end of story."

"Why don't I believe you?"

"Because you're a romantic at heart. Heather, you know I'm not up here for that."

"Yes, but if you happen to find love while you're there, how is that a bad thing?"

"Love is messy, Heather, and, to be honest, I have no faith in it."

"Faith in love with the little 'l', now that would be dumb, but faith in God is faith in Love with the big 'L'. Don't go slamming any doors, okay?"

"Yes, ma'am," Katherine said grumpily, and Heather mercifully let it go.

A few hours later she was done for the day and walking the half-mile from her cabin to Pete's house for dinner. He'd caught a salmon and offered to grill it if she took care of the rest. She felt a bit like Little Red Riding Hood, walking along the side of the road with a basket full of salad, bread, and a blueberry pie. The walk wasn't a long one, and when she was almost there, a large pickup truck slowed to a stop next to her and the window rolled down. Mac's voice floated out through the window.

"Where are you headed?"

"Pete's . . . for dinner."

"It's nearly sundown." His voice was stern. "If you're planning on walking back, you should be wearing something reflective and carrying a flashlight." His expression made it clear he wasn't joking. He really did want her to find something reflective to wear. *This guy* . . . she thought and managed not to roll her eyes at him.

"Relax, 'Captain Safety'. I've been crossing the street on my own for a long time. I think I can handle the half-mile home without getting hit by a car."

Mac didn't seem to appreciate her sense of humor. His eyes narrowed, and his jaw tightened.

She could tell that he wanted to start in on a lecture, and she was not in the mood to hear it. "If you're so worried about picking my carcass off the side of the road, I'll ask Pete for a ride home. Okay?"

Instead of looking happy she gave in, he seemed angry. With a shove, he put his truck into gear. "Good night, Kate." He nodded his head at her and drove off.

Katherine walked the rest of the way to Pete's. *Great.* He was standing on his porch, probably watching the whole thing.

"What exactly is his deal?" she asked when she was close enough.

"Well, today it would be the job, not the man. Doug Carter had a heart attack. Mac was first on the scene. He was alone, administering CPR, waiting for the EMTs to get there, with Doug's wife in hysterics. When they finally got there, it was too late." Pete's matter-of-fact tone took not one iota of tragedy out of what he'd shared.

Katherine didn't know the Carters, but she could only imagine what it would have been like for Mac to work desperately to save a man's life with his wife looking on. And failing.

"That's . . . I don't know what to say." But she was sorry she'd mouthed off to him as usual and not taken a second to try to understand him. She thought of herself as an empathetic person, but she had given not one thought to Mac's feelings. Not even once. It was an uncomfortable recognition of yet another of her faults, and she quickly said a silent prayer that God would be with him and give him comfort.

"It's the hard part of the job. Though, if anybody was the right person to be there, it was him. He's good with people." He paused. "Most people."

Katherine gave him a look, but he added, "C'mon back. I've got the grill going."

Pete led her through his house. He had decorated it in 'Modern Log' – log lamps, log tables, log chairs – but it was a comfortable space since he'd also added plenty of soft furniture and an overstuffed recliner in his living room. In his backyard he had a table and chairs set up on a patio. The yard was beautiful, a gentle slope that ended in a meadow with the forest beyond. He explained that the meadow stretched all the way to Mac's property, and that a wide, flat trail ran through it. He showed her the map; that same trail ran right past her house. "Is it good for running?"

"It's okay, but there are rough stretches. Mac takes his horses over that trail, and with how careful he is, I imagine it has to be in good shape, or he'd never let them put a hoof on it. Speaking of which, I was surprised you said yes to dinner tonight; I expected you to have plans. What with you juggling the affections of Sweet River's bachelors."

Fighting a smile, he pulled out a printed page that looked like the Sweet River Lowdown. She snatched it out of his hands and saw a picture of her with Dr. Dan Connors, the church pastor. Connors had barely made any impression on her at all. They'd had a ten-minute conversation about the vespers program he did at the school and his position as volunteer basketball coach—that was it. The picture was from their meeting when he'd shaken her hand and, out of context, it looked cozy.

"For pity's sake, how did they even get this shot?" She read the caption, dread settling in her stomach. She couldn't tell if it was because gossip made her life difficult and her soul hurt, or if she was dreading what Mac would think when he read it.

Drs. Katherine Grant & Daniel Connors share a special moment

Well, it looks like our preacher may be stealing a march on our favorite lawman. It wouldn't be a bad match, since they're both so brainy, but we doubt that Dr. Grant would want to be a pastor's wife. We find ourselves still rooting for Mac. Besides, we all know who pines for Dr. Connors.

"I cannot believe this," she said in dismay.

"Oh, it's in fun, nothing to be worried about. Of course, that picture does make it look like there's something happening there. Is there?" Pete asked.

"No way," she said emphatically. "I mean, he's a nice guy, but . . . no. Second of all, he was being friendly. He wasn't making a move. Whoever took that picture . . . this kind of press is the last thing I need."

"Hey, don't worry about it. Last month they had a picture of one of the new deputies and one of Maria's waitresses. They probably picked you since you're new and therefore news. I only have a copy of it because the dispatcher up at the station – Annie – she got a hoot out of teasing Mac with it. She gave him grief over that first post about the two of you as well."

"Ugh, I bet that did not improve his mood."

"Probably not. So . . ." She had a feeling Pete was warming up to asking her something embarrassing. "Do you have someone at home?"

"You mean like a boyfriend?" she asked and Pete nodded. "No. To be honest," she said while dishing out the salad and bread, "I haven't had one of those in a long time."

"Has that break been as long as your church one?" She was not surprised he'd guessed it right. Pete was almost dangerously perceptive.

"Yes." She took a bite of the fish on her plate. "Pete, this is so good! I've never had fresh-caught. Wow, the difference is huge."

He smiled and let her change the subject. While the sun set they ate and talked about how it was going at the school, and then Pete told her a story about the three months he spent hiking the Appalachian Trail.

"I would never survive."

"Sure you would. You have to start small with day hikes, getting your skills up. Most people work up to it. There've been a few who strap on sneakers and hit the trail, Grandma Gatewood for one, but she was made of tough stuff. Had to be, considering she had eleven kids and survived a husband who talked with his fists.

She said she found peace in the woods. On the AT that isn't hard. Stress can't find you."

"Sounds pretty great, and I love the woods, but I'm not really outdoorsy."

"You grew up riding horses, though."

"Not the same thing as sleeping under the stars and pooping in the forest."

Pete threw his head back and laughed.

Mac pulled on the reins, bringing his horse to a halt. He could hear Pete's laugh coming over the meadow. He turned Misery for home. This ride was supposed to clear his head; instead, all he could think about was how much he'd pay to trade places with Pete. He wasn't stupid enough to think anything romantic was going on. It was the easy manner they had between them he was jealous of.

To him, Kate was sweet one moment then caustic the next. She was a trigger he kept tripping no matter how easy and careful he went. *Liar.* He hadn't been easy or careful with her. What he'd been doing was pushing her away while trying to get near all at the same time. He didn't want to be attracted to her; he didn't want to watch her like he did. A cure was what he needed, something to banish her from his thoughts, because think of her he did—daily.

Last Sunday had been the hardest day so far. Sitting in the service, he'd prayed for patience and relief. Instead, halfway through a hymn he heard a beautiful voice behind him and, turning around, he saw her singing. Of course it was her. Kate's voice was like the rest of her: attractive, appealing, and beyond his reach. A woman like her wouldn't be interested in settling down in a tiny town in the mountains of Maine. He was only wasting his time, because there was no way he was moving off the mountain. He'd found the place he felt he belonged. If she didn't feel the same, there was nothing he could do about it.

Mac nudged Misery onto the flat ATV trail, the only stretch where he dared let the horse run, and Misery opened up into a gallop. The stallion needed it, or he'd get restless and mean. Tonight Mac felt the same.

It was over dessert that Pete broached the topic again. He'd been nudging the conversation to her childhood, what it was like to grow up with a famous painter for a mom and an equally famous DA as a dad. Then he'd finally hit the question of why she was single, couching it as gently as she'd ever heard it. "Katie, you are a heck of a cook, beautiful, intelligent, and successful, so can I be rude and say that I'm surprised you're not in a relationship?"

"That's not rude, it's observant." Katherine smiled. "Besides, you gave me, like, five compliments in one sentence; how could I object?"

"Well, I'm glad you're not offended, but you didn't answer the question." They were still outside at his patio table, overlooking the meadow that was his backyard, and the last rays of the setting sun glowed in the distance. The night was growing cold but he had a fire going in a stone pit nearby, so it was almost comfortable.

Katherine sighed and tried to think of a way to answer honestly. Pete was her closest ally in town, but he'd also become her friend. He deserved the real answer, not the usual spin she gave people about how she was content in her singleness.

"I'm broken, Pete." She paused and tried to get up the courage to explain. "Let's just say that no man with any sense of self-preservation would get near me if he knew the depth of that brokenness. I'm not . . . I can't give them what they think they need." She shook her head. "I know I'm not making any sense, but a long time ago I trusted the wrong man and made a terrible mistake. Huge. And I suffered for it. The consequences of that spread, and anyone who tried to protect me or loved me in the smallest way ended up suffering with me. I'm not up to another round of that, so I steer clear of eligible men. Or I did until I got here," she said with a smile, trying to make it a joke.

Pete didn't play along. "I'm guessing you need to keep the details to yourself, and I'll respect that. But I gotta wonder what could have been so bad to make you swear off ever having love or a family or . . ."

"See this?" she interrupted, touching the scar on her face. "This is from a car accident that both saved and ruined my life." It sounded so odd to say it out loud, but it was true. The accident had almost killed her, and what had followed it was equally painful, but it had led her fiancé to abandon her, and marriage to him would've been a horrible mistake. He had proved that he was a man with no love in his heart for anyone but himself. The fact that he was a seminary graduate about to be ordained was a wretched kind of hypocrisy. These were the details that even after ten years proved too painful to share.

"You can't tell me," Pete said softly when she didn't go on to explain.

"I speak in riddles because it still hurts, and I'm still afraid of what people think of me when they hear the story. They change their minds about me, they judge me. I'm from a town not much bigger than Sweet River, and I can tell you that there were maybe ten people who didn't openly hate me by the end of it all."

"Katie," Pete admonished, "I could never hate you."

"No, of course not. Pete, you're the kind of Christian who actually believes what he says and lives his faith. You're a lot rarer than you might think. But I don't want the way you see me to change. I'd rather live in the present."

"Child, how could the way I see you change?"

"I've made big mistakes, and I've suffered for them. I know on the outside I look like I've got it together, but inside . . . I'm kind of a mess." She felt like her soul had broken into pieces, and she'd cemented them back together, but they'd never be whole again. He leaned across the table and took her hand. That simple gesture made her eyes moisten and her nose sting. She looked up at the rapidly darkening sky, trying not to burst into tears.

It was his voice, soft and low, that brought her eyes back to his. There was nothing but kindness in how he looked at her. "You know, there's a good brokenness and a bad one, too." He said it solemnly. "The good kind keeps your heart open and your pride humbled; it allows you to feel friendship for people you'd want nothing to do with otherwise. It helps you be more like Jesus and less like a sinner. But the bad kind, that's what it sounds like you mean. The bad kind keeps the hurt alive; it keeps you cautious, like a dog that's been beaten over and over. You bite the friendly hand, growl at everyone, and hide in your den."

She almost laughed. "You're not wide of the mark, but it's been a long time, Pete." She slid her hand out of his, getting a grip on her emotions again. "My hiding in a den days are behind me."

"Oh, I know you've probably let some of it go, but you're still growling. Only God fixes that kind of broken, and only when you let Him. Part of that is letting go of the pain caused by what those people did to you, or what you did to yourself. It makes you bitter, closes you off." Pete fell silent.

Katherine let those words sink in, past the pain of hearing them. They sat together in silence, watching the night close in around them as the stars came out.

"You know what's amazing, Pete?" she asked thoughtfully.

He shook his head.

"If anyone else said those things to me, I would've bitten their head off—figuratively, of course. Seriously, I would have ripped right through them and laid waste. I'm thinking you've had a bit of experience with wounded dogs."

Pete was quiet for a moment then said, a gentle kind of humor in his tone, "Had one move in a few years ago. A big ol' shepherd. Barked at everybody. He'd bite, too, if you got too close."

Katherine smiled, thinking that was a pretty fair description of Mac.

"It took a long time for him to come around – in fact, he still barks now and again."

"I think I know that dog."

"You sure do," he said with a smile.

CHAPTER TEN

KATHERINE HEARD THE PING ON HER phone, opened it, and read the email from Stephanie Campbell. It was after hours and Katherine should have known better than to look. As usual, Stephanie had sent an impertinent challenge in electronic form. She took a steadying breath and tried to rein in her impulse to reply with something scathing. She dropped the phone on the table and bent to tie her sneakers, keeping her thoughts fixed on how well things in general had been going.

She'd gotten almost immediate approval from the board to hire a weekend kitchen crew for the boarding students, as well as a custodian. The kids were thrilled and the dorm parents were relieved. It was a win all around, since it employed three locals who had been out of work for months. Elaine and the other administrative assistants were more cheerful as well. There was a feeling of optimism amongst the staff, with the exception of Stephanie; the only dark spot in what was otherwise a pretty shiny start.

At every possible opportunity, Stephanie stood in her way. It didn't matter what the hill was, so to speak, Stephanie planted her flag and went to battle. Every small change Katherine recommended, the director attempted to block. All that was nothing compared to the downright war going on over the athletics department. Bill Swift was the director and, although a nice guy and Stephanie's brother-in-law, it was looking like he was far short of competent. He was a great coach, but the budget was a disaster.

In an attempt at building some goodwill, Katherine actually let a few of the small skirmishes go, thinking she'd be able to get traction on the larger issues, but it was all for nothing. Even when Katherine willingly gave up the field, Stephanie trumpeted the victory and marshaled more forces. She'd had uncomfortable meetings with Mindy from the board of trustees, the athletics director, and two sets of parents. The woman kept forcing confrontations. Last week it was a dustup over uniforms, this week it was the annual sports banquet. The last thing Katherine wanted to do was to throw down with her, since she was still investigating the budget mess. She needed Stephanie's help in sorting it out, since Swift was proving useless. She had to find a way to communicate with her that didn't end up in another pitched battle or, worse yet, create more opposition.

To combat the stress, she'd found the trail Pete had shown her on the map and began running it as often as she could. The trail started as hard-packed dirt through the woods, then out through the meadow and back into the woods, through a clearing that looked like a fairyland of felled trees and funky mushrooms, before rounding back out to the road and passing right by her cabin. That last bit she always did at full speed, and the burn felt great and helped banish whatever uptight feelings she was hanging on to.

Today she was in an especially foul mood, and after vacillating between running it off or eating a whole pan of double-chocolate brownies, exercise won. After work she'd put on her shorts and a t-shirt, with the intention of taking advantage of the warm afternoon, maybe even sitting in that fairyland-like clearing and listening in 'God's cathedral' for a while. Although it had been getting progressively colder, today was downright hot. Probably the last warm day for a while, considering it was October. She'd put her earbuds in, started one of her playlists, and double-timed it through the flats to feel the burn in her legs and get the endorphins to deal with her rotten mood.

About halfway through the meadow, she looked up and almost screamed. A figure astride a large black stallion emerged rather dramatically from the mist right ahead of her on the trail. She stopped and caught her breath while they rode nearer. The rider was a tall man, sitting confidently in the saddle with a firm grip on the reins. It only took a second for her brain to match that rigid posture with the only man she knew capable of it: Captain MacAlister. Ignoring the strange feeling the recognition gave her she stood off the trail, waiting for him to pass. Close up he barely looked like himself, since he was dressed in beat-up jeans and a Henley. Katherine had to suppress the flutter of attraction she felt that threatened to make her say or do something stupid.

It wasn't fair to combine his lived-in good looks and a horse – it just wasn't fair. She wouldn't get so . . . whatever she got when he was around if he were five-foot-five, bow-legged, and homely as a hedge fence. As he slowed to a stop in front of her she told herself, *he's not that good-looking. Don't say anything mean or stupid.* By the time his stallion was close enough to give her a good sniff, she felt ready to be polite. She waited while the horse settled down and then she moved to his side to stroke his shoulder. Since she'd been raised around horses, she could tell that this one was well cared for and not as high-strung as he had seemed at first. He definitely seemed like a handful, but one that Mac was having no trouble controlling.

She glanced up at Mac. As usual, he didn't look pleased. "Hi." She nodded towards his mount. "He's a beauty." The horse bumped her with his nose, and she resumed stroking his shoulder.

"That he is. He's also conceited, stubborn, and has a bad sense of humor." There was enough affection in his tone that she guessed Mac liked having the challenge of a spirited horse more than he let on. "He was trained to the track, so a leisurely ride isn't really his thing. He's been fighting the bit the whole way. Speaking of which, you shouldn't be running out here either." He frowned down at her like she was a misbehaving child.

"'Speaking of which?'" she asked, cocking her head to the side, feigning confusion. "Did you mean the 'fighting the bit' part?"

Mac's jaw tightened, but he didn't take the bait. "The trails that run through Martin's Meadow are uneven at best. You're gonna snap an ankle."

"I only run when it's a hard surface; the rest of the time I walk it." *And why do you care?* she almost added.

"Those are running shoes. They're not made for this kind of terrain." Katherine looked down at her sneakers, and they looked fine to her. *Such a nag.*

"Those clothes aren't doing you any favors either."

She crossed her arms and gave him a glare.

Mac looked uncomfortable for a moment then clarified, "I mean, it's too much exposed skin . . . there's thorns all along here, and—"

"I'm nowhere near any thorns, and it's warm."

"Okay, it's warm, but not that warm. Those are . . . too skimpy," he said, gesturing at her with his reins and causing his horse to stomp a bit with impatience.

"Skimpy?" she asked, her voice rising. "Running shorts and a t-shirt are not 'skimpy', grandpa, and it's not like anyone is going to see me out here anyway."

"I'm seeing you," he pointed out.

"Not for long," she snapped back, and she stepped wide of him, pushed through the knee-high weeds, and went around the horse and up the trail.

"You're gonna need to check yourself for ticks since you're wading right through their feeding ground," he bellowed, and when she looked over her shoulder she saw that he was twisted in his saddle, frowning at her. She saluted him rather mockingly, and then half-jogged down the trail. As soon as the trail changed to firmer ground, she broke into a run in case he was still watching, and she could defy him further.

The very next day the temperature plummeted, and Katherine

was glad that she had taken her run. When she got home from work that afternoon, she took a shorter trail so she could make it through the meadow while the light lasted. Autumn had finally arrived, and the trees all around were engaging in their yearly show. Her cabin was mostly surrounded by pines and oaks, so not exactly a thrill, but here and there were beech, birch, and maple. She planned to go into town where the trees were truly gorgeous and hunt up good leaves to press. Maybe she'd even get out a sketchbook. That would shock her mother, if nothing else. Her mom always lamented that none of her girls took to art.

At the moment, the only creative juices that Katherine felt flowing were the culinary kind. She had a pile of apples that needed to be made into something, and tonight felt like a pie kind of night. After dinner she put an apron on over her usual nighttime garb of yoga pants and a t-shirt. She had made the apron herself. It was a forties-style blue gingham check – pretty, but not frilly. She loved old aprons and tea-towels, and almost all vintage fabrics. They reminded her of visits to her grandmother's cottage and happier times for her family.

Getting out the flour, shortening, and butter, she got to work on the crusts. They were always the toughest part. Once she had them lining a few pie plates, she got down to the fun part. She had purchased an old-school crank peeler at the orchard she'd visited to pick the apples. It was fun to jam an apple on the end and then watch it spin, the peel flying off in one long strand. A pleasant, almost happy feeling filled her as she worked. It was a quiet kind of contentment, and it lifted her mood far better than yesterday's run had done. After assembling the pies, she slid them into the oven. In no time at all the smell of baking apples began to fill the cabin.

About an hour later she was putting an apple crumble into the oven to take to school the next day, when she heard a knock at the door. Since she had finally put up curtains, she could only guess who it might be. Pete always called first, and no one else ever visited. No one except her grumpy landlord, that is. She wiped her hands on a kitchen towel and headed to the door. She drew back the curtain, but it was Jake, the boyfriend of Erin Sullivan's daughter Brittany. He'd have no reason to be this far off campus or at her doorstep.

Rather than let him in, she opened the door and moved out onto the porch. "Hi. Do you have an emergency?" she asked him in her stern teacher's voice. Jake was one of the vocational students, and had resumed his internship with the construction company he had told her about at the beginning of the year. Like most days, he was in 'work clothes'—jeans, a t-shirt under an unbuttoned flannel, and work boots. He was a bit grimy, but it didn't look like he was injured.

"I'm . . . it's totally out of line for me to come by, but I've been putting in a retaining wall at Captain MacAlister's place, and we finished a few minutes ago. I figured since I'm right here, this might be the only time to speak to you outside school."

"Is someone going to pick you up?" she asked, looking around for a car.

"I am." Katherine jumped as the voice answered from behind Jake. Mac had come around from the driveway, but she hadn't even heard him. "Sorry about that. I didn't mean to startle you." He was dressed like Jake—jeans and flannel covered in a bit of dirt. "Jake shared something with me today, and I told him he should take it to you."

"Business hours would have been better," she said to Jake, "but c'mon in and let's talk." She let them into the cabin. Mac and Jake took noticeable deep breaths as they stepped in, clearly smelling the dessert that she'd been cooking. Both of their faces made it clear that they hadn't had dinner. "Do you guys want a piece of pie?"

"Oh, I don't want to trouble you, Dr. Grant, if you had that for someone . . ."

"Nope, I'm using up some extra fruit." She cut into the mostly-cooled first pie and set a piece in front of each of them. Going back into the kitchen, she put coffee on since her usual tea didn't go with pie. Once the pot was brewing, she turned back to see that they had already finished off their pieces. "Was that a race, gentlemen?" she asked with one eyebrow lifted. Mac looked a bit sheepish, but Jake grinned. She didn't really mind since she was pleased they liked it; pleased enough to cut two more pieces for them.

When the coffee was ready, she poured them all a cup and finally sat down. "So, what's going on?"

Jake was a tall kid, probably six-foot-two, with a strong build no doubt from the manual labor that he did. His hair was brown, but bleached blond by hours spent outdoors. He was attractive in that easy way, like it was simply his nature, nothing intentional. She could see why Brittany was hooked on him despite her mom's disapproval. He sat back with a sigh. "It's about hockey. Dean, Mike, and me have all been told there isn't enough money this year, and that we're off the team because we don't have a parent or guardian to pay the equipment fee."

Katherine reined in her knee-jerk reaction to shout, "What?" and took a moment before asking, "Who told you boys that?"

"Mr. Swift."

Katherine wanted to pound her head against something. "To be clear, Mr. Swift said it was a fee that was preventing you from playing?"

"Yes, ma'am."

Katherine took another moment to control her temper. Jake was the wrong audience for a diatribe on the battles she'd had with Stephanie Campbell and her cohorts. She wanted to be sure he knew that she'd find a way to get this fixed, but there was a limit to what she could tell him.

"You are not off the team. Your athletics fees are paid by the state as part of your tuition, and this is likely a misunderstanding. Leave this with me until Monday, okay? I'll sort it out, and you three can plan on returning to practice. I need a few days to make sure we're all set."

"Thank you, really, it's just . . ." Jake trailed off, as if trying to find a way to put it.

"You're gonna need to explain the rest of it, kid," Mac said.

Jake looked even more uncomfortable. "Mrs. Campbell and Mr. Swift run the shuttle up to the ski resort, and he does the lifeguard certifications for the summer camp at the lake. I know how the world works. You run your mouth and make someone's job harder, they're going to find a way to make it hard for you. I can't afford to tick anybody off. I work the ski resort during winter breaks, and I lifeguard at the camp in the summer. It's the only way I can get to stay here year-round. The resort gives me housing. I'm eighteen now, so it's not like my social worker's gonna send me off someplace, but there's still Christmas and Easter break for this school year. I won't have anywhere to go."

"So that's why you needed to see me off campus?"

"Yeah, Mac said if anybody could help, it would be you."

Katherine felt a strange mix of pride and surprise hearing that. She didn't know Mac thought much of her or her work. "This is probably an administrative issue, Jake," she reiterated. "The school has already received funds from the state for this school year; nothing can be revoked. Those funds cover tuition in addition to fees."

"I tried telling Mr. Swift that, but he told me Mrs. Campbell said it goes into a pool and doesn't count for me. She said it gets spent on books and stuff. It's the way it is when you're in the system."

"How so?"

Jake looked pensive for a moment and then spoke. "My aunt got paid to take me; money for clothes, money for books and stuff – I never saw any of that. I didn't have a single thing that wasn't someone else's before it was mine. Christmas was a joke, my birthday was just another day. I figured out pretty quick that she'd taken me on for the money. When she dumped me back into the system when I was ten, I was glad. I thought I'd get a real family, but nobody wants older kids; it was more of the same, only with strangers this time." He shrugged as if to imply that it was nothing. "I guess that's the way it is, and usually I get past it, but this time . . ." He shrugged again. Katherine had to resist the urge to reach across the table and hold his hand. "But you're not going to see me mouth off or act ungrateful. I know what I got at the school is good. I know my only chance to have a good life is to finish school. I'm not throwing that away."

Mac sat back, and his expression was full of something Katherine couldn't translate, but in his body language she read that what Jake had said hit him as hard as it had hit Katherine. He handed a set of keys to Jake. "Go warm it up, and I'll be out in a minute."

Jake said goodnight to Katherine and headed outside.

Katherine waited until she heard the truck start. "I feel this terrible urge to go back to every foster parent that kid had and smack them silly. He's smart, do you know that?"

Mac nodded.

"Bright – really, really bright. He could easily go to college. In fact, I tried to talk him into it at the start of the year when I saw his test scores. He laughed and said there was no way he'd ever have the money. I tried to tell him there were grants and student loans specifically for kids who exit care, but he said it wouldn't be enough, and frankly he's not wrong." She thought of all his struggles, all the challenges that would still be ahead. "I'd like to kick something or someone, even though I know I shouldn't."

"Anger is sometimes the emotion that lets you know something is wrong. What you're feeling, these kids need that, but you have to direct it, not let it turn inward. You have to use it, not be consumed by it."

"You're not wrong."

"Kids with Jake's kind of story rarely reach adulthood whole and hardy. The way they get treated leaves them with scars. He is smart, yah, but he's also tough and determined; I've never seen anyone work harder. He's got a goal, too. Granted, she has blue eyes and blond hair." Mac smiled at Katherine's frown. "His endgame is marriage and family, so I'm not about to judge him for it."

"I don't have a problem with Jake's goals, but they're so young and there's so much out there in the world to see and learn before settling down. I don't understand the rush. The two of them, Brittany and Jake, could easily go to college first, then they'd be better prepared to be partners and parents."

"I don't see a benefit to four years spent among kids intent on not growing up — c'mon, even you have to admit college kids are immature," he said when she tried to object. "It's paying the bills and keeping a job that makes you grow up."

Katherine shrugged her reply.

"While he might be able to do college, in the end it's not for him. He does have a bright future ahead of him, but not what you'd consider 'bright'."

"You think I'm wrong to encourage him to go to college?"

"Not every kid who can go to college should. Some kids are destined for the kind of success that comes with a tool belt, and there's nothing wrong with that. Jake's aiming high. He'll make a great general contractor. He's got both the intelligence it requires and the creativity, not to mention the people skills. Coming from where you do, your background, I can see that you'd think he's wasting his potential, but really he's not."

"Ugh, that again?" Her temper was about to get the better of her. "You think I'm narrow-minded, don't you? You think because I had a privileged upbringing that I can't empathize with or understand someone who didn't?"

Mac shook his head and held up a hand before she could get another word in.

"No, I don't, and I'm not fighting with you tonight, Kate." His tone was both stern and frustrated. He got up from his chair and headed for the door, but turned back and stared at her a moment. "I wanted to say, about yesterday, on the trail . . ."

"Don't worry about it," she interrupted with a wave of her hand. "I know I annoy you to no end."

Mac looked at her blankly for a moment before putting his hand on the doorknob, as if he was simply going to leave. She caught the tense mouth and narrowed eyes that meant he was angry, but she didn't get angry words when he finally spoke.

"I'm sorry for the misunderstanding. But, then again, you seem determined to misinterpret everything I say." For a second she thought he was going to launch into another lecture, but instead he stared at his boots as if he was trying to control his temper. As stone-faced as usual he barked out, "Thanks for the dessert and coffee, Kate. Have a good night." The door didn't quite slam, and his boots on her steps didn't quite stomp as he left, but it was close.

Katherine sat in silence after they were gone. Some unexpected thoughts were settling in, and she didn't like them one bit. When the apple crumble finished baking she set it out to cool, cleaned the kitchen, and still felt unsettled. She needed advice and perspective. Grabbing her cell phone, she took it up to bed with her and settled in under the blankets, waiting while the phone rang on the other end. "I'm screwing this up," she said as soon as Heather picked up.

"Well, hello to you, too," Heather laughed. "Are we talking about the job, because that would not be true."

"No, this connecting with people thing. I think I'm kind of a jerk."

"You've always been kind of a jerk; in mortal circles that's called 'assertiveness'."

"Ha, ha. No, seriously. I was just mean to someone who was trying to apologize to me. Why would I do that?"

For a long moment Heather said nothing, and Katherine began to panic thinking that she was about to hear some unpleasant truth about her miserable personality that her best friend had been hiding. "The truth is that you've been showing the world one particular face for a very long time, but it was never you. That Katherine was warm and accessible, but remote. That Katherine didn't need people, never felt lonely, never wanted any deeper connections. She was the lie you were telling yourself. Honey, I think the minute you decided to take this job you also decided to leave her behind and I, for one, am so glad you did. But deciding to leave her behind doesn't mean that everything is hunky-dory now. You've still got work to do."

"Heather . . ."

"I'm going to say this, Katherine. I've been wrong not to say it before. But I never thought you were ready to hear it."

Katherine braced.

"It's time to forgive him. You will never be whole until you do."

"What?" That was not what she was expecting to hear.

"He'll never ask for it. He probably still thinks he did nothing wrong. I didn't tell you, but I heard years ago that he married that woman, and they live in Pennsylvania somewhere. I've resisted the temptation to Google him and engage in a little schadenfreude, since I'm guessing he probably cheated on her, too. The point is that he doesn't deserve your forgiveness; and none of us deserves God's forgiveness, yet He gives it."

"Uh, because He's divine; I'm not."

"Doesn't matter. What do we pray? 'Forgive our debts as we forgive our debtors'."

"But Tom . . ."

"Doesn't deserve it and will never ask for it, but you still need to give it. It's how you avoid the bitterness. It's how you heal, how you become whole again."

"Way to lay it out, Heather," she said, feeling like she'd been kicked in the gut.

"Do me a favor. Read Luke 6 tonight. There's a strong message there about forgiveness." She was silent for a moment then asked,

"Who were you mean to at this hour?"

"Captain Wonderful, who else?"

"Oh," Heather said. "I get it."

"Could you share with the class then, 'cause I don't."

"You're attracted to him and don't want to be. Do the math. Poor Mac isn't going to get your good side, is he? You give that to your work, going overboard to win people over, going out of your way for others, but not for him because he doesn't need anything from you. He's a man, your equal, who happens to be interested in you. And that scares the pants off you, doesn't it?" Heather chuckled and Katherine repressed the urge to hang up on her. "I looked up Captain MacAlister. Did you know he was a detective for the NYPD? He had a number of seriously high-profile cases. And his picture is . . . wow. Nice eyes. How could you be mean to this man?"

"Apparently, it's a new skill," she said ruefully.

"Hang on." Katherine heard a baby cry in the background and guessed that Mirabelle, Heather's youngest, was up again. "There she goes. Teething is torture for both of us. I have to get her because Michael has the early shift and . . ."

"Of course; I'll let you go."

"Don't forget that I love you and I'm here for you . . . well, electronically."

"I love you, too. Goodnight." Katherine ended the call and stared at the wood ceiling a few feet above her head. She didn't hate the loft anymore and had finally stopped hitting her head when she got up. It was almost like they had a truce. She'd like a truce with Mac, if for no other reason than that she actually liked him—part of the time. Remembering that Heather had given her homework, she reached over to the pile of books on the floor beside her bed, picked up her Bible, and began reading, but it wasn't sinking in.

She could actually feel her heart resisting what her head was reading. So she prayed. None of this was easy. None of it. She wanted God to wave His hand and fix her, but she knew it didn't work that way. After praying, she felt more peaceful and tackled the chapter of Luke again. When she got to verse twenty-seven, she felt it. 'But I say to you who hear, Love your enemies. Do good to those who hate you, bless those who curse you, pray for those who abuse you.' There was a feeling of . . . not condemnation or even scolding–but a nudge on her conscience.

Katherine was in the habit of going to war for a cause she believed in, and she gloried in being right. She wondered how much of that was because she relished each battle she won, loved proving someone wrong, as well as the thrill of vindication. Some more hard-to-take truths were dancing around in her head. For a woman who considered herself a Christian, she had to admit a lot of her behavior wasn't so Christ-like. Thinking it over, she knew the exact day when things had started to change.

It was the day she'd been discharged from the rehabilitation hospital, finally able to walk with crutches, and ready to return to teaching. When she'd first been injured, the elders had assured her that her job at the church-run school would be held for her. She hobbled up the steps of school that day only to be confronted by the principal, who whisked her down and into the nearby sanctuary where he proceeded to tell her that she was suspended pending a review. And then it got worse. Tom had lied to protect himself and left her alone to deal with the fallout. The accusations hurled at her still burned even now. She could feel that burst of righteous indignation. It was the one wrong she'd never been able to right.

That day she'd turned her back on her town, her friends, and in some ways, on God. Heather was the only friend who stuck with her, even leaving the church because of what they had done. Her mother had left, too, writing to the board and to the pastor that Katherine had been judged unjustly. It didn't matter, though. It all followed her anyway. Katherine didn't get how forgiving Tom for all he had done would somehow redeem the past. It was what it was.

CHAPTER ELEVEN

Mac sat in his truck with Pete beside him, and watched for movement in the distance. For the last three nights they'd been staking out the trailhead on Dave Wilson's property right off the highway, trying to catch his trespassers as they exited. Mac and Pete both knew that there was only one reason they'd keep coming back at night to this exact spot: there was something in the woods that they wanted. It was either illegal baiting or a marijuana grow. Either way they had to take care of it before Dave went hiking in with his shotgun.

The wardens had tracked two groups of men using the ATV trails. One they lost track of and had to give up on. The second set of tracks led straight to an illegal bear stand over a pile of bait. Pete was pumped to catch the poachers, and they knew the men would return at daylight. What they didn't know was where the other group went or why they were in the woods. It was posted property, so no one had any legal business in there. That was problem two, though. Tonight they were waiting for problem one.

Normally Mac didn't mind backing up the wardens on stakeouts, since he usually got to hang with Pete. The old man would either be quiet or he'd be telling stories, great either way. But tonight he would not shut up about Katherine Grant. Actually, for weeks he would not shut up about Katherine, and what with Mac's own thoughts straying to her far too often for comfort, it was almost painful.

After the pie and coffee with Jake, which had gone well for the kid and not for Mac, Katherine had thrown down with Stephanie Campbell, and it got ugly. Katherine had found what Pete described as 'accounting irregularities' in the athletics department. Money was being spent stupidly, and some of that was state money, so now they'd had to call in an outside auditor for an official report. Stephanie, instead of cooperating, was defending her brother-in-law, but Katherine wasn't having it. That woman was not afraid of a fight. As he well knew.

"You should see her with those kids," Pete was saying, "I've been working a few hours a week up at the school lately, and I've seen how she is with the kids from foster care. She's got a good way with them. Meets them where they are, but holds the line, makes them show respect. It's a tough thing to do, you know? You push too hard, they break. If you don't push at all, they never move. Katie seems to understand that."

"Well, she has all those degrees; you'd expect she'd be good at it," he said, not intending to dismiss her talent, but desperate for Pete to stop talking already.

"It's not her education, Mac; it's her. See, you were raised different. You didn't have it easy, but you didn't have the knocks these kids did. I had some of the same ones, and I'll tell you, trust someone in authority? Or, at all, for that matter? Not gonna happen. Katie gets it, walks that line the right way."

"You sure are a fan," he grumped.

"And you aren't 'cause she don't like you," Pete said, laughing. "If you'd stop acting like a bear with a burr on its butt every time you get near the woman, you might be able to change that."

"Pete, don't you have anything better to do than to talk about Katherine Grant? Give a man a break."

Pete was quiet for a few minutes then chuckled. "You're falling for her."

"What?!" Mac blurted, spilling the coffee he'd been holding in his hand.

"Yeah, I figured that was the case."

"You are out of your mind." Mac cleaned up the coffee as best he could. "You didn't tell her that, did you?"

"No, course not. I can't help seeing it, though. Just give in. She's a wonderful girl. She'd make you a perfect wife. Keep you well fed. She makes these cookies . . ."

"Pete," Mac interrupted, "Katherine Grant hates me. She's made that clear several times."

"No, she don't; she just don't like you. It's different."

"Okay then, she doesn't like me. Either way, I'd have to be a fool to even consider it."

"I didn't say you were doing it on purpose, but doing it all the same – falling for her. I'm advising you to go ahead and let yourself. Be a little nicer to the woman, and then ask her out. She'll probably say no a few times, but you can get over that. Maybe put in that wood stove you promised her. That would help."

"It was delivered today, and I'll put it in tomorrow," he countered, then made a mental note to actually do that, realizing now that he hadn't even told her it was being delivered. Another strike against him. "Pete, you're way off here. Katherine wants nothing to do with me."

"Ah, but I noticed that now you're not arguing with me about whether or not you're sweet on her."

"'Sweet on her'?" Mac asked sarcastically.

"I'm old. Old people have old sayings," he said, adding, "You like her," then laughed like he remembered something funny. "I knew it weeks ago when she said you passed her on that trail she runs and gave her grief about her gear. Then you scolded her about needing new tires on her car. Then, what was it, last week? You went over there to fix the light on the back porch and ended up yelling at her because she had a space heater running on an extension cord. And, of course, there was Sunday at church when you laughed at her new boots."

"I what?" Mac snapped, out of patience with Pete.

"Laughed at her new boots. She ordered them over the computer; the furry ones with the little pompoms on them."

"They were laughable, Pete." And they had been. Granted, she'd looked cute in them, but they were no good for the fast-approaching weather. It was only November, and it had already snowed hard once. Next week was Thanksgiving, and a huge storm was supposed to come in. Katherine didn't seem prepared for what the winter was going to be like on the mountain, and she was going to get herself hurt. She needed someone looking out for her. Mac keenly wanted to be that someone, but he knew that was a bad idea. He'd been fighting the temptation of her since the day she arrived.

"Face it; if you didn't like her, you'd leave her alone."

"Shut up, Pete. You're killing me here," Mac said, rubbing a hand over his very tired eyes. They'd been at this for hours. He hadn't had a good night's sleep in forever. He wanted to catch these guys and be done with it, not listen to Pete giving him grief.

"Be nice to her, Mac. Not only does she need it because she's had a pretty rough go of it, but the reward for you would be immeasurable," he said solemnly. "I know you buried that part of yourself to avoid temptation, but Katie clearly got under your skin anyway. The way I see it, you two are perfect for each other. God Himself moved that woman up here for you, so stop being stupid."

"I'm tuning you out now, Pete," Mac said, leaning back in the truck and watching for any sign of movement at the edge of the woods.

"You do that. Don't mean I'm wrong, though."

"For the love of . . ." Mac started, but Pete hushed him, and pointed out the windshield into the dark as the flicker of a flashlight shone through the woods. They both slowly opened the truck's doors and slid out. Waiting there in the silence, Mac felt the familiar rush of adrenaline, his hand automatically running over his holstered weapon, and his heart kicking up its rhythm as they slowly approached the head of the trail where three men emerged.

Don't be stupid . . . don't be stupid rang through his head, although he knew it was highly likely that they would be. The three men were all dressed in camo, as if they were hunters, but with no guns in sight. That didn't mean they weren't armed. He raised his flashlight, clicked it on, and shone it on the men.

"Game warden!" Pete called out. "Fellas, I'm going to need you to stop right there. If you've got weapons, you need to put 'em on the ground." They halted a few feet from a waiting truck with the woods at their back, but they seemed to do as instructed and two shotguns were on the ground. Before they could get any closer, Mac heard a tell-tale mechanical sound and shouted, "Drop your weapon!" In the time it took to blink, a shot split the still morning air, and chaos erupted.

CHAPTER TWELVE

KATHERINE STARED AT THE SQUAT BLACK stove sitting on her hearth. The delivery guys had dropped it off yesterday, saying they didn't know who was installing it, only that it wasn't them. Mac was probably planning on it, but he hadn't said so, and hadn't warned her that it was arriving either, which was so typical. She had been pretty busy lately, so maybe he had tried. He used to track her down in person, but since his last visit when they'd argued over the space heater—which she had gotten rid of—he'd made himself scarce.

That should have been a relief, but it wasn't. She began to look for his cruiser unconsciously when she drove through town. When she was home and his truck would drive past, she'd look out, and part of her hoped he'd stop by, which made no sense at all. He drove her nuts, and she returned the favor, so why was she wishing he'd come by again? All her weird longing combined with Pete's constant drumbeat of "Mac's a nice guy, give him a chance" was beginning to make her think that she might have misjudged him.

His scarcity probably wasn't personal or intentional, anyway. She knew he was busy, and considering all she had on her plate, it was a wonder she had time to even worry about it. The last few weeks had been a trial. She'd had a few wins, like the calls and emails that she had made to verify the funding for each student coming from the state. She was able to get all the kids who wanted to play onto the teams that they wanted to be on. Morale among the boarding students was pretty high, but she had utterly burned the bridge between her and Bill Swift. The bridge to Stephanie was aflame as well.

By the end of the week she was stressed out and grumpy, so last night she'd bought the boarding students pizza as a surprise, just to be around people who were happy for a while. Pastor Dan Connors had come over for vespers a bit early and joined in. She got to see him interact with the kids, and was impressed by how good he was. He'd stuck around for cleanup, and they'd had a chance to talk as well. He seemed the genuine article, a man of God through and through.

Working with Dan was easy, but they both had to be careful that people didn't jump to any conclusions about them again. That handholding picture in the Lowdown had been enough. For his part, Dan had been clear that he wasn't in the slightest bit interested. He had called her after the blog reported on them, and apologized for the drama. "I willingly yield the field to Captain MacAlister, the better man."

Her last mission before the Thanksgiving break was to get the board to rule on the official termination of Bill Swift as Athletics Director. His errors went beyond mismanagement, kissing the edge of fraud. The board was ten members' strong, and including Pete she knew she had eight on her side, but now it was both female members of the board she consistently found herself up against. Mindy had been pro-Stephanie from the start, and now she had Cindy Daugherty on her side. Of the two, Mindy was the more strident. She didn't think it was a coincidence that Mindy handled the school's real estate and was the one to rent Erin Sullivan the house promised to Katherine.

In a turn of events that surprised even her, Katherine was seriously considering Erin for the hopefully soon-to-be-open position of Athletic Director. Dan spoke highly of her, and with an undergrad degree in education and her work as a personal trainer, Katherine felt she was perfect. She was almost ready to approach

Erin, but she had to be sure Swift was gone and somehow get over the awkwardness of their first meeting. After all, Erin had essentially called the cops on her.

Stephanie wasn't letting Swift go quietly, though. Katherine suspected that if it was up to him, he would have resigned by now. But Stephanie seemed to be forcing a fight. That left Katherine spending most of the week navigating figurative minefields, careful not to tread on anyone's feelings, lest she make things worse. After all of that, she was close to emotional exhaustion, definitely not in the mood to deal with anything, and that included tracking Mac down to figure out what was up with the stove. She'd called him twice—no response. She called Pete and got no response either, but she knew that he was working. Finally, she gave up staring at the hunk of metal, since that was hardly helping, and decided it was time for lunch.

It was Saturday, so she took the time to make something warm and comforting rather than default to salad. She put vegetable soup on the back burner of the kitchen stove to simmer, and pulled a loaf of bread out of the oven. There was something heart-warming about the smell of fresh bread. It wasn't the easiest thing to make, but required more patience than skill. The reward was worth the effort. Cutting off a hunk, she slathered a shameful amount of butter on it and took a huge bite.

With perfect timing, a knock came at the door. She could see out the part in the kitchen curtains that it was Pete and Mac, both still in uniform. She chewed and swallowed her mouthful of bread as best she could and headed for the door, opening it with a smile, along with a puzzled sort of "Hi?"

"Stove came today?" Mac asked her, and once again he hadn't bothered with pleasantries like 'hello.'

Pete rolled his eyes. "I think what Mac wants to say is, 'Hi Katie, how are you? I heard that the stove was delivered today, and I'd like to go ahead and put it in for you. I know you've been pretty cold out here.'"

She smiled at Pete while Mac stood there like stone, as usual. "You both look like you came straight from work. Honestly, this can wait. You can come another day; I'll survive."

"No, Kate, we've got to do it today," Mac insisted impatiently. "You can't use the fireplace with all the supplies sitting there," he winced as he gestured to the hearth where the stove and stack of pipe sat. His face looked a wee bit pale, and she wondered what sort of day they'd had.

"It's fine. I have my electric blanket."

Mac slowly closed his eyes in what looked like frustration. "Please tell me you don't use that thing on an extension cord."

"Why do you always assume I'm going to do something stupid to burn your cabin to the ground?" she snapped. "It's battery operated, Smokey the Bear, so you can relax."

Mac looked relieved at that, but he also appeared to be exhausted, and he didn't fight back. Normally he'd never let one of her sarcastic names for him slide by. Feeling a bit concerned, she took a good long look at him.

"No offense, but you look terrible."

"Aw, he's fine; he just got shot," Pete said, and Katherine couldn't suppress her gasp of dismay. She immediately reached out to Mac to support him, as if she thought that he might drop to the floor. "Where?" she asked as she held onto him. Mac looked down at her with the oddest expression: a mix of confusion, surprise, and something a good deal warmer. For a moment, that look held her there, fixed to the spot while she drank it in, but then she realized what she was doing, dropped her hands, and stood back.

"Shoulder," he said, and his voice was a bit croaky. "Only a graze."

"Are you okay, though?" she asked, her heartbeat returning to normal.

"Yes. Just tired."

She could hear it in his voice. He sounded done-in. "Forget the stove; I'll be fine." And, whether it was compassion or some strange need to take care of him, she found herself saying, "Why don't you stay for lunch? I've got plenty for both of you."

"Sounds great," Pete said, wasting no time and steering Mac towards the table. He sniffed at the air. "It smells fantastic in here."

Katherine helped Mac off with his coat.

Pete settled himself in a chair. "What is that?" he asked, pointing down at her soup with an expression of clear disdain.

"Veggie soup. And don't make a face; you'll like it."

"Well, at least there's bread, and the butter is real, right?" Pete asked, clearly not thrilled.

"Pete, you cannot exist on diner food, take-out, and canned chili. You have the diet of a twelve-year-old. Grownups eat veggies," she scolded, and he chuckled. "Sit and I'll serve." She got two more bowls out. By the time they were actually eating, Pete grudgingly admitted the soup was good.

"It's a bit spicy."

"Secret ingredient," she said, smiling. "So how did you get shot?"

Mac sat back in his chair, wincing a bit before saying, "It was no big deal."

Pete expanded on Mac's customary monosyllabic answer with the details. "We confronted trespassers who turned out to be poachers. Each of them was armed. They were pretty surprised to see us and, even though we got the drop on them, they fired on us."

Mac shook his head. "Pete, you gotta stop telling the story." He was sounding less exhausted now and more exasperated. "It wasn't that big a deal. Only one of them failed to put down his weapon when directed, and he actually dropped it on his own foot. It discharged a wild shot. I got grazed in the shoulder, which is more like a bad burn than a bullet hole. The guy had been trying to set the stupid thing down, not shoot me. This wasn't the crime of the century."

Pete cuffed Mac upside his head. "I was trying to make you some points here."

"Seriously?" Mac asked him, and Katherine smirked into her soup.

A short while later, Pete got up and said that he was going to head home, promising to help Mac with the stove the next day. Mac stayed right where he was, slowly finishing his second bowl. Very slowly. Katherine sat and waited, wondering if he had something on his mind. "This is really good, Kate. Pete's always praising your cooking skills, and for once he's not exaggerating."

"It's great to have time for cooking. It's one of the nice things about being in the middle of nowhere. Fewer distractions. Before I came up here, I hadn't baked or sewed this much in years."

"I couldn't help but notice what you did to the couch. It looks good." Katherine had taken the time a few weeks ago to take the sheets she'd thrown over the couch and turn them into a cover. It wasn't perfect, but it made the thing a bit less horrible.

"That couch is nasty, Mac."

"I know. I've been meaning to update this place for a while. It's usually hunters who rent it, and they have different expectations."

"Right, they wouldn't expect a dryer, dishwasher, or internet."

"No. I've done the research, though, and I've decided to upgrade it, something like how I did my house."

"I've never seen your house."

"I'll have to give you the tour. You can meet the rest of my animals, and I think Misery misses you." Mac smiled at her, a rare full smile.

Katherine felt her pulse pick up a little. He really was attractive when he smiled. "I'd like that." They lapsed into silence again.

Mac didn't let it last. "Kate, I wanted to talk to you about something. See, Pete has this crazy idea . . ." Mac trailed off and then tried again. "He sorta pointed out to me that I . . ." He laughed and sat back in his chair, rubbing a hand over his forehead. He looked heavenward for a moment before catching her eyes again. "What I'm trying to say is that I'd like it if we could get to know each other better." And then his phone rang.

Mac muttered something under his breath about timing and pulled the phone out of his pocket. He answered and immediately his whole aspect changed. He was 'Mac the Cop' again, stone-faced and stiff-jawed. He stood up and grabbed his coat, wincing as he pulled it on. "Give me twenty, and I'll be there," he said into the phone as he headed for the door. Katherine got up, and he stopped short, turning back to say, "Kate I've . . ."

"You've got to go," she finished for him, feeling unsettled. She wanted him to finish what he was about to say even if the very idea of Mac asking her out scattered her brain. Before she could make up her mind if she wanted him to or not, he reached out and slowly cupped her cheek in the palm of his hand. Despite watching him do it, she was so surprised by the gesture that she stood fixed to the spot, her eyes on his, unsure what to do.

His hand felt warm and a bit rough on her far softer skin. It had been a long time since someone had touched her like this, and it was . . . confusing. Without understanding why, she leaned her cheek into his palm, quietly soaking in the affection. She watched his face as the tension of the phone call faded away, replaced by tenderness. He breathed out what sounded like a regretful sigh, and she let her eyes drift closed. She felt his thumb stroke her cheek.

He stepped back. "Tomorrow, Kate," the words came in a low voice, and then he was gone.

CHAPTER THIRTEEN

TOMORROW CAME AND WENT, BUT NO MAC. No call or text either. From Pete she learned that Mac had been called out of town. She kept telling herself that it wasn't like he'd promised her anything, and who knew what he had meant by that 'tomorrow.' Ignoring her stung feelings, she went about her weekend as usual, helping the ladies at church set up the senior luncheon and, since she had nothing better to do, staying for it and sitting with Mrs. Beasley while she talked about her days as a waitress in a dive bar the next town over. Mrs. Beasley was a hoot, but Katherine wasn't as diverted by her stories as usual.

Sunday afternoon, Katherine got into her car and drove an hour out to the nearest Target for some retail therapy. She came back with three new lipsticks, a chenille throw, two new books, and scented candles that she probably didn't need, but smelled like Christmas so were irresistible. They would also annoy Mac—a bonus. When Monday came and went without a peep from him, Katherine tried not to take it personally and reminded herself that she was basically nothing to him but a tenant. She'd probably misinterpreted that look on his face and the words he'd said. Why would he want her anyway? She'd been nothing but trouble for him.

One bright side, grades came out, and she wasn't ashamed to have actually danced with happiness when she reviewed them. Not only were most students up in all grades, but the new kids coming in had decent marks. There were a few trouble spots but they were among the day students, and that wasn't where the state or the board would be looking. She and Elaine celebrated by grabbing three trays of cupcakes at the grocery store and making sure each and every staff member got one. Stephanie had been out, so the good cheer lasted all day.

Tuesday was the last day before the kids were dismissed for the Thanksgiving holiday, and even with good report cards to take with them they were predictably horrible. By the time the students went home she was ready to collapse, and she'd only been observing. She imagined the teachers were more than ready for the break, short though it was. Pete took her for dinner at Maria's. It was Chicken Pot Pie night, his favorite. Katherine didn't tell him that, while Maria's was good, hers was better. She used puff pastry to top hers and nothing beat that flaky, buttery goodness.

After listening to her vent about her day, Pete tried to bring up Mac. She redirected the subject, but he did it again. After three failed attempts to discuss their mutual acquaintance, he put down his fork and swiveled on his stool to face her. "Katherine Grant, that's beginning to get on my nerves." She looked up sharply. "And don't pretend that you don't know you're doing it."

"Sorry, Pete," she said, although she wasn't, not really. She didn't want to talk about Mac because her feelings were still pretty hurt and worse, she didn't feel like she had any reason for it. He hadn't made her any promises, and she felt all out of whack, pining for a man she didn't think she liked until yesterday.

"He's up in Albany, dealing with something real serious. I know you don't think much of him." She tried to argue this, but he shut her down. "But Mac is the officer with the highest investigative skills this state has. It's not even his job, but they pull him in on the tough stuff. I don't know the details, but I know he's been flat out since he got up there."

"Whatever it is must be pretty serious to tie him down so he can't even call or text. I suppose he hasn't stopped to sleep or eat? Grab a cup of coffee? Send a quick text to you?"

Pete opened his mouth, thought better of whatever he was going to say, and promptly shut it.

Katherine felt like a jerk for mouthing off to Pete. She did think Mac's job was important, terribly so, but why couldn't he have called? She sensed Pete was ticked at her so she bumped his knee with hers. "Sorry." He gave her a shake of his head, but there was a small smile on his lips, so she understood she was forgiven.

When Katherine got home, she grabbed a book, her electric blanket, and sat in her rocking chair in front of the fireplace that she still couldn't use because it was covered by stove parts. The cabin was cold, but with the baseboard heaters in the kitchen and bathroom cranked, it was about fifty. It was frosty, but fine if she was under the blanket. That thing put out some serious heat.

After drowsily re-reading the same page for the third time, she realized that she lacked the gumption to take herself to bed. Instead, she closed her eyes, rocking the chair with one foot, thinking about her holiday plans. Tomorrow she was leaving early to drive down to Cape Cod to spend Thanksgiving with her mother and sisters. They planned to have a post-Thanksgiving, pre-Christmas crafting weekend–her sisters' obsession with Christmas crafts had no limits–and catch up with each other. Katherine was looking forward to having time with just them—no kids, no husbands. They hadn't done that in years. She loved her sisters' families, but having girl time with them was something she missed.

As she was drifting off under her warm blanket, a familiar knock sounded on her door. *Mac.* She quickly did the cost-benefit analysis on answering it and decided to stay right where she was. Essentially, she was already in bed, so it wasn't like she was ignoring him; he'd just come by too late. The knock came again, and she looked at the time on her phone. It was only nine. Half of her wanted to sprint to the door, throw it open, and make sure he was okay before asking him why the heck had he been ignoring her. The other half was afraid of what she was feeling and what he might say. He knocked one more time and, still a house divided, she did nothing. The sound of his footsteps leaving the porch brought twin pangs of regret and relief. She went to bed with her stomach in a knot. . Her conscience was needling her, but she brushed it off, thinking it was all for the best that she had ignored him. A relationship with Mac was a huge mistake anyway. The guilty suspicion that she was being cruel in an effort to protect herself snuck through her defenses and sank in.

"I'm such a jerk," she whispered as the cold night wrapped her in sleep.

"So, is it that Captain MacAlister you're thinking of?" Katherine turned at the sound of her mother's voice.

"What?" Katherine had gotten up early with things on her mind she'd rather not have, and tried to banish them with strong coffee and the gorgeous view of the Atlantic Ocean out her mom's kitchen window. It hadn't worked. Her sisters were still asleep after last night's lengthy Scrabble tournament, which eventually became Boggle, which finally turned into Yahtzee when they were too tired to spell anymore. Her mom had gone to bed before them, and being only the three girls again had been sweet. Her thoughts this morning were not.

"The only time a woman gets that particular look is when a man puts it there." Her mother sat down at the table with her. She tried to argue, but Mac had been on her mind. It was Sunday. There hadn't been any communication from him over the holiday, and he hadn't left a message when she'd sent his call to voicemail that night he came knocking on her door. She was worried that whatever overture he'd tried to make, she'd killed, and strangely that really upset her. It was like she'd been offered something precious, and she'd thrown it to the ground, stomping on it before realizing what it was.

"Uh . . ."

"That's a lot of feeling for one syllable." Her mom reached out and brushed the hair off her forehead, her eyes lingering on Katherine's scar. "You're so fearless, so strong, that sometimes I forget all you've been through. I forget you're as fragile as the rest of us."

"No. You know me, Mom." She took a sip of her coffee. "I'm solid as a rock."

"No, you aren't." Her mom reached out and held her hand. "Don't forget that I was at the hospital. I watched while Tom ripped your heart out and walked away. And I was at the church when those awful women said those terrible things to you. I've been here through it all, and I've waited, hoping that one day you'd be able to put it behind you. If I thought your singleness was by choice or conviction and not fear, I'd celebrate it with you. I think we both know it's not. Tom's lies and his faithlessness all but ruined your life. The one you've rebuilt is a good one, but it's so remote." Katherine looked away, unable to contradict a thing her mother was saying.

"You're still in a season of bitterness."

"No, I'm not," she automatically replied.

"I've struggled with it, too," she admitted. "Your father leaving me, the divorce . . . it wasn't the same as what Tom did to you, but it was still soul-crushing."

"Oh, Mom." Katherine squeezed her mom's hand, her heart aching.

"I've been reluctant to bring any of this up, because I could see you had a life you enjoyed, but now I think it's finally the time; you're clearly in pain, and it's not just this man you're interested in."

Katherine began to regret telling her mom and sisters about Mac. She had tried to work him into her whole description of the folks up in Maine, but clearly her mother had worked it out.

"It's time for you to heal." She reached out and touched the scar on Katherine's cheek. "It was so hard to see you in that hospital bed. All those surgeries, all that pain. When your child suffers, so do you. I felt it each time they opened you up again, chasing after yet another complication. I thought I'd lose you." Her watery eyes fixed on Katherine's. "It was worse once I knew all those rumors were starting. He should have stayed and stood up for you."

"Water under the bridge, Mom."

"No, it isn't. Not for you, is it? Physically, you healed, but I think your heart never did. It's time to let it heal. It's time to try again."

"But . . . What if Mac wants children? He's still young enough to want a chance at a family. I can't give him that. Not every guy is okay with adoption. What if he wants babies of his own that I can't give him?" It sounded stupid to say it out loud, but she remembered Tom's words: 'God wouldn't give me a broken wife'. The words he used to justify leaving her.

"I think you need to discuss it with him and see what he wants. A woman's ability to give birth to biological children should not be on the list of things that make a relationship work."

"It's hard to let that old dream die," she confessed. "I wanted to have as many children as God saw fit to give me. We'd have a big house, and a huge yard with a tire swing. I'd have a garden and chickens, a barn to homeschool from. I'd take them hunting for fireflies on summer nights and make them cocoa in the winter." Katherine smiled a little ruefully at the vision she'd had ten years ago, when she'd worn Tom's engagement ring and her whole future seemed to be filled with family and love.

"He took that away from you," her mom whispered. "But when you hold on to the pain, you take that hope of having a new dream away from yourself." Ouch. Her mom was in tough-love mode. "That dream is dead, yes. But there's no reason you can't find a new one. You said you've been going to church? That's a step in the right direction, and one I'm proud you've taken. Considering all the grief you were given by our own church, I worried you'd never set foot in one again."

"Almost didn't. Pete nagged me, and eventually I caved."

"I think I like Pete," her mom said with a smile.

"No question, you'd love him. You ought to come up with me at Christmas and stay for a bit. I could always take a weekend and drive you back."

"Maybe. That's a while to be away. We'll see."

CHAPTER FOURTEEN

EARLY MONDAY MORNING, KATHERINE DROVE BACK up to Sweet River. The drive was a long one, so she went straight to the school instead of stopping at her cabin first. She was barely in time for the first bell. The day was predictably convoluted, and when she finally got back to her cabin that night it was ice-cold and completely dark. She turned on almost every light she had, and then spotted the little woodstove, fully installed, patiently waiting on the hearth, with an entire stack of wood nearby arranged neatly. There was a kindling bucket, matches up on the mantel, and an instruction booklet left on the top with pages tabbed and highlighted.

"That man is a control freak," she said aloud, but she felt a warmth spread through her at the evidence of his caring nature. Mac hadn't simply installed the stove; he wanted to be sure she was able to run it. It was an incredibly kind thing to do, when her parting shot certainly hadn't been. It was also practical, exactly like him. He was probably the sort of guy who would give his woman snow tires for Christmas. Once again she regretted her temper and the way she bristled around him. How could he be so nice to her now when she'd been so nasty? She put down the instructions and decided to tackle it after she'd unpacked.

It looked like Mac had taken down her Christmas lights, but she didn't mind. Her mom had given her a small fake Christmas tree that was actually quite nice, and she'd planned to put them there, anyway. She took it out of the box and set it up in the corner away from the hearth, where she wrapped the lights around it, and then she hung the felt ornaments she'd made that weekend. The cabin instantly felt more cheerful, although not a bit warmer.

Katherine picked up the instruction book, and after a few minutes of reading she tried her best with the newspaper and kindling. No joy. She wasn't sure what she was doing wrong, but it wouldn't stay lit for love or money. It made no sense, since she'd used the fireplace often enough. What could the difference be? Her phone rang and, seeing that it was Pete and maybe this meant a rescue, she answered.

"Hey, Pete!"

"I saw you'd finally come home." His voice was grumpy but sounded glad all the same. "Did you get the message from Greg? Bill Swift thought things over and submitted his resignation this evening. We met tonight by phone to accept it. Guess he decided to take the high road and do the right thing in the end. You won, kiddo."

Katherine didn't jump up and down with glee, but she did feel a whoosh of relief run right through her and said a quick prayer of thanks. It certainly wasn't her efforts that changed Bill's heart. "That is a load off my mind. The fight was getting ugly, and I was really worried it would spread. Thank you for telling me. Today was so busy I haven't had the chance to go through my messages."

"You just got home?"

"From school, yes. I got back from my mom's this morning. I did kind of stay to the bitter end, but my family was really glad. That's probably the most time we've ever taken off at Thanksgiving." She paused, giving the wood stove a hard stare. "By the way, any chance you can help me figure out how to run this new stove?"

"You didn't get it lit yet?"

"No, and I'm freezing."

"Okay, I'll get Mac to come right over."

"Oh, that's not necessary. Pete, wait!" But he had hung up. She felt the flutter of butterflies mixed with dread. What would he think? Called in to rescue her ungrateful self again. "Rats!" she shouted. Running around the cabin, she quickly put her things away and straightened up. She was stuffing her bags in the closet when she heard the familiar knock. Katherine opened the door with a smile, but Mac was back to all-authority. Her smile froze in place at the sight of the cold expression on his face. She knew she deserved it, but it hurt to see it all the same.

His face was stony as he walked in and surveyed the scene. "Pete said you needed help with the stove." He took off his coat and frowned when the cold hit him. "Kate, it's freezing in here. You should have called sooner."

"I . . . well, yes, but I just got back."

Mac's eyes moved to the brand-new, fully-decorated Christmas tree then back to her. "Right this second?" he asked in his cop voice and, as usual, it ticked her off.

"No, Dick Tracy," she sniped and immediately regretted it. Taking a breath she tried to remember that this was the man who had been so kind to her and that she liked, when she would let herself. There had to be a way to fix things with him. "I did some stuff before I tried to light it . . ." she pointed to the stove, "but it wouldn't go."

He stepped in front of her and seemed about ready to tell her off for not reading the manual he'd put together, and she actually wished he would, but he stopped himself and got down to getting the stove lit.

She should have felt relieved, but she didn't. While she was glad to skip a lecture, not getting one felt a little like he gave up on her. It reminded her of how she'd felt that morning at her mom's house, like she'd let something precious slip through her fingers.

He crouched in front of the stove and began layering kindling and twisted up newspapers, explaining each step as he did it, little of which she heard. Instead, she was taking in all the wrong information, like how adept he was at making a fire, how down-to-earth he looked in his jeans with his shirt-sleeves rolled up. He seemed so different when not in uniform, more approachable. Although right then he was all business, she knew if she hadn't messed it up she'd be seeing the softer side of him. Again she felt a rush of regret and wondered how she could fix it. Before she had a chance to clear her head and start paying attention, he was shutting the little door on a roaring fire. His careful explanations were lost while she was staring stupidly at him.

"There you go." He stood up and brushed his hands off on his jeans. "Keep this going until you go to bed. In the morning, get it going again, and when you leave for school, check the dampers. The way this is set up, you should be able to come home to a reasonably warm house, and then stoke it up again to get it warm enough to last overnight. But you have to mind the dampers and burn the right wood. I took my seasoned logs and cut them down to fit this stove. They're stacked for you out back. You have a cord to start with." So he'd cut and stacked an entire cord of wood for her after she'd ignored him and dodged his call. Katherine's heart melted right there, but Mac was still standoffish, his face still stony.

He turned away from her to pick up his coat and leave. "You should be all set now. Good night." Clearly he had received the unspoken message she now wished that she hadn't sent. Katherine went to war with herself over whether or not to try to repair the damage. The war lasted about three seconds.

"Please wait," she said so softly that she wasn't sure he had heard her. He stopped at the door, and she caught up as he slowly turned to face her. "I thought I'd have more time to think of something clever to say, but . . . can you imagine that I've apologized? Really nicely? Because I do want to apologize. Dodging you last week was a lousy thing to do."

Ever so slightly, his expression softened. "It was an emergency. If I could have come back to see you, I would have."

"But you didn't call or text."

"There's times I can't."

"For three days?"

"I'm out of practice, Kate," he admitted. "I haven't had anyone to care whether or not I called in a long time."

Katherine felt another squeeze on her heart.

"Pete clued me in when I got back, and I would have explained that had you actually answered the door . . ." He took a breath. "Do you think you can stop assuming the worst about everything I do and say? Because that's what it's going to take to make any kind of relationship between us work. Kate, you are the most beautiful and intelligent woman I have ever met."

She felt a burst of warmth at his compliment and then steeled herself for the likely caveat.

"But you're also the most stubborn, the most . . . defiant. I keep going wrong here no matter what I do. I need to know if you can give this a real chance."

She took a deep breath, trying to answer in a way that was entirely honest. He leaned on the doorframe, his arms crossed over his chest like he was waiting for her to sort it out. He wasn't encouraging her with one of his rare smiles or soft expressions either. He was leaving it up to her. This was her move. She knew that if she faltered here it would be the last time he tried. Even as conflicted as she was about him, she didn't want him to walk away.

"Mac, I'm up here to do this job, but also to get some stuff worked out, and a relationship is not part of the plan." She paused and moved a step closer to him, almost unable to stop herself, like a little moon caught up in his gravity. He watched her move, but said nothing, did nothing, only waited for her to go on. "But then there's you, and you're a good man; one I actually like when you're not lecturing me or being condescending." The edges of his lips lifted as if he was fighting off a smile. "I had it all planned out, a few months up in the middle of nowhere to get my life sorted, but you're kind of blowing that up."

"Your life isn't sorted?"

"It looks good from the outside, doesn't it?" she said with a rueful smile.

"Are you here to find yourself?"

"Not really. I know where I am, and I don't like it. I came to where the pace of the world couldn't distract me from trying to change it."

"Am I a distraction?"

"Definitely," she said with a sigh, and for some reason this answer seemed to please him. He didn't look like the big bad cop right now, not with his blue-green eyes focused intently on hers, waiting for her to decide. "I'd like to be distracted." And with her finger and thumb she measured off an inch. "A little."

He smiled for real then, and, standing away from the door, he took a step closer to her. "Okay. Let's try this again." His voice was low and soft.

Katherine felt her pulse kick up a notch as he took another step nearer.

"Tomorrow, Kate." He reached out and took her hand, raising it and kissing the back of it, his eyes on hers, and the look in them gave her fluttery feelings. "Don't go disappearing on me." She shook her head. "And answer if I call." She nodded. He turned her hand over and kissed her palm, the stubble of his chin against her skin giving her goosebumps. "Goodnight, Kate."

The door shut; she heard his feet on the porch, then down the stairs, and then gone. She was still frozen to the spot, stunned by his sweetness and gentleness. "I am out of my mind," she said aloud.

CHAPTER FIFTEEN

MAC LOOKED DOWN AT THE WOMAN in front of him and took a breath to steady himself before he spoke. "Ma'am, there's not a lot I can do if she doesn't turn herself in."

"Please." She looked up at him and he saw it there in her eyes, the desperation, the helplessness, and the fear. Something he'd felt a hundred times. He struggled not to react, not to feel at all. Mrs. Fontaine was probably in her late fifties, the silver in her hair more an accent than a take-over. He could see years of care worn into her skin. Her hands were clasped in front of her, her fingers white from holding on so hard.

"There are programs . . ."

"She won't go. I've tried."

"Maybe if her dad . . ."

"He said she's dead to him," and her voice broke. She blinked in rapid succession before continuing. "I know she's using again. She won't answer her door. I don't have the key, and the landlord won't let me in; he said it has to be a cop."

"I've got no probable cause."

"I put an app on her phone that tracks her." She held out her own phone. "She left work thirty minutes ago, and that's halfway through her shift. That waitressing job is all she has, and she'd only leave it if it was to get high."

Mac inwardly sighed. This was all too familiar, but not enough, not nearly enough to warrant him breaking her door down or getting the landlord to open it.

"Please," the woman said again, and Mac felt the swell of emotion he was fighting break over the wall that was holding it back and wash over him. "Wellness check. You said you haven't spoken to her in days, and that she's not answering her door?"

"Well, yes, but the app says . . ."

"You said it's been three days," he interrupted, repeating it with emphasis.

"Yes." Hope lit her face. "I need a wellness check on my daughter," she told him, like they were speaking in code. "That's what I should have said. I haven't heard from her, and I'm concerned." The woman gave him the address, as well as the name and number for the landlord.

It was a man he knew, Mike Thomas, so at least getting into the building wouldn't be too difficult.

Mrs. Fontaine looked up at him with such relief he wanted to warn her not to get her hopes up, but it seemed to be too late. "Please save my daughter from herself. Please."

Her words were a kick in the gut he didn't need. He knew what he'd likely find when he went into the apartment and had been steeling himself. She was probably long past saving.

"I'll do what I can, ma'am, but you should know —"

"I do," she interrupted. "This stuff is . . . she was such a good kid." Shaking her head, she closed her eyes for a moment. "It's been three years. I know what you might find."

Mac nodded. Turning away, he pulled out his cell and called the landlord. Ten minutes later he was parked in front of the apartment building, waiting for Mike. Mac didn't have a good feeling about this, but, then again, when it was heroin, he never did. Looking up, he saw Mike arrive and get out of his truck. Mac got out of his cruiser and met him at the front steps. "Mac."

Mike held out his hand and Mac shook it. "Good to see you even if the circumstances are . . . well, she's a nice girl, but I had a feeling there was trouble."

"The mother asked to be let in?"

"Couple times in the last few months. Told her I couldn't, but she could call the cops. Glad she finally did." He held up a key ring and nodded to the front door. "She's 2B, second floor. C'mon up."

Following Mike, he entered the building and climbed the stairs to the second floor, feeling apprehensive the further they went. The building seemed decent, carpet in good shape, sufficient lighting, looked like good locks. Whoever the daughter was, she'd been together enough at one point to have taken care when she chose where to live.

Mike knocked on the door and called "Ms. Fontaine?" There was no answer. "Ms. Fontaine, I have Captain MacAlister here from the county police. We want to be sure you're okay." He opened the door and then stepped back.

Mac entered, and at first glance it seemed empty and relatively neat. There wasn't the usual physical evidence of addiction. There was no pile of dishes in the sink, no random clothing tossed everywhere, no half-eaten food left on the counter. "Ms. Fontaine, are you home?" he called as he moved through the apartment. The super stayed at the door. He probably knew the drill. Mac called for her again before checking the bathroom and the first bedroom. Again, it was all relatively neat and completely vacant, but it felt as still as death. The apprehension he was feeling with every step had changed to alarm. Something was off. He walked down a short hallway to the master bedroom.

She was on the bed. At first it looked like she was asleep, her long brown hair covering the pillow, the blanket pulled up to her chest. One arm was hanging over the edge of the bed. Stepping closer, Mac saw her eyes were open, her mouth slack. Moving quickly he felt for a pulse, for breathing, as he checked her over. He found the syringe on the floor and another wave of emotion washed over him: a mix of pity, regret, and anger. He grabbed his radio, called dispatch, and then began CPR, praying that somehow a miracle would occur and this girl would live.

Pete walked into Mac's office and took a seat in front of his desk. Mac saw the expression on his friend's face, and as much as he loved and respected the man, he wasn't ready to talk.

"You okay?" Pete asked.

"Nope." There was no point in trying to lie about it. Pete knew what responding to a heroin overdose would do to him. He didn't have to put on a brave face, but he wasn't about to spill his guts over it either.

"Heard the call and figured you'd be feeling it."

That was the understatement of the year. He should have let someone else handle that call. Tonight he'd probably relive it, caught in the 'what if' loop for hours. Then he thought of Mrs. Fontaine and the look on her face when she'd made it to the hospital. He knew that look. He'd seen it in the mirror often enough. It was the anger and helplessness that made the loss that much harder.

"It's not your fault," Pete said, interrupting his thoughts. "Like Cindy wasn't your fault."

"Pete, I appreciate the concern, but . . ."

"Shut my mouth, right?" he asked with a rueful smile. "Okay, then let me give you some information that might ease whatever it is you're feeling." Pete leaned in. "I think I know the dealer. I think the Sawyers have graduated from pills and pot. I caught Buddy Sawyer's two boys trespassing on that stretch of land beside the highway off Western Avenue. Do you know it?"

"Before the exit; it's posted, right?" Mac asked.

"Sure is, and the owner called me to report ATVs tearing up one of his fields, but they weren't joy-riders. It was the Sawyer brothers, and they weren't tearing up his fields; they were crossing them over and back a couple of times a week. This owner lives at the far end; if there was something back there he'd never know."

"What are you thinking?"

"I thought they might be cooking meth, but now I think they may have their hands on industrial-strength heroin. I'd heard something about them playing with a variety of chemicals and planning to sell it all, but I've never had any evidence."

"So, how's this helpful?"

"Last night, Buddy Sawyer was seen night-hunting. There's evidence he poached a deer, and that means I've got grounds for a search warrant. Thought I'd hit them by surprise, search the compound for deer meat, and see what else we find."

"That sounds iffy at best and hazardous to your health at worst. Buddy Sawyer is a nasty piece of work, and his boys are worse. You better go carefully and don't go alone."

"I got this covered." Pete sounded confident, but Mac knew with a family like that things could go south in a second. He'd have to be sure Pete was really getting back up. The man relied way too much on his ability to play the good cop, the nice guy. The Sawyers would see right through that.

Mac's phone chimed, and he pulled it out to see Kate had texted. He smiled and Pete chuckled. Looking up, he couldn't miss the satisfied grin on his friend's face.

"What?"

"I'm guessing I know who that's from."

"Shut it, Pete."

"Be sure to invite me to the wedding." In a far more serious tone he added, "You'll need to go carefully, you know that, right?"

Mac sighed. Pete wasn't going to let it go and, in a way, that was a good thing. He clearly cared for Katherine and didn't want Mac to make a mess of things.

Pete leaned forward, his hands braced on his knees. "The thing about Katie is that she looks like she can handle herself, take any hit, meet any challenge, but that's all her way of protecting herself.

The real Katie is in there, but she protects that like a lioness. You want in there, you're going to have to fight whatever it is that makes her bare those fangs and claws."

"I'm acquainted with those claws, Pete."

"I don't think so. The closer you get to what it is that hurts her, she'll do more than just call you a sarcastic name and walk off in a huff. She'll freeze you out. Hold on when it gets rough, both hands, because it'll get rough."

"Aren't you a ray of sunshine?" Mac knew any relationship with Kate would be complicated, but Pete was putting a serious dent in his happiness to finally get to find out exactly how complicated. "I will be careful, Pete. Don't worry. I know what I'm in for."

"I'm glad to hear that. I honestly believe that she needs you, probably more than you need her. And I'm really glad you didn't give up." Mac had no answer for this, just nodded. Pete gave him a chin lift and headed out of the office. Whatever it was that she was protecting, whatever in her past made her so cautious, it had to be something huge if she hadn't shared it with Pete. They were thick as thieves. All the way over to the school to pick her up, Mac silently prayed for both patience and discernment.

Katherine sat in her office, contemplating the text on her phone. She'd received one earlier that simply read: *Busy today. But can do dinner. Six. I'll pick you up. Text me where.* Despite last night's rather sweet goodbye, and the hint of more sweetness to come from the Captain, he was still cold and abrupt in his communication. But she had two choices: she could hold it against him, or she could get over it like a big girl and realize that a man who'd been a cop for most of his life and alone for a decade would need some understanding.

Understanding he'd get, but not without a little bit of a nudge. She'd texted back: *Hi! Thanks for asking if I'm free tonight. Dinner at six sounds great. I'll wait for you here at the school. I hope your busy day goes well.* She'd received a reply. *Affirmative. She chuckled.* That man was too much.

Outside her office she heard a commotion; shouts were turning into screeches. "What on earth . . ." She stepped into the hall to find two senior girls in each other's faces. One of them was Brittany Sullivan.

"You shut your mouth!" Brittany all but screamed at the other girl, whose expression was not angry at all. It was sly.

"You think I'd say anything?" Her tone was sickly-sweet and almost sing-song. She was egging Brittany on.

"Problem, ladies?" Katherine asked, and their heads whipped in her direction. The other girl blushed and shook her head before dropping her gaze to her toes.

"Okay, then it's ten minutes past dismissal, so I'd like to know what you two are doing in the hallway shouting at each other."

"I think this is in my purview, Dr. Grant." Katherine turned around to see Stephanie Campbell coming up the hall, her long gait eating up the distance. Brittany's shoulders slumped, but the other girl was back to looking sly.

This was not good. If there was one thing she definitely knew about Stephanie Campbell, it was that she was terrible with teenagers. She was likely to scream at these two and, in doing so, never discover what their beef was to begin with. Also, it was now common knowledge that Katherine had suggested Brittany's mom Erin as an emergency replacement for Bill Swift, and it was possible Stephanie held a grudge. Looking at Brittany's face now, maybe more than possible.

"If you don't mind, I'm all over this one, Mrs. Campbell."

Stephanie's face indicated that she did mind.

Katherine felt that it was worth burning through whatever patience the woman had left with her to save Brittany from her wrath. "The girls and I are going to have a chat in my office, and if there's anything that needs addressing, I'll let you know. Thanks." She nodded to Stephanie and motioned for the girls to follow her back into the office. Elaine gave her a big-eyed look, having clearly seen the exchange. Katherine mouthed to her 'Call Erin.'

The girls were sitting in the two chairs in front of her desk before Katherine had to ask. She shut her door and pivoted. "Now that everyone's had a chance to take a breath, let's talk about what it was that got so heated."

"I'm really sorry for shouting, and for arguing with Jenny in the hall," Brittany immediately offered. "I lost my temper, it wasn't Jenny's fault." Katherine didn't miss the look of surprise on Jenny's face. Then again, Katherine wasn't expecting Brittany to take all the blame either.

"I heard two voices raised," she countered, and the girls didn't speak.

Then, again Brittany tried to take the blame. "It really was me. Jenny . . . She . . . It really was me, the way I reacted, and I apologize. If you need to suspend me—"

"I'm not suspending anyone over an argument in the hall, but I'm also not hearing one word from Jenny." She faced the other girl. "What got so heated?"

Jenny shrugged. Whatever it was seemed to be a secret, and from the pleading look on Brittany's face it was a big one. Katherine began to feel uneasy. It went against what she'd normally do in this situation, but she pressed again. "What's going on, ladies?"

"I promise it's nothing to do with school." Brittany's voice shook like she was in a full-blown panic. "Please, Dr. Grant. I promise we won't argue again. I promise." Her voice was barely more than a whisper.

"Nothing you say here is going beyond these four walls." She tried to reassure Brittany, but it wasn't working, and Jenny was looking smugger by the moment. It irritated Katherine to the point she made a terrible mistake. "That's enough of this. Out with it,

Jenny."

"Brittany's pregnant."

Katherine's jaw dropped open as Brittany collapsed in her chair and burst into tears. Jenny sat smirking, seeming to enjoy the scene.

"Wipe that smile off your face," Katherine said, leaning forward. "Who else have you told?"

"No . . . No one," Jenny stuttered, and Katherine was glad she finally understood the seriousness of the situation.

"You are not to spread this information, you are not to let it slip, no anonymous posts on her Instagram, no tweets, no emails. You should never have known this to begin with, and I can only assume, since you're clearly not a friend of Brittany's, that you got this information by eavesdropping or gossip."

Jenny paled.

"I want your word that you will keep this to yourself."

"I promise." Jenny's voice was soft and contrite.

Katherine knew that she meant it for now, but there was no way she'd keep that promise. There was also no way Katherine could force her to keep quiet. "You're dismissed, but for the next two weeks you are not to be on campus unless school is in session. Is that understood?" Jenny nodded and got out of her chair. "That means no games, no clubs, not even vespers. You are not here unless you're in class." Jenny nodded again and practically ran from the office. She left the door open.

Elaine popped her head in. "Mrs. Sullivan is on the way." She ducked back out and shut the door.

"You called my mom?" If possible, Brittany looked even more distraught.

"I called her when I thought I might be hearing that you'd cut class or any number of far less serious things." She tried to keep her voice gentle. "I never imagined that something so personal would be shared." Brittany twisted her hands in her lap. "However, that being said, I can't let you leave without speaking to your mom. I'm guessing you haven't already told her." Brittany shook her head. "Then I'd advise you do it now. We can do it together if you like."

"Okay."

"How far along are you?"

"That's what Jenny overheard. I was telling Jake that I think I'm already twelve weeks. That means I'll never be able to graduate." Her voice broke on a sob.

She was right. Even if Jenny hadn't been eavesdropping and was certain to eventually spread the rumor, she'd be showing long before graduation. Per the school lifestyle conduct rules, both she and Jake would likely be disciplined, if not expelled. "And Jake can't . . . this can't happen to him. That's why I was trying to get Jenny to shut up about it. This is going to ruin all his plans."

She ducked a hand into the neck of her shirt and pulled out a long silver chain. At the end was a gold ring with a small diamond. "He asked me this summer, and I said yes, but we had to hide it because my mom would freak. We wanted to get married after graduation. He was gonna find a place near me and commute to work. We had it all planned out."

The door opened and Erin, looking more than a little concerned, walked in, took one look at Brittany, and then shut the door behind her.

"What's going on?" Her voice was somewhere between anger and fear. Brittany responded by bursting into tears again.

"Would you like me to help you tell your mom what we talked about?" Katherine asked, and Brittany nodded. "Erin, today I overheard Brittany and another girl arguing in the hall. I had them come to my office to explain what the difficulty was, and discovered that the girl had overheard Brittany confess that she's pregnant."

Erin's knees gave out and she stumble-stepped into the empty chair, her face pale.

"Brittany is very upset, obviously."

Erin said nothing.

"I can assure you that I had the other girl promise that she would keep this to herself."

"Right." The word from Erin was both sarcastic and tearful. "Sure she won't. In a week the entire town is going to know."

Katherine wanted to say 'no, of course not' but they both knew how the world worked.

"Brittany, we need to go home." She stood and Brittany followed. They huddled together for a moment, emotions playing over Erin's face. She was angry, but she also loved her daughter. "I'll come back for her stuff in her locker."

"You know she doesn't have to drop out. Not until you decide it's time or until--"

"Until that girl runs her mouth?" Erin shook her head. "No, she quits now so we can avoid that drama. Maybe she can get her GED or . . ." she trailed off and looked up at the ceiling.

Katherine could see the tears in her eyes, and her chest clenched with empathy. "I can help." Katherine stood as well, coming around the desk so she could give Erin's hand a squeeze. "We'll have you file to homeschool. Legally you can pull your child out at any time. I've got all kinds of information, and I can even tutor Brittany in the evenings. She's already so bright she really could probably take the GED now, but you don't want to go that route. You can homeschool this last year and still apply to all the colleges you wanted to. It won't change a thing. They're looking at your junior year transcripts anyway, and they're great."

"But how can she do college with a baby?"

"Lots of people do it. You're due in June?" Brittany nodded. "Then she has the whole summer to get a routine in place. Colby is not that far and, Brittany, with your grades I know you could get in."

"Why?" Erin asked, and Katherine didn't understand the question. "Why do you care?"

Truth was needed here, but this wasn't the time for it.

"Can I come by, tomorrow night maybe, and explain?"

Erin looked puzzled and a bit suspicious.

"I want to help. And not only Brittany. I know right now you're probably thinking about taking a shotgun to him, but I care very strongly about Jake's future, too. If there is one thing I cannot stand above all others, it would be what the world does to unwed moms."

Erin seemed to accept this. It was the truth, if not all of it.

Kate pushed to her feet. "Tomorrow then?"

"Yah, I guess. Come at seven so my boys will be done with dinner."

"I'll bring brownies."

Erin gave her a look that indicated she didn't think much of that suggestion, but she nodded anyway and they left the office.

Elaine wasted no time once they had left the building. "Everything okay?"

"Not even a little bit." Katherine sighed and motioned Elaine into her office. "I need to ask you not to mention this incident unless someone directly asks, and then to send them to me."

"Oh no problem, I'll act like I didn't see or hear a thing."

"Did you?"

"Well . . ."

"Elaine." Katherine gave her a hard look, and she crumbled like usual.

"Your door is sort of thin. But I had already guessed it anyway."

"What?"

"For the last month Brittany's worn nothing but sweatpants and hoodies, and for a girl who likes her clothes skintight, it was a red flag. When I could hear her screaming at Jenny to keep her mouth shut, I put two and two together. Jenny has always had a crush on Jake."

"Oh, the tangled web . . ."

"High school; it's a soap opera every day."

"So will Jenny keep her mouth shut?" Katherine asked the

question, fearing that she already knew the answer.

"Not a chance."

CHAPTER SIXTEEN

MAC PICKED KATHERINE UP AT THE school and took her to The Smooth Moose. "It's a little gritty, but they serve the best grilled cheese sandwiches I have ever tasted, and I know how you like grilled cheese," he explained with a wink.

The sandwich was as good as promised. Hers had tomato and pesto, something she would never bother with at home. Mac had gone with bacon and cheddar, not exactly a surprise. "After the day I've had," Katherine said with a sigh. "This is perfect. Comfort food."

"Bad day?"

She nodded her answer.

"Is it something you can share?"

"No." She took a drink of her iced tea, noting Mac had ordered the same. "You don't drink?" she asked, pointing at his glass.

"No. My father did. I decided pretty early on not to go there."

"'Did'?" She caught the use of past tense and wondered if he had lost his folks.

"He died when I was twelve; on the job, actually."

"He was a policeman, too?" It totally made sense that Mac was a second-generation cop. That authority seemed to be in his DNA.

"Dad was a patrolman. The night he was killed he and his partner were responding to a domestic dispute. They thought they had it under control. Boyfriend ends up pulling a knife out of nowhere, got Dad before his partner could even react. The knife nicked an artery, and Dad bled out."

Katherine reached across the table and laid her hand on his. "I'm so sorry."

Mac turned his hand over and held hers before she could take it back. "It was a long time ago. My mom had a tough go of it, but she always knew he wasn't going to die in his sleep at eighty. My uncles stepped up and tried to make sure we didn't feel it. They took me to Yankees games and fixed Mom's car, or shoveled her walk, that kind of thing. My mom was a rock. I still felt the loss, but she took a lot on herself to lessen it. Too much probably."

Katherine looked up sharply, catching the past tense yet again, and he nodded the answer to her un-asked question. "I lost her three years ago. Complications from pneumonia."

Katherine murmured another sorry.

He held her hand tighter. "Thanks. She was always overdoing it. I told her that a hundred times, but she was pretty stubborn. Insisted on staying in New York, insisted on working even when she could have retired. Mom was made of iron."

"Not the Grant women. My mother says we're like reeds to the winds of fate; pushovers."

"It's better to be a reed. You bend rather than break."

"Sometimes you break." Katherine looked down at her plate, afraid she was sharing too much.

The waitress came by and interrupted them with a refill of their drinks. Mac ordered dessert–Indian pudding–and she made a face. "Trust me on this one. It's incredible." When it arrived it looked like bread pudding with a scoop of vanilla ice cream melting into it. "Try it," he insisted, so she did.

Mac wasn't exaggerating; it was really good – warm, spicy, and sweet. It was so good she spoon-wrestled him for the last bite. After the dishes were cleared she said, "Now I've got to ask you the one question that has been on my mind for ages."

"Fire away."

"What's your first name?"

As soon as the words were out of her mouth he frowned, looking puzzled, as if the question was completely out of left field. "Didn't I ever tell you?"

"No, that first night at the cabin when we got around to the names part, you just told me to call you Mac—rather dismissively, come to think of it."

"I was distracted by those Christmas lights masquerading as a fire hazard you had wrapped around a completely flammable hearth," he said flatly, but his eyes were full of mirth.

"Okay, you get a pass, but you still haven't told me."

"Kyle Patrick MacAlister. Now you have the whole thing."

"Kyle is a great name; why do you use Mac?"

"I used to think it was a guy thing. Nicknames. First it was the boys in the neighborhood, then it was the guys I was friends with at college, then the academy . . . But I think it's more my last name, instant nickname. Even my wife called me Mac."

Whoa. Mac had been married. She tried to hide her shock at him slipping that in with no warning. He was older than she was, after all, good-looking, and successful. It made sense that he would have had a wife. "I didn't realize you'd been married."

"Got married right out of high school." Clearly it was the theme of the day.

"That's pretty young,"

"Too young. I wasn't ready, she wasn't ready. Where we were from, though, that's what you did. You finished school, got a job, got a wife, and got on with it. All of our friends had pretty much the same story."

"There's nothing wrong with that," Katherine insisted, thinking about Brittany and Jake.

"There is if you're not prepared to be a husband, and I wasn't. All I had in my head was getting my shield, making it past my old man. I thought she was happy at home, so I left her there. By the time I looked around and remembered I had a wife, she was lost."

Katherine waited for him to go on.

"Drugs. I never saw it, not until it was too late."

"Some people are really good at hiding it."

Seeing the guilty look on his face, she wanted to say something to change it, but pressed her lips together, waiting for him to continue.

"Yes, and Cindy was a master at it, but it got bad because I wasn't paying attention. I was working all the time, never home, never there for her." He took a drink like he needed a break. "She wanted kids. I told her we had to wait. It takes a while to make detective, and I wasn't aiming to only be a burglary guy. I wanted the prestige spot—homicide. That meant busting my . . ." he smiled. "That meant a lot of work. She would ask me every once in a while if we could start a family, and I'd tell her no. After a while she stopped asking. We moved to Manhattan when I made detective, and she fell in with a group of friends who partied a bit hard, but I thought they were okay. She was happy, always going out. I was actually glad." There was bitterness in his words. "All that time she was moving from alcohol, to prescription drugs, to heroin, and there is nothing like that last one for destroying a person." He shook his head. "I came home one night and found her passed out. Finally, I clued in, but it was too late." He paused for so long that she wasn't sure if he was lost in a memory or gathering courage.

"What happened?" she asked softly.

"She overdosed." Katherine reached out again and took his hand. "I'm really sorry. I can't imagine how much that must have hurt."

"It did, but I felt like I deserved it."

"You must know that her death was not your fault."

"Yes and no."

Katherine tried to read his face, but he wasn't giving anything away.

"I neglected her, and that both fueled her addiction and enabled it. The overdose was Cindy choosing the high over everything else: her family, me, life itself. In the end, she destroyed herself, but it's not like I'm blameless." With a bleak expression he looked down at their clasped hands, his thumb gently stroking the back of her hand.

If they'd been at her house, Katherine would have cleared the table to hug him by now, her desire was so strong to wipe that look off his face.

"It was a rough few years after she died. I thought that I deserved to suffer, that it was my penance. As if you could ever atone for something like that." He squeezed her hand a little tighter. "In the end I had to leave. Everyone thought I was nuts for going from Manhattan to Maine."

"You left the suits behind for a uniform?"

"I brought a few of the suits with me," he said with a wink. "I don't mind being back in uniform, though, and it's second-nature now. I've been up here for ten years."

"Really? How long ago did she die?"

"Fifteen years." He paused. "I'm sure you're doing the math and figuring out I'm a geezer. Turned forty-two this year."

"Wow, you do *not* look your age."

"Good." He sounded relieved. "I was a bit worried I was too old for you."

"Uh, no, Mac, I'm thirty-five."

He sat back, his turn to look surprised. "I thought you were thirty at most. I should have done the math on you, I guess; with all your degrees and accomplishments you'd have to be older than that."

"A very elegant compliment, thank you." She toasted him with her glass, "But one undergrad, one Master's, and two doctorates aren't actually a lot in my field. In education you typically have to get multiple degrees if you want to be an administrator."

"Is that what you were aiming for all along?"

"No. I was aiming for wife and mother," she said before she could stop herself.

Mac raised an eyebrow and she knew he'd have some

questions she really didn't want to answer. Luckily, while she was panicking, his phone rang. He sat back to answer, letting her hand fall away. The conversation was brief and ended with the usual, "Give me twenty and I'll be there."

"You've got to go?"

"I'm sorry. I'll get the check. You'd think that with two new deputies . . ." he trailed off and got up to find the waitress. Once Katherine was settled in his truck and they were on the road, Mac looked at his watch. "I only have a few minutes until we get to your car, and I was going to try and be smooth, but you already know I'm not."

Katherine laughed.

"I like you, Kate, and I want to see more of you, on a regular basis."

"Dating," she said solemnly.

"I can tell you're not thrilled with that idea, and I suppose it's because you're out of here soon. I'll be honest; it's what kept me from asking you out the first day I met you. It's also why I was such a jerk. But the other night I was thinking we've still got months, and it's worth taking a shot at it. Man, that sounds stupid, but I think we might have something worth exploring," he said, dividing his attention between her and the road.

"Okay."

"Now I know that . . . wait," he said, his eyes darting back to her. "Did you say 'okay'?"

"Yes. I sort of surprised myself with that answer," she admitted.

Mac laughed, but went right back to it. "How about dinner Friday night? There's a restaurant over in Lovell; it's a bit of a hike, but they do this farm-to-table thing that's out of this world, even in winter."

"Wow—cop, rancher, and foodie?"

"Not a foodie, but I do like good food. And rancher? Honey, I've got two horses, a goat, and one lonely cow. Not exactly ranch-

levels."

"I've been meaning to ask you. How on earth did those horses get named 'Misery' and 'Agony'?"

"Their owner up in Saratoga had a bad sense of humor."

"C'mon there's got to be more than that."

"They had the usual sorts of names for race horses until one day they finished a race tied for last. He lost his temper and renamed them."

"That seems kind of harsh."

"Turns out he'd bet the farm, literally, on them finishing first and second. He went bankrupt pretty soon after, and an old friend of mine got in touch when the horses couldn't find another home."

"Why didn't you rename them?"

"They didn't seem to mind." He shrugged. "Anyway, you didn't answer my question. How about it? Dinner, Friday night." He pulled into the parking lot next to her car.

"I'd like that."

"Great," he reached out slowly and laid his palm against her cheek.

A shiver, the good kind, ran through her at the sensation of his warm hand against her skin. That touch felt so tender that once again she leaned her cheek into his hand. His eyes dropped to her mouth as his thumb stroked her bottom lip. He was fixed on it for a moment, and she wondered if it was because he wanted to kiss her.

"Good night." His hand dropped away. "I'll call you tomorrow."

She got out, waved goodbye, and got into her car, not minding that he hadn't kissed her. First kisses were special, and she loved that he was saving theirs for someplace other than the front seat of his truck.

CHAPTER SEVENTEEN

"RUMOR HAS IT YOU HAVE A date," Erin said as Katherine walked into the Sullivan house the following night.

It wasn't the opening line she expected to hear. She handed the tray of brownies to Erin who took them to the little kitchen, which was every bit as cheerful and perfect as she remembered it from the photos the school had sent. An unavoidable pang of jealousy coursed through her before she was able to dismiss it and remember that Erin had three kids. They deserved this nice house, considering what troubles lay ahead.

"How on earth would you know that?" she asked.

"Town blog? Duh."

"The Lowdown strikes again," Katherine muttered.

"And Anne, the dispatcher. She's one of my clients. She said Mac threatened her with night shifts if she let anyone call him in, and she wheedled it out of him that he had a date—although he wouldn't say who—not like he needed to."

"Are you . . . I mean I know you, well I don't know . . ."

"Stop with the brain stutter." Erin held up a hand. "I'm fine. Mac is a friend, has been for a long time. If he was ever going to be something else to me, it would have happened already. He's always careful about that, never gives anyone the wrong idea."

"And you're cool with it?"

"Listen to you with the hip slang. Yes, I'm fine." She started hacking up the brownies. "I knew it that first day. I've tried to get him to look at me like that for ages. Here you come, actually ticking him off, and he still looks at you like he's seeing home for the first time."

Katherine gave herself a second to absorb that, and the little thrill that ran through her along with it. *Nope, can't do it.* She'd have to file that comment away for later examination. "How could you tell with his sunglasses on?"

"His face, it softened." She shrugged. "Mac has like, two expressions: stern cop face, stern guy face. Even when he's in a good mood or laughing, it's still pretty hard. He looked at you, and it softened."

"I have no idea why since about all I do is annoy him."

"Good, he needs more of that." She arranged the brownies on a blue Fiestaware plate. "Enough about Mac. I'm fine, but I'm not giddy over it, so let's drop it. Besides it's time to feed the beasts." And she walked into the dining room. At a large dining table two boys sat with books open, papers strewn about, and pencils raised in a sword fight. "Hey!" Erin shouted and they stopped. "I have brownies, but only for boys who finish their homework."

They instantly dropped their heads and began poring over their work. "That's better," Erin said, laying a brownie on a paper towel next to each of them. "Don't make a mess." She walked Katherine back out to the living room, and they both took a seat on the couch, the plate of brownies between them. The boys came in right after, but she shooed them upstairs to brush their teeth and go to bed.

"Brittany is at my sister's house tonight." She paused. "She needs some distance from Jake right now so she can have a clear head. I was going to have Mac talk to him, but that's putting him in an awkward spot."

"What about Dr. Connors?"

"Why didn't I think of that!" Then her face sort of fell. "That man completely intimidates me."

"Why? He's so nice."

"I can't explain it; it's just one of those things. You wouldn't understand."

"Try me."

She sighed. "He's the church pastor, and I'm . . ."

Katherine waited, hoping that Erin would feel safe enough to share whatever it was with her.

"I'm a single mom with three kids and a drunken idiot of an ex-husband, a late ex-husband actually, or did you already know that?"

"Yes." Katherine said as gently as she could. "I looked up Brittany's records when we spoke. I'm so sorry. That must be hard on the kids."

"Yah, they take the brunt of it in messy stuff like this. Jimmy wasn't anyone they could respect while he was alive, and once he was dead . . . it took them a long time to forgive him for not being a dad they could be proud of. Longer than me."

"And you've forgiven him?" Katherine was surprised. She didn't know a lot of women who forgave their ex-husbands for being jerks.

"That's actually due to Dr. Connors—another reason for me to be intimidated by the man. One Sunday he was talking about forgiveness, and it was like he had written that sermon for me. Luckily I was doing nursery duty that day, and they have the audio feed over a speaker down there, so only the babies saw me cry." She laughed. "It was that convicting. It was like he had looked into my heart and seen that giant-sized pile of hate I had for Jimmy. I wish I could remember what he said, but basically it was that you will never heal until you let go of it and forgive, even if the person doesn't deserve it. And Jimmy didn't. That's for sure."

"For a young guy, Dan can be really eloquent."

"Oh, he's not young," she immediately answered. "We're the same age, thirty-five. He spent ten years working in India, Bangladesh, and all these third-world countries where he worked at youth camps. He pretty much went right into missions after college. Never even married. He said God called him, and he responded. He only moved home when his mom got sick. Her stroke was really bad. He's stuck by her side, doing everything he can. I guess he's one of those guys who is too good for this earth."

"And you're into him?" Katherine said plainly, since it was obvious in the way she spoke about him, but with the shocked and almost frightened look on Erin's face, she instantly regretted pointing it out.

"What?" Erin sputtered.

"You . . . it just seems like you really like him. I mean, like him-like him." Katherine smiled and Erin picked up a brownie and threw it at her. "Hey!"

"Don't say anything." Erin sounded like she meant it.

"Of course I wouldn't. But I think you would make a good couple. Just saying," she added as Erin gave her a dirty look. "And thank you, Erin, for letting me come over and I hope, forgiving how we first met?"

"I changed my mind about you ages ago. I hadn't had the chance to make nice."

"What changed your mind?"

"You're wearing my earrings—the ones I made for the market in August. Nancy said you made a bee-line for them the second you saw them and asked her if she had any more. Then, of course, Mac told me how much you liked his bracelet."

"I love your work. Seriously." Erin laughed and Katherine added, "You have to tell me when your next show is or craft fair or whatever, because I'm probably going to buy everything there."

"Thanks. It's something I do to relieve stress, so hearing it makes you happy is a nice bonus." Erin shifted on the couch until she was sitting upright. "Much as I would like to sit here and talk about how talented I am, we need to talk about my daughter."

"I meant what I said yesterday. A baby does not shut the door on college." Katherine wasn't sure if she was pushing so hard for Brittany's sake or that even now she was wishing she could change the past.

"I think it's too late for that. She's determined to marry that kid and... I'm trying to understand what the right thing is to do. Part of me says that she should leave the baby with me and go to college, and then the other says she loves that boy and the two of them should try to make a go of it."

"Okay, but whichever way you go, she needs to finish the school year and graduate, either homeschool or public, so that if she decides later on that college is something she wants, she has a shot at it."

"That's the easy part. I took a look at the forms to fill out, and I think I can swing homeschooling."

"Great, and I can help you with that, too." Erin's brows rose. "Can I ask why? You don't know us from Adam and getting involved is drama you probably don't need."

Erin deserved a truthful answer, the whole truth, but Katherine still couldn't explain. "I grew up in a small town, too. I know what it's like to be shamed and discarded. I don't want that to happen to either Brittany or Jake. I want to help them start off right. Whatever way I can."

"You've got a story to tell, don't you?" Erin asked, but not like she was expecting an answer. "Some day when you're ready we can swap stories. Mine's a doozy, too."

"Thank you for understanding."

Erin waved off her thanks. "Of course. But, you'll talk to Dan for me, right? Set it up for him to talk to Jake?"

"If you'd really rather I do it, yes."

"I really would. I'll get the forms filled out for homeschool and you can look them over for me. Then we'll . . ." She stopped, closing her eyes for a moment before continuing. "Then we'll deal with it. Because what else can we do?"

"I know rough waters are ahead, Erin. I'm here in whatever way you need me."

"See, now that's why I can't hate you—not that I ever did. I'm stubborn and occasionally sarcastic; can you handle that in a friend?"

"Absolutely."

"Good. I have a feeling after this gets out I'll be down to only the one."

Katherine's stomach sank, knowing from experience that Erin was probably right. Depending on the kind of friends she had, they'd either stick with her or judge and avoid her. She leaned forward and hugged Erin.

Erin was still for a moment but then softened and hugged her back. "Don't make this a habit." Erin pulled back, her eyes a bit misty.

"Hey, can you do me a favor?"

"Depends." Erin narrowed her eyes.

"Mac is taking me to a restaurant in Lovell, does farm-to-table food. I have no idea what it's like, and I wondered if you'd ever been there. So I can know what to wear."

Erin looked at her with a slightly curled lip. "Are we seriously going to have the Rom Com moment where I help you pick out an outfit so you can go on a date with the guy I crushed on for years? Ah no. That's a bridge too far, sister."

"Shame. I do love your style."

"Flattery will not get you any help from me." Katherine gave her a frown and Erin huffed. "It's upscale, but not fancy. Wear a dress because that says you're serious, but don't go crazy; a church dress is fine."

"Got it. Thanks, Erin."

Erin hopped up from the couch, and Katherine followed. "I've got to go upstairs and deal with the boys. Remember to talk to Dan. Tonight, if you can. I don't know how long that girl will keep her mouth shut, so Jake's days at school are pretty much numbered, like literally."

"I will. I'm going to advise him to write a letter to the administration and the board together, rather than just going to

Stephanie. If he does that he might catch a break, and they could suspend him or confine him to campus."

"Whatever happens, happens." Erin shrugged her shoulders.

Katherine could tell Jake had a long, steep climb to regain Erin's good opinion. If he'd ever had it at all.

CHAPTER EIGHTEEN

FRIDAY NIGHT KATHERINE STOOD IN FRONT of the mirror and rethought her outfit for the gazillionth time. It was her favorite dress, her go-to, never-fail dress. From its warm brown color to its wrap-style, it was usually perfect, but tonight she was second-guessing everything. It was her first official date in nearly a decade and nothing was probably going to look right. She'd worn her hair down instead of up, and now she was even rethinking that. At least her boots were a no-brainer. It had snowed a foot yesterday so, whether she liked it or not, she had to wear her snow boots, even though they were the ones Mac laughed at. Why, she had no idea. They were cute, not funny.

Looking at the clock, she realized she was out of time. Mac would be there any second, so no more wardrobe changes. She grabbed her purse and chucked lip gloss and her phone inside. As she walked towards the door, he knocked, and she had to take a steadying breath. *Cool, calm, collected, this is no big deal*, she told herself. *He's just a guy, this is just a date.*

When she opened the door all of that flew right out the window. Mac was standing there with the hint of a smile on his lips, looking like a more handsome version of himself. A much more handsome version. Like her, he hadn't gone over the top, but he looked so different. He had to have picked up his clothes in New York since they were sophisticated and downright stylish. He had on a black turtleneck sweater, charcoal slacks, and a wide black leather belt all topped with a black overcoat he'd left unbuttoned.

The slight lift of his lips increased, and she realized he wasn't missing her drooling over him. *Nice.* She stepped out onto the little porch and shut the door behind her. "Ready," she announced.

He laughed lightly. "I think you'll probably want to get a coat on first."

"Right," she said, feeling her cheeks heat. Stepping back inside, she grabbed her coat, threw it on, and belted it tight. "Moron," she said under her breath before stepping out onto the porch again. Mac took her hand and escorted her out to his . . . muscle car? "Hey, this is sweet."

"It's a '69 Mustang Fastback. I thought for a first date this would be nicer than the truck. Usually it's under a tarp in my barn, but since we've got clear roads tonight, I thought I'd break her out."

Katherine smiled as he handed her in and shut the door. It was good to know she wasn't the only one worried about making a good impression.

Mac got into the car and turned to face her. "You're beautiful every day, Kate, but tonight you look incredible."

Katherine's heart melted a wee bit, and she was pretty sure she was blushing right up to her hairline. "Thanks. You kind of look like Steve McQueen. You know, with the black turtleneck and the car."

Mac laughed out loud. "Okay. That's a first." He started the car.

She felt the rumble of the engine in her chest. There was nothing like that sound. The drive to Lovell was about forty minutes, and she was looking forward to it since his car was awesome, but he drove it exactly like he did his truck. Boring.

"This car was built for speed, buddy. You could at least let it loose on the highway."

"The speed limit is there for a reason, Kate," he said sternly.

"Okay Dudley Do-Right," she said under her breath.

He gave her a stern look. "You are impossible, Dr. Grant."

When they got to the restaurant she was surprised to find it was in a large, barn-like building attached to a nineteenth-century inn. There was a huge hearth at one end and the kitchen at the other. Instead of individual tables for two or four, they had several long tables with bench seats. It went well with the Civil War-era building and décor, but it made for less intimate conversation.

The food was a set menu based on what was locally available. At first she was prepared for meat and potatoes, but the chef was far more creative. Each dish was spiced and seasoned perfectly, and there was fish, chicken, and some rather interesting veggies in the mix. Mac's taste in restaurants rivaled his taste in cars and clothes. The man had depths she had not expected.

They talked a bit about her work, a bit about his, but stayed away from the personal stuff. Mac saved that for the trip home. A few minutes into the drive, he said, "I had a great time tonight. I think this might be the best date I've had in . . . well, ever. Talking with you is a pleasure."

"Likewise, Mac," she said honestly. They'd discussed everything from politics to theology and hadn't argued once. It was probably a record for them.

"I'm glad we have the drive home to talk some more, because there's something that I want to bring up and it might be a bit awkward."

"I knew it couldn't last," she sighed.

"What couldn't?"

"Us not arguing."

"It's nothing to get your back up, or at least I think it's not." He paused. "I haven't dated anyone in a while."

"Pete said as much."

"What he probably left out is that before . . . let's just say I was kind of in a tailspin after Cindy died. I took comfort where I could find it. I'm not proud of that, and when I made the decision to come up here I meant it to be a clean break from who I'd become, all of who I'd become."

"If you're worried that I'm going to judge you—"

"No, it's not that. I wanted to give you a reason for the rules."

"Rules?"

"The rules I need to put in place for us going forward. We're both in public jobs, and we need to avoid any drama, but it's more than that. I know my limits, and I need to respect those and you. This is how I can do that. They're pretty simple."

Mac might say that, but Katherine didn't like anyone making up rules for her to live by. She tried to suppress her knee-jerk reaction, though. Mac wanted to respect her and their fledgling relationship, and she should hear him out.

"The first is that I won't be in your house with you alone, and I won't ask you to my place unless it's as a guest with others joining."

"Oh," she said softly, a bit disappointed this meant no cuddling in front of a fire or movie nights at his place. Then again, maybe he didn't have a TV, either.

"Being alone with you is something I'm looking forward to. I've got a snowmobile track practically out my back door and even in all this snow there's places we can take the horses. Pete told me you can ride," he added as an aside. "I'd like as much time with you as possible, but making love to you is something I intend to save for our wedding night."

"Wedding night?" she choked out. "Aren't you sort of accelerating things?"

"No. The whole purpose of dating is to see if the attraction you feel can turn into something else: love. If it can't, there's no point in still dating, is there?"

"I guess not," she said flatly, feeling a bit overwhelmed.

"It's another one of the rules—I state my intentions so you know where you stand. I also assume that this is exclusive." He chanced a glance at her here, and she nodded. "Good. And I'd like it if we made a habit of going to church together. People in town are gonna talk like there's no tomorrow, so I don't want anyone getting the wrong idea about what this is."

"What is this?" Katherine asked.

Mac reached out and took her hand, but kept his eyes on the road. "It's dating with a purpose, and the purpose is marriage."

Katherine stared at the side of his head, completely floored. What on earth was he thinking? Marriage? She returned her attention to the road in front of them and tried not to let on that he'd freaked her out. They'd had a tiny handful of civil conversations, never even kissed, and he was talking about forever. Who did that? She took a quiet breath, slow and steady, trying not to have a panic attack.

When they finally got back to her cabin, she walked up the steps of her porch, turning back once she reached the door. "So . . ." she said, trying to think of what to say and drawing a complete blank.

"I freaked you out, didn't I?" he asked, standing close, and she nodded. "I don't see any point in us dating if marriage isn't my endgame. Otherwise it's torture."

"See, that I do not get."

"You're not a guy," he said with a little laugh, running his hand through his hair, making her fingers itch to do the same. He caught that longing look, and she could see it returned to her two-fold as he moved a little closer, his face bare inches from hers. He stroked her cheek, lifting her chin to tilt her face up to his. "You blow all my safeties, Katherine Grant," he whispered and his lips touched hers for the very first time.

As first kisses went, his was off-the-charts good. He made it even better by putting his arms around her and holding her against him. She didn't think one second about the fact that this was the first time anyone had kissed her in years. She didn't worry about what he was thinking. She didn't obsess over what her breath might smell like. The kiss and the warmth of his arms around her made her head spin like a DVD failing to load. Before she realized what she was doing, her arms were around his shoulders and one of her hands in his hair. It was an absolutely perfect moment.

When his arms fell away and the kiss ended, it took her a second to come back down to earth and let him go. He slowly stood back from her, his eyes lingering on her face, and she knew why he was being cautious. It wasn't like they were teenagers. They both knew exactly how good that kiss was and what that meant for all that could follow after it. "I think I'd better say goodnight." Katherine nodded in agreement, words pretty much beyond her power, and fumbled in her pocket for her keys.

Once she had the door open, he said, "I'll wait here while you get safely inside."

She rolled her eyes at this, but appreciated the gesture.

"Goodnight, Kate."

"Goodnight, Mac," she answered before closing the door. As soon as she was in and she heard him leave, she got into her PJs, took her phone, and climbed up into the loft. Under her covers, she dialed Heather and immediately launched into a recap, ending with a repetition of his rules. That kiss, and her reaction to it, she kept to herself. "How weird is that?"

"Oh, I don't think it's weird at all. I think it's sweet."

"He said marriage. We've known each other a few months, that was literally our first real date, and he said marriage."

"Sweetie, this is a good thing. He's letting you know he's serious, that he wants something real."

"What if what all he wants is a reboot? Another shot at a happy family? I can't give him that."

"You need to talk to him in the same honest way he spoke to you. And you need to do it soon."

CHAPTER NINETEEN

CHRISTMAS BREAK ARRIVED, AND FOR ONCE Katherine was not thrilled to be spending two weeks with her sisters, mom, and Heather's family. Part of her wanted to stay on the mountain and have Christmas amongst the snow, pine trees, and her new friends; or if she was honest, Mac. As much as he still frustrated her, she was getting used to spending part of nearly every day with him. They'd only been official for a week, but he'd show up on her steps in the morning with a to-go cup of coffee exactly how she liked it, and twice he'd brought her lunch at school and stayed to eat with her. At night, if they didn't spend time having dinner at Maria's or the Moose, he'd call her and they'd talk for an hour.

How she got to that place with him was a mystery, since he still nagged her every chance he got, including today.

"You need to garage this car and get a 4x4 for the rest of the winter." This was Mac's way of saying goodbye, apparently. They were standing in her driveway, and she was expecting a tender moment before she had to drive for hours to get to her sister's house.

"I told you, Henry is good in snow."

"No rear-wheel drive car is good in snow." He was in lecture-mode again, his face stern, his hands on his hips.

"Don't get all . . ." She waved a hand to indicate his stance. "I've had this car for years. We've been through multiple winters together, Captain Careful." She was going to tell him exactly what she thought of his over-protectiveness, but he'd pulled her into his arms and kissed her. It was a very effective way to win an argument since his kisses scattered her brain, especially the ones where she found herself wrapped up in his arms.

Still holding her tight, he lifted his head, brushing her lips with his softly. "Come home to me in one piece." His voice was quiet, but gruff. Those words echoed in her head for days.

The first week of vacation she spent with her mother and her two sisters and their families. She loved every minute of it, soaking in their happy chaos. The next week she stayed with Heather, Michael, their three boys, and baby Mirabelle, and it was more chaos, but still the good kind, the kid kind. Katherine got as much snuggle time with the baby as she could before her break ended. As she and Heather sat together one night, Katherine rocking Mirabelle and Heather curled up on the couch, her friend asked a question she wasn't prepared for.

"Are you going to come home in February as scheduled, or is Captain Mac tempting you to stay in Sweet River?" *Come home to me . . .* floated through her head.

Katherine ceased her rocking and stared at Heather.

Heather sat up and stared right back. "You do realize that your contract is almost up. In order for things to work out with Mac, one of you eventually has to relocate. I would think it would be you since your roots aren't that deep out on the Cape. You've rented that place out for years and could keep right on doing that, maybe keeping a month free in the summer to visit us."

"I keep forgetting that I'm almost done and he's . . ." Her head was suddenly filled with questions she hadn't thought about. How would she earn a living up there? He lived in the middle of nowhere and traveling to and from Sweet River was a pain; there was no airport she could fly out of any closer than Portland. Mac didn't have the kind of career that would allow for time to pursue a long-distance relationship. It dawned on her that if she didn't do something, her relationship with Mac had an end date stamped right on it, and it was barely more than a month away.

"Probably time to start thinking," Heather said quietly as she sat back again.

Katherine cuddled Mirabelle's pudgy little body closer and kissed her silky head. The baby's warmth and weight was comforting when thinking about the possibilities, both scary and thrilling, that might lie ahead. "What if I can't do it?" she asked aloud, not really expecting an answer, but she got one anyway.

"Sweet River is good for you. I've seen the change in you in just the last few months. You're more open, sort of…softer. I don't think it's just your new boyfriend either." Heather gave her a smile.

"Do you think I should stay up there?"

"I can't tell you one way or the other. I think you need to wait and listen for God's will."

"Well, waiting I can do. Listening I'm trying to be better at."

"Go sit in the woods or something."

"It's snowy in the woods."

"You know what I mean." Heather nudged her with her foot and Katherine started rocking with Mirabelle again, her head full of thoughts that left her heart confused.

As he'd asked her to do, Katherine came home to Mac in one piece, but he wasn't there to see it. He'd been appointed some kind of training coordinator and now would be traveling frequently. There was something of a silver lining, in that he hired Jake as his 'ranch hand' since he wouldn't have as much time to take care of his animals. Jake was still at school, but it was only a question of time before the news broke and he was expelled. Dr. Connors had begun counseling him on his options and was steering him towards a full confession. Dan was telling him it was the right thing to do, and

Katherine agreed since Jake had violated the lifestyle conduct rules.

Things with Stephanie were now so tense that Katherine had begun to brace anytime she had a meeting with the woman, like she did now. Looking up at the clock she saw that, as usual, Stephanie was late. Not enough for Katherine to make an issue of it, but enough for Stephanie to make her point. Katherine already knew the woman had no respect for her, she didn't need the reminder.

At five after three, Stephanie walked into Katherine's office and stiffly took the seat in front of her desk without a word.

"Hi!" Katherine said cheerfully, shifting aside her irritation.

"We'll need to get going," Stephanie skipped any pleasantries. "I have another appointment after this."

"No problem." Katherine decided not to point out that it was Stephanie who had arrived late. "Elaine provided me a copy of the spring schedule, so if you've got yours we can dive in."

Stephanie leaned over and pulled a single sheet of paper out of the bag she'd brought with her as if it was an imposition.

"Great. So first up is the formal. I know that previously it's been held in the gym, but there's been a request from this year's planning committee that it be moved to Harper's Farm, and I think it's a great idea. I know the barn is popular for weddings, so it's perfect for a formal."

Stephanie's expression hardly changed. It was still stuck at disdain.

"You know, one of the parent volunteers told me they used to have dances at Harper's barn a century ago."

Stephanie was not impressed.

"I think that's great, sort of a connection with the past and the town's history. Good for local good will, as well."

"I suppose." Stephanie sighed and looked down at her schedule.

Katherine stifled her own sigh and began again. "So after the formal we have two prospective student weekends, and you'll want to be thinking of a few parents we can ask to be tour guides. We need to choose these carefully because they and their children end up being walking references for the school."

"Well then, Erin Sullivan is out." Stephanie lifted her eyes and met Katherine's stare. "After all, we can hardly call her a good reference."

"I think that's—"

"What you think, *Kathy*," and Stephanie emphasized the nickname she knew full well Katherine hated, "isn't the point, is it? It's what a prospective parent will think."

The dig at Erin was nothing but bait for a fight that would reveal more than Katherine wanted to, so she didn't take it. "I doubt Erin has the time, so it's beside the point. Rebecca Allen would be a good choice. She's very outgoing and enthusiastic about the school. She also has the time. If you can come up with one or two others we'll be all set."

"What about Holly Markham?" Stephanie asked and Katherine frowned, trying to place the name. "Jenny Markham's mother." Jenny who had eavesdropped on Brittany to begin with and started all the drama? "Of course, she might not be the best choice after you disciplined her daughter for that fight with Brittany."

"I believe it's best if we choose parents of students in good standing, since the students lead part of the tour."

"Jenny's standing is fine with me." Stephanie's tone was caustic. "She's always been very helpful and respectful of authority. Proper authority," Stephanie added.

Katherine had no doubt that the director had either coerced Jenny into talking or she was bluffing. Again, she didn't take the bait. "I'm glad you've had positive experiences with her. As it is, she's not a good choice for the student tours at the moment. Do you have no other suggestions?"

Stephanie shook her head and Katherine moved on to the next item. The rest of the meeting was fraught with tension. When Stephanie finally left, Katherine felt exhausted and strung-out. It was time to call it a day. On the way home she got a call from Mac, on his way back from training.

"You, sir, have rotten timing."

"Why?"

"I'm busy tonight."

"Who said I was calling to ask you out?"

"Weren't you?"

"Yes," he chuckled and then added "Busy with . . ."

"Pete. I'm cooking for him tonight."

"So I'm getting thrown over for the old man?" Mac didn't sound like he minded. "Fine, but one of these nights you can come over to my place and make us both dinner. How about that?"

"I'd like that." She'd watched a Patriot's game there with him and Pete one afternoon. Mac had a huge kitchen, with beautiful appliances he pretty much never used. He also had a sunken living room with a big leather sectional and a flat-screen TV that took up the better part of one wall. When she'd needled him about it, he said it was to make up for not being able to go to Yankees games anymore. Apparently on his side of the hill he could get a satellite signal. Halfway through the game she'd fallen asleep and woke up cuddled against Mac, a blanket thrown over her. "Maybe no football this time?"

"Yah, I noticed you're not a fan. We'll make it a movie. You got a preference?"

"No horror, no war movies unless it's something epic. Like no Rambo stuff. No Chuck Norris either. Bruce Lee I can do." She heard Mac laughing. "What?"

"Bruce Lee?"

"I'm trying to compromise here."

"Okay, I'll get creative. Might be some complaining from Pete, but I'll find something you both like. Tell him Sunday night is good if he's available."

When she arrived at Pete's, her heart was still heavy despite Mac's call. She was thinking about Brittany and Jake's troubles and what might lie ahead. Pete's radar was up from almost the minute she walked in, so she got down to cooking dinner to keep him from asking any questions. She made roasted vegetable frittata, and he gave it the side-eye until she assured him it had plenty of cheese and therefore he'd love it.

After dinner he cleared the dishes, served the coffee, and then launched right in. He hadn't missed the mood she was in, but he picked the wrong cause. "Everything going okay with Mac?"

"Surprisingly, yes."

He raised an eyebrow at her answer.

"All things considered."

"What kind of things?"

She shifted on her chair thinking of a way to put it. "I don't have the greatest track record with relationships, and Mac isn't interested in keeping this casual. I'm honestly not sure I want to be married. I know that sounds ridiculous because we've only been dating a few weeks, and for half of that I was on vacation, but the idea of that kind of permanence worries me. Once bitten…" It hurt to admit that. It was like the scar she bore. It had faded, sure, but it was still there, always would be. The scars on her heart were the same, faded, but not gone. A feeling of inadequacy settled over her. "I don't know where he gets his confidence. I'd like to have half of it."

"I think it comes from the fact that he's done this before. Love, that is. For all the mistakes he made, he loved Cindy something fierce. He'd know it if he felt it again." Katherine was about to object before he held up a hand. "I'm not saying he's already in love with you, but I think he's headed there."

That shook her.

Pete didn't miss her reaction. "Why does that scare you?"

"That's part of the 'all things considered'."

"It's that story you can't tell me." Pete seemed to be disappointed, as if she couldn't trust him.

She didn't want him to feel like that. She did trust him, thought the world of him. Slowly he seemed to retreat, and she could feel a kind of pressure build inside her. Trying to ignore it, she searched for something to say to explain, but she floundered in silence.

"I was engaged once," she blurted out, and the story almost began to tell itself. It seemed to spill out of her. "His name was Tom. We grew up together, worked at the same church. He was finishing up at the seminary and I was in my first year of teaching. Four months before the wedding everything went horribly wrong, and he left me. For the longest time I've wondered if he ever loved me to begin with. Honestly, when I think about Mac's love for Cindy, I know . . ." She balled her fists in her lap as the emotions she had kept buried for so long began to fight their way out. "My mom always says that no one can fall out of love. You either love someone or you don't, and she's right. Tom and I . . . Everyone said we were so perfect together, but . . ." She could feel her control slipping. *Just the facts,* she told herself, thinking she could keep it all down if she concentrated hard enough.

"But what?" Pete asked.

"The feelings we had were too simple." She looked up at Pete. "Does that make sense? They were too small, too shallow." She felt a wave of regret rise and wash over her. There were so many things she'd do differently if she could.

"What broke you up?"

"This." She pointed to the scar on her face.

Pete's expression grew puzzled.

Katherine didn't want to explain. This was the story she never told anyone because she was afraid of what she'd buried so deep, afraid of what she would feel. But she wanted Pete to understand.

"A few months before the wedding, I got pregnant."

Pete draw in a sharp breath.

"I know . . . Smart People Making Really Bad Decisions could be the title for our entire engagement."

"I'm not sure what to say."

"There's nothing to say; we messed up. And Tom," she huffed out a laugh, "he lost it."

"He blamed you?" Pete said, disbelief evident in every fiber of his being.

"Oh yeah." The words held all of the bitterness she'd lived with for so long. "It was my fault. I had ruined our future because no church was going to take him on as pastor with a wife he'd knocked up before the wedding."

"That's ridiculous."

Katherine didn't give Pete a chance to say anything else. She didn't want his defense. Even now, she still felt the bitterness and anger over the way Tom had treated her mixed with the soul-churning guilt and grief for all that came after. "I was worried about what people would say, but I didn't think it was the end of the world. So we'd be forced to admit that we weren't the perfect Christian couple after all? I didn't see that as being the end of his career. We'd acknowledge our mistake; ask forgiveness of our church family. It seemed so simple to me, and Pete," she leaned in, her words deliberate, "I wanted to be a wife and mother more than I wanted my next breath. I had this dream of having a family and sure, we hadn't gone about it the right way, but it felt so close I could touch it. The day I first felt the baby move was one of the happiest of my life." Katherine's voice broke, and she sat back, a hand over her mouth like she could hold back the rest of it.

Pete's expression was full of compassion. He would probably let her off the hook, not insist on hearing what happened, but she couldn't stop. "One night we were driving home, and he starts in on me." She could still remember the look on Tom's face, the sneer, the utter hate that spilled off him until it seemed to fill the car. "He said I had failed him in every way and then he let it slip; there was someone else."

Pete shook his head. "Why am I not surprised?"

"I dunno, Pete, because I sure was." She'd been gutted, devastated, and she still felt it now, still wondered what she had ever done to Tom to deserve how he treated her or the way he spoke to her, like she was nothing. "For me, he was still the father of my baby. I still wanted that dream, even if it was a bit . . . tarnished by then; it was all I could think about. That's when he got nasty. I believe he wanted to make me leave him so he said the most terrible things." She had to break off, her throat clogged with tears. She finished in a whisper. "He was so busy destroying every hope I had of a future together, that he never saw the car in front of us."

The night was silent while Pete waited for her to be able to go on. Katherine wasn't sure she could. The memories of that night were surfacing all around her, bringing emotions with them she hadn't dealt with in years. It was overwhelming. She felt like she was sinking into them, dragged back into the pain.

"Katie, what happened?" Pete's words snapped her out of it.

"Tom lost control of the car. It crossed the median, and we were broadsided by a pickup truck," she said the words in a rush.

Pete winced like he could imagine the force of that hit.

"The driver of the truck was okay, Tom was okay, but I wasn't. My side of the car was crushed, lacerations to my face, legs broken, shoulder separated." She rattled off the facts, hoping they'd keep the emotions she couldn't handle at bay.

"And your baby?" Pete asked, and all at once the detachment she'd called up disappeared. The feelings rushed in again, and she was drowning in a grief so acute it took her breath away. It was like she was back in the crumpled car, covered in broken glass. The firemen rushed towards her, their hands lifting her broken body. She felt the ripping pain, heard herself screaming, begging them to save her baby. The tears formed in her eyes and spilled over her cheeks in a rapid freefall.

"There wasn't anything they could do," she managed to say past her tears. "If she was a few weeks older, she would have survived, but . . . she was too little." Katherine finally broke. Dropping her head into her hands, she wept. She heard Pete's chair scrape as he pushed back from the table and then felt his arms around her. He sat on the chair next to her and held her while her grief stormed inside her. After a while she pulled back and he got up, grabbed a box of tissues off the side table and handed them to her. "Thanks. I can't believe I'm being such a—"

"Human," Pete interrupted. "You're being human. You lost a child, Katherine. Something I can't even fathom. Something I'm not sure I'd survive."

"When they told Tom, he was relieved."

Pete gasped in surprise.

"I know it's unbelievable, but he was. In the ambulance he kept saying it was God's will. That this was God putting things right."

Pete just shook his head, as if he couldn't take it in.

"And after . . . There was a lot of damage, and in the second surgery they had to take drastic measures. I can't have children," she said and then stopped as the tears clogged her throat again.

Pete's eyes slowly closed, his expression pained.

Katherine took a breath and went on. "After he heard that, Tom disappeared for two whole days." She pulled out another tissue. "I thought he was grieving and that he would come back to me." She hated how pathetic that sounded, but it was true. Lying in the hospital bed, she had mourned for her baby, facing a future where there would be no other babies, knowing no new life would grow inside her; she'd never feel those gentle flutters in her belly again, no nursing a soft little bundle. Yet even then, she'd wanted Tom. "When he came back, he asked for his ring." She caught the next few tears with the tissue before they fell. Tom didn't deserve them. "It was his grandmother's, and since I wasn't going to wear it as his wife, he wanted it back."

"What?" Pete asked.

Katherine tossed her tissue aside and went digging for another. After drying her eyes and wiping her nose she tried to steady herself, to find that steely calm she drew on whenever she was in a spot, but it wasn't there. She was in pieces. "Tom told me that the accident, all it did to me, all it took from us, was God's will because our whole relationship was a mistake. He said that had to be it because God wouldn't give him a broken wife." She ended on a whisper.

Pete reached across the table and took her hand, squeezing it tight. "That may be the worst thing I have ever heard a man say."

"He couldn't have loved me, could he?"

In a quiet voice Pete said, "No, he didn't love you, honey."

Katherine nodded. She'd known it was true, but hearing it from Pete was oddly comforting, as if he was proving she wasn't wrong to think it. She took a drink out of the mug in front of her and made a face. She'd left her coffee to get cold.

"Let me get you something else." Pete jumped up and took their cups inside, returning with two full mugs of what smelled like tea. "This is the herbal stuff. Supposed to be good for you."

Katherine held her mug and inhaled the sweetly floral scent of chamomile. They quietly drank tea for a few minutes, and she tried to get ahold of herself. "After Tom, I tried dating again, but . . . I couldn't give them what they wanted. They'd be settling for damaged goods and at some point they'd start resenting me for it. I didn't want to marry someone who'd eventually learn to hate me."

"Child . . ." Pete began.

Kate shook her head—he couldn't understand what that had felt like. All those great guys hoping for a date to turn into something real, a relationship that would end in marriage and children, something Katherine couldn't give them. She'd never felt more broken, more worthless. "I've made some real mistakes."

"Yes, but he never should have touched you if he hadn't meant to keep you." Pete spat out the words. "And babies are blessings, even ones who arrive to unmarried parents. No baby dies as a punishment for its mama. I've never heard anything worse." He ran a hand through his hair in agitation.

"Looking back now, I see it. Then, I felt like a door had been slammed in my face and locked forever. And I lost my job, of course."

"What? Why?"

"Oh, that's the second half of the story I never tell anyone." She tried to make it a joke, but her heart wasn't in it, and Pete, rightly, didn't find it funny. "Tom needed the recommendation of our church's board of elders to be ordained. That same church owned the school where I taught. It was a small town and, like all small towns, word traveled fast. Tom wasn't acting like a grieving father-to-be, and the church noticed. They hauled him in and demanded an explanation for his behavior." She paused, the familiar righteous indignation rising, but this time it was tempered somehow. In the past when she felt the grief, the anger at Tom always rose, making her feel steadier, but this time it was different. It was as if she understood it better now.

"What did he say to them?" Pete prompted.

"He said that he wasn't grieving because the baby wasn't his."

Pete swore out loud, a creative string that made Katherine snort out a laugh. "Sorry, Katie, but that's pretty bad."

"Yes, and it was enough to get me fired. They dismissed me without once asking to speak with me." She shrugged her shoulders. What was devastating at that time was now beginning to feel like another piece of the past she could make peace with; the deep wound didn't burn anymore. In her heart she could feel a kind of mercy covering it like a salve, and she knew it was God's mercy covering her. He was coaxing her broken soul to let the wound heal. Holding onto the sins of others, and to her own, had done nothing but break her apart.

It was as if telling Pete was some kind of confession. It hurt to say these things, to feel them again, but at the same time she felt light, unburdened. Years of guilt, grief, and anger had spewed out of her and she didn't want them back. She prayed that God would take them instead and that He'd forgive her for holding onto it for far too long. All those years she'd been hiding away from God, and now it felt like she was stepping into the light, happy to be found.

"I can't believe a church would act like that." Pete's words brought her back to the moment.

"They were already prepared to believe him."

"Why?"

"My parents had separated the year before. My dad had a mid-life crisis of epic proportions and left my mom for a paralegal. Up to that point my dad was Mr. Perfect, as far as they were concerned. He was a deacon, donated to everything, son of one of the church founders. They liked the cache of having the famous DA as a member. So when he left and my mom stayed?"

"They resented her," Pete gave a slow nod.

"They had to pick a villain. It couldn't be Mr. Perfect. They ignored his actual sin and assigned all sorts to my mom, instead. Mom's not the most conventional human. She's an artist, for one, and they viewed that with suspicion. And she's pretty progressive in her politics. When the rumors started, it didn't take much for them to spread because there were a lot of people, mostly women unfortunately, who were thrilled to have something bad to say about us."

"Human nature." Pete shrugged.

"But I honestly think Tom was only trying to save his own skin when he lied, not destroy me. I doubt he knew it would go so far."

Pete shook his head. "Did he check it when it did? Did he set the record straight?"

"No," she admitted. "It wouldn't have been so bad if those women hadn't wanted to hurt me, to humiliate me like they did. They were almost gleeful about it. When they were done they went for my mom, my sisters, and even my friend Heather. The gossip about me was like poison, working its way through the congregation. Anyone who stood up for me was covered in it and then rejected."

"I understand now why you weren't keen on churches," Pete said, rubbing at his forehead like he couldn't take it all in.

"I'm telling you, Pete, if this were two centuries ago, they would have had stones in their hands and I would not be standing here. And I never went back. To this day they still believe that I am pretty much the Whore of Babylon."

"I wonder what they think when they see you on TV?"

"No idea. They probably assume I'm a godless communist or something. Seriously."

Pete barked out a laugh. He reached out and took her hand in his, giving it a squeeze and looking her over thoughtfully, like he was choosing his next words carefully. "I think I understand your fear of relationships a bit better, too, but you can't let that rule your life."

"I'm not afraid, really; it's more like . . ." But she couldn't say because she really didn't understand it herself. Mac was pretty great. Her heart was certainly tangled up with him, but love?

"Love," Pete began, answering the question she was too afraid to ask. "The kind that lasts isn't a smooth, straight path. It's a broken trail, full of switchbacks and rough spots. You have to fight for it. I think what Tom did was lie to you by giving you smooth and safe when it was anything but. What you've started with Mac seems like the real thing. You've both got a lot of reasons to be cautious, and if I know one thing, Mac will not lie to you. I think that's all I can promise. The rest is up to the two of you."

"Quit it, Pete," she muttered.

"Quit what?"

"Being so perceptive and wise. It's annoying." She gave him a smile. "The only problem with all of that is I don't trust anyone but myself."

"That's a lonely place to be." There was empathy in his tone that took the sting out of his words. "What about trusting God?"

"That's still a work in progress. I feel like I'm miles away from where I was when I got here, but still not where I should be."

"Then start by putting your full faith and trust in God and see what that does for your trust in others."

CHAPTER TWENTY

SNEAKERS SQUEAKED ON THE PARQUET FLOOR as the students did their sprints. Erin stood nearby with a stop watch and clipboard. She was in her athletics director 'uniform' of warmup jacket and school track pants. Even though she'd had the job for a while, it was still odd to see her out of her usual stylish outfits, her hair up in a serviceable high ponytail. Katherine headed to the bleachers and took a seat as Erin wrapped up the class. "Nice times!" she called out as they finished. "That's all for today. Hit the locker rooms. You have ten minutes before lunch." The kids filed out as Erin spotted Katherine and joined her on the bench.

"Looks like the PE classes are going well."

"That your professional opinion?" Erin cocked a brow.

"I'm not technically observing you, no, but I like your class management skills thus far."

"I was dismissing them for lunch. Not exactly a tough task."

"Do you ever take a compliment?" Katherine asked with a smile.

Erin looked like she was going to say something and then shrugged. "I'd have to like myself first."

Katherine wasn't sure how to respond. It was a revealing thing to say. She was discovering that Erin was a far more complex person than she presented to the world. On the surface the woman was beautiful, outgoing, and funny, but below there was pain, self-doubt, and even bitterness. It was something God had been showing Katherine in her own heart over the last few months. Old wounds left more than scars, and the only thing that healed them was God's mercy, love, and grace. Since her talk with Pete she'd been feeling free, unburdened for the first time in years. It was a feeling she wanted to share.

"Sorry," Erin began to apologize.

"Don't you dare."

"What?"

"Don't apologize for being real with me," Katherine explained. "Too many of us put up this pretty front, like nothing's ever wrong, like Christian women never struggle, as if we're not allowed to have a bad day."

"Or bad hair," Erin countered with a smile.

"Or skip a Sunday service."

"Or a signup sheet."

"Or say no to anything."

"Or say that we're the ones who need help."

"Right, because admitting I need something is admitting I'm not perfect," Erin hunched a shoulder. "That's not how I roll. There are people lining up hoping to see how imperfect I am. If they only knew the half of it." She sighed—a defeated sound, at best.

"No one is perfect, and that's why I don't want the 'Erin is Just Fine Thanks' façade. I'd much rather have the real Erin."

"Okay." Erin gave her a sharp look. "Then I get the real Katherine as well. Not the super annoying 'I'm Perfect at Everything' Katherine. She gets on my last nerve."

"Hey!"

"Truth hurts." But then Erin gave her shoulder a friendly shove. "Dr. Katherine Grant can be a bit much, but plain ol' Katherine seems pretty good."

Katherine blinked hard, a bit overwhelmed by how those words affected her. She'd been so closed off for so long it was almost hard to handle.

"You're not seriously going to cry on me, are you?"

Katherine mustered a smile. She should have known Erin wouldn't let the moment get mushy. "Keep it up and I might even hug you," Katherine admitted and Erin leaned back. "All kidding aside, your friendship means a lot to me. Thank you."

It was Erin's turn to look touched, but she didn't let it last long. "Are you done with the squishiness?" She got up from the bench rolling her eyes.

Katherine nodded, trying not to laugh. At the far end of the gym the doors banged open and the students for the next class began to file in. Erin gave Katherine a mocking salute before jogging over to meet them.

"This is . . ." Mac trailed off, unable to find the words for what they were seeing.

Pete nodded as they both stared at the scene before them.

The trailer was in a state Mac had never seen in his entire policing career. Every last inch of the place was covered with something: debris, discarded food, clothes, garbage, you name it. It had taken Pete an hour to find the weapons he came to confiscate. Buddy Sawyer's house had been relatively clean, but the trailers his sons lived in were so far from it, there wasn't a word that described them.

Sitting at a table with drug paraphernalia in plain view was Buddy's daughter, Molly Sawyer, high as a kite. Her hair was stringy and, although her clothes were decent, they were rumpled, like she'd been in them for days. There was something off in how she was interacting with them, and Mac didn't think it had to do with her chemical impairment. She appeared to be young, barely twenty, and far too thin to be healthy.

"She's got developmental delays. Years ago she was in a

mental hospital," Pete whispered, answering his unasked question. "I didn't know she was living here, or I'd have brought a social worker."

They had timed delivery of the warrant for when they'd hoped to have only Buddy to deal with, but they'd pulled up to find the whole family home. The two deputies Mac had brought with him were keeping an eye on the men while they executed the warrant. "What's the story on the mother?"

"Long gone. Left Buddy three years ago. I thought she'd taken the daughter with her."

Mac couldn't stop the memories from flooding his mind, memories of Cindy at the end when she'd disappear for days at time. He'd find her in some flop-house, dirty, her beautiful blond hair matted, her clothes . . . Mac rubbed a hand over his face.

"Someone needs to be held accountable for this."

The girl looked up at him, her head cocked to the side like she couldn't understand the malice in his tone.

She seemed so sweet and innocent. She deserved better than this. A gentle soul like her needed a gentle life, not to be drugged into insensibility by people who were supposed to love her. The anger that had been stewing since they'd walked in the place flared inside him. "Look at her!" He started for the front door.

Pete grabbed his upper arm and with surprising strength, pulled him away from the doorway and into a back hall. "Get a grip," he said, releasing Mac's arm.

"I'm fine."

"No, you're not," Pete insisted. "You've been wound tight since we got here, and if you walk out there like this you're gonna do something stupid."

"Don't be ridiculous." Mac tried to move past the old man, but Pete blocked his way.

"If I had known this would be like stepping into a flashback for you, I wouldn't have called you in. I'm sorry, but now that you're in you've got to remember that the world is not yours to save. You need to keep your head and do your job."

"If you'd get out of my way, I'd get to it." Mac was having trouble reining in his temper. His head wasn't in a good place. His heart was a swarming mess of emotions he thought he'd given to God a long time ago.

"Vengeance isn't your job. Right now," Pete raised his voice as Mac tried to object, "it's written all over you. Take a breath." Pete stepped back but remained alert.

Mac knew his friend was right. A minute ago he was ready to go out that front door and take the first Sawyer he could get his hands on and beat the life out of him. It had been a long time since he'd felt that kind of anger. He closed his eyes and leaned against the wall, silently praying for God to take control, utterly powerless to do it on his own.

"We're not gonna get a charge for the sister to stick," Pete said softly. "You know how it goes. At least we can get her out of here and, God willing, get her straight. You charge them with what we found."

Mac grimaced. "That wasn't much. A few dime bags, some traces of meth; we missed the big stuff."

"You did your job, and I got the deer meat and guns I was after. I'll take Buddy in on the poaching charge; your deputies can run Ryan and Sean in on possession while you take the sister to county."

Mac nodded, eyes on the floor, the words of his prayer still fresh in his mind.

"It's that or you leave and we get another deputy. You want me to make a call?" Pete asked.

"No." Mac stood up and shook his head. "I've got it together."

Pete looked him over and then stood aside. Together they went back into the room and managed to get Molly onto her feet, and found what seemed to be her purse. When he took her arm to lead her out, she slid her hand into his and smiled up at him like he was an old friend. He swallowed hard against the lump in his throat and headed for the door.

Pete was the first out the door, with Mac and Molly behind. Buddy and his sons were standing in the driveway, smoking and giving dirty looks to the two deputies keeping an eye on them. Then they caught sight of Mac leading Molly to his cruiser.

"Hey!" Ryan yelled, flicking his cigarette into the yard and rushing at Mac. Pete stepped in front of him, hand out. Ryan stopped, but Sean was right behind him. Pete shifted to block them both.

Standing six-foot-two and weighing, by Mac's estimation, at least three-fifty, Buddy was a bear of a man. The deputies closed in, one focusing on Buddy Sawyer, who had headed straight to the cruiser. Mac opened the rear door and got Molly in, trying to keep an eye on Buddy charging his way and Pete confronting the brothers.

"You got no cause to take my girl—" was all Buddy got out before Mac closed the distance between them.

"Not another word," Mac spat out. "You got that, Sawyer? Not another word."

Buddy's expression was defiant.

Mac leaned in closer. "This is the only warning you get. That girl is high, emaciated, and filthy. Nobody deserves to live like that. And you know it," Mac finished on a harsh whisper.

Buddy didn't react, but he didn't open his mouth again either.

Mac turned to his deputy, who had been hovering as if unsure what to do. "Deputy Cruz, I believe Warden Coleman needs to speak with Mr. Sawyer concerning the deer meat found on his premises." Mac wanted the man gone, out of his face, before he did something stupid. "Escort him to the—"

"On the ground!" Deputy French shouted.

Mac watched French take a struggling Ryan to his knees. The Sawyer boys were resisting arrest. Pete was trying to get cuffs on Sean, but the man was fighting him, hard. With Molly safe in the cruiser and Cruz taking care of Buddy, Mac ran over to help.

Pete struggled to keep the one wrist he'd already cuffed behind Sean's back. He swept Sean's leg out from under him and got him to the ground, but the man rolled, got his hand free, and punched Pete in the temple.

"Whoa!" Mac shouted. He grabbed Sean's arm before he could get off another punch as Pete fell to the side. Mac flipped Sean to his stomach and put a knee in his back. Once he had Sean cuffed, he turned.

Pete was sitting on the ground with a hand on his forehead, blood dripping through his fingers.

"Call it in!" Mac shouted at Cruz, who already had his radio off his shoulder. "Pete, you okay? Talk to me, buddy."

"I'm fine," he said weakly. "Just got my bell rung."

"You're bleeding like a stuck pig." Mac got up off the ground. Sean tried to get to his knees and Mac shouted, "Stay down! You're already looking at possession, resisting arrest, and assault on an officer of the law. Don't add stupid."

Sean put his head on the ground.

"Head wounds bleed like crazy, Mac, you know that. I'm fine." Pete tried to stand.

Mac pushed gently on his shoulder. "You stay down, too." Mac jogged back to his cruiser, checked on Molly, and returned with a first aid kit. Pulling out a bandage, he handed it to Pete. "I'm going to secure these idiots while you try not to bleed to death."

Pete gave him a wave and stayed seated as Mac pulled Sean off the ground and moved him towards French's cruiser.

Hours later Mac was finally home, out of uniform, and in a place where he felt he could process all that had happened. Standing at the sliding glass doors to his back deck, he looked out at the last of the sunset. It was a thing of beauty, lighting the tips of the trees with color, painting the distant mountaintop purple. His eyes could see the beauty, his mind could understand it, but his heart couldn't take it in. He was still troubled.

Pete was going to be fine, according to the ER doc, and the social worker had showed up in record time and officially took custody of Molly. There was no telling how that would end, but he had to remember that it wasn't his responsibility. He'd done what he could.

Closing his eyes, he prayed. In the quiet he heard the gentle reminder that he was the servant, not the master. He needed to surrender his control to the One who controls the universe. Mac felt the load on his heart lighten. With a last look at the setting sun, he headed to the kitchen where he'd left his phone. He wanted to call Kate, knowing that her voice would soothe the restlessness he still felt, but he heard a knock at the door and went to answer it instead.

"I need to talk to you . . . sir." Jake stood on his doorstep, an odd look on his face.

Mac let him in. Jake had never been inside Mac's house.

The kid took in the high ceilings, barn beams, and stone hearth. "Wow. Your house is sah-weet!"

"I'll take that compliment. What brings you out this way?"

Jake sighed, and Mac guessed that this wasn't going to be pleasant. Considering his whole day had been unpleasant, he was ready for it, whatever it was.

"Okay, I'll just lay it out. I screwed up. I wanted . . . I wanted to do this the right way, but I—" Jake shook his head. "There's no other way to say it. Brit's pregnant."

Mac sucked in a breath.

Jake shoved a hand through his hair. "I know I messed this all up, but I wanted you to know that I didn't mean . . . but I'm gonna do the right thing now."

"You're gonna marry her?"

"I already asked her over the summer, and she said yes, but she wasn't eighteen yet, and she didn't want to make her mom mad, so we were gonna wait."

"But you couldn't?"

"I messed up." Jake sounded devastated. "I . . . We . . ."

"I get it." Mac held his shoulder. "What does it mean for school?"

"Dr. Grant is trying to work that out. She found out, and Brit said she's workin' on a solution."

"Well, she would." He knew Katherine thought a great deal of Jake and would try everything she could to keep him in school. "But you still need to man-up. That means coming clean at school, too."

"I will. Brit asked me not to for now, but, sir . . . I'm ready. I don't care what it takes. She's my wife in all but name. That baby is mine. I want to name it. I want to get on with it. But Brit wants—"

"You do what she wants until she tells you otherwise." Mac gave him a hard look.

Jake nodded.

"Give it the time she needs, since she's the one who's gonna take the brunt of it. May not be right, but the girl is the one to pay when this particular mistake is made."

"I know. And it's killing me."

The way Jake said it, Mac didn't doubt it. "For now, it's good that you came by. I'm gonna be out of town again and might need you even longer. Maybe we can work out a deal with the school. I'll do what I can."

"Thank you, sir." He sounded relieved. "I was worried that . . . I thought you might . . ."

"I didn't hatch at forty, a fully-formed cop and model citizen, Jake. I understand."

"Thank you. You have no idea how much I appreciate that. And whatever you need, I'm your guy." Mac saw a lot of himself in Jake. He hoped—no—he prayed that a better future was ahead for this kid.

CHAPTER TWENTY-ONE

KATHERINE STARED AT HER SCREEN, NOT believing what she was reading. "Heather . . ." she whispered into the phone and got nothing back. It was enough to render her oldest friend mute.

Sweet River Lowdown

People up at the Sweet River Academy better get their heads checked. Turns out their consultant is nothing but a liar. Dr. Grant has been helping one student hide her pregnancy and the other student hide that he's the father. And to make matters worse, Pastor Dan Connors, who should know better, has been helping them.

It should come as no surprise that the pregnant student is Brittany Sullivan, considering whose daughter she is. Jake Dawson, a foster kid and fellow student, is the father but has not come forward or been expelled. He's still enrolled and that's not right. Jake is a rough kid from a very questionable background. He has no business being in this town. He's not even from this county. Let his own people take care of him.

For weeks now, Dr. Grant has been campaigning to have Stephanie Campbell removed as director. She's already gotten rid of Bill Swift and replaced him with Erin Sullivan. We have no idea what's going on up at the school, but it's some dirty dealing. The board needs to clean house, but it will have to start with itself first.

Is this how a Christian school is run? We think not.

"Heather, what do I do?"

"Give me a second. I literally cannot see straight right now. I am that angry."

"Where do I even start with this?"

"We'll have to—" Heather was cut off by the sound of Katherine's office door banging open. It was an hour before school started, and she'd come in to get a head start on her budget report. The auditor had found further inconsistencies. Not fraud, but definitely gross mismanagement. It meant that Stephanie would likely be called before the board and asked to resign, something she had warned the woman about yesterday afternoon. Stephanie hadn't reacted at all.

"That's not the real Lowdown!" Elaine shouted as she burst through the door. "I'm the Lowdown! That is, I write it. But that was not me!" She was out of breath, red-faced, and looked like she'd thrown on her clothes and run out the door.

"Elaine?" Heather asked in her ear.

"Hang on." Katherine put the phone down, and Elaine slumped into the chair in front of her desk. "You write the Lowdown?"

"Yes. I know . . . but it's like my hobby and it's more for information, but it's been so fun to follow you and Mac's story."

"But you didn't write this." She pointed to the computer.

"No. I was hacked. I've asked my nephew to look into it; he does all the tech stuff, I only write the posts."

"Can you get this down?"

"I already did from home." She leaned forward, almost bonking heads with Katherine. "Refresh the page; it should be gone." She did, and it disappeared.

"That doesn't really get rid of it."

"I know, I think she might have emailed people copies of it."

"She?"

"Stephanie. Who else?"

An hour later, and the second-floor conference room was filled with the entire board including Pete, Erin and Brittany Sullivan, Dan Connors, Jake Dawson, Katherine, and Stephanie Campbell. The very air held malice. It was like a poison, and Katherine wanted to open the windows and stick her head out. For her part, she wasn't angry. She felt pain for Erin, Jake, and Brittany, and for Dan as well, but the anger that should be coursing through her right now was completely absent. She'd been praying pretty much constantly since the call from the board, so God was clearly at work. She needed to trust Him.

"Okay, now that we've got everybody, we need to get right down to it," Greg said from the head of the table. The board chairman was a reasonable guy, very even-handed, and Katherine held out hope that he'd listen and understand why they all had acted to protect Jake and Brittany. "Dr. Grant, I would like to hear from you first."

Katherine nodded. "As you know by now, Brittany is pregnant and Jake is the father. This information came to light when she was having an argument with another student. I had Erin come in, and she decided it would be best for Brittany to withdraw, and she did so. She had no obligation to state the reason, and as I'm not an employee of the school and have not signed any agreement to provide information on students to the administration or board, I kept this to myself."

"But you did involve Dr. Connors."

Katherine shot him a look, and he seemed perfectly at ease. Erin, sitting a few seats away, did not. She looked mortified. "Jake needed counseling. Erin and I discussed that need and determined that Dr. Connors was the best choice. We asked him to guide Jake on what to do."

"I already know what I'm doing. I'm marrying my fiancée, and I'm going to provide for her and our kid." Jake stood defiantly, daring anyone to doubt him.

"Sit down, son. We'll get to you," Greg barked.

Jake took a seat but didn't look happy about it.

"Dr. Connors?" Greg asked.

Dan sat a bit forward, adjusted his glasses, and spoke loud enough so that each person in the room would hear. "I spoke with Jake on several occasions. I'm not obligated to share the details of those conversations, so I will not do so."

"That's fine; I didn't figure a pastor was going to talk to us about counseling sessions." Greg spoke as if it was ridiculous that Dan had even been called.

Katherine began to feel real hope that Jake might be allowed to stay.

"Okay, young man," Greg continued, "let's get down to it."

Katherine looked across the room at Pete, who gave her the slightest of winks. The alarm she'd been feeling began to ebb.

"You violated your conduct agreement by, well . . . we all know by what. No need to get into the details." He waved a hand around and most of the board looked like they agreed. "There are a few different paths here. The first is, of course, expulsion. The second is suspension, and the third is campus confinement. That means you'd be limited to the dorms and classrooms for the duration of your enrollment. What I want to hear first is if you're sorry you put yourself and Brittany in this spot."

"I'm not sorry for loving Brittany, but I'm sorry for not showing her the respect that waiting until we're married would have done. And I know this sounds like too little too late, but when I signed that agreement I meant to keep my word."

There was such a tone of solemnity in the way he said it, Katherine knew he meant it.

"I'm sorry for breaking it. I didn't get the chance to do any of this the right way. Coming forward was what I wanted to do, but I was working up the courage . . ." He shook his head like he was disgusted with himself. "It took too long."

Dan smiled ever so slightly, and Katherine guessed that some of what Dan must have said sunk in, and he was pleased with that.

"Okay, now do you understand and accept that we need to address your failure to abide by the terms of the agreement?"

Jake sighed and glanced once at Dan before saying, "Actions have consequences. These are mine, whatever you decide."

Nicely said, she thought, and hoped that the board heard his submission and understood what it took for a kid like Jake to actually say those words.

"Alright, then. Before we go to a vote, does anyone have any questions?" No one spoke up. "If everyone's prepared, may I see a show of hands for expulsion?" Katherine held her breath while only Mindy raised her hand. "And now for suspension?" Two hands rose.

Katherine wasn't sure if Jake would mind suspension over confinement, but it looked like he wasn't going to get a choice.

"And finally for confinement?" Every remaining hand rose. It was a clear majority. "Jake you are confined to campus until graduation on May seventeenth or such a time as you are married. You will be allowed to continue your internship, but all other off-campus activity, even if it's a job, will cease. This may seem harsh, but the punishment you are receiving is light compared to expulsion, which your actions merited. You are shortly to become a father, and that's an awesome responsibility. I'd like to see you take this time to reflect on what's ahead. Please continue your sessions with Dr. Connors." He turned to Dan. "Assuming you don't mind coming to campus."

Dan shook his head.

"That's it?" Stephanie was on her feet, her cheeks flushed. "It's all okay now? We're going to ground him and hope he reflects on his actions?" Her voice was rising in both pitch and volume. "And not only are we going to let him stay, but if he marries her all is forgiven? They get to move on as if nothing happened?"

"No, they get to be parents. What did you think was going to happen here?" Greg asked.

"I expected them to be punished. I expected the board to hold Dr. Connors and Dr. Grant responsible for the way they've misguided these children."

"We already looked at that and determined that no—"

"That's because you don't have all the facts," she interrupted. "Dr. Grant lied on her résumé."

Katherine's stomach clenched.

"I know for a fact that she was fired from her first job for adultery." The room seemed to still as Stephanie went on. She had all eyes on her and she knew it. "The church that employed her discovered that she was pregnant and, although engaged at the time, it was by another man."

Katherine was frozen in place, unable to react, utterly shocked that Stephanie would go this far.

"The worst of it?" Stephanie asked. "No one even knows what happened to the baby. But I think we can all guess."

Pete leapt to his feet in defense of Katherine, as did Dan, and the room exploded in sound, Stephanie fixing her expression into one of innocent confusion, as if she didn't understand what the fuss was about.

"Enough!" Greg roared, banging the gavel on the table.

Stephanie sat down and Dan followed.

Pete collapsed in his chair across the room, his eyes on Katherine, his expression pained.

"First of all, this is not a place for insinuations and accusations." Greg shot a look at Stephanie, but she didn't react. "We're not here for what amounts to gossip. What happened years ago at Dr. Grant's first position is hardly germane in this situation."

"It is if it shows a pattern of bad behavior and lack of judgment," Stephanie countered.

Katherine felt the urge to throw something, but instead she

said a quick prayer for the right words and cleared her throat. "Could I address that, please?"

Greg nodded.

Taking a steadying breath, she began. "In all of that there were two true things. I was engaged, and I did become pregnant."

Surprised faces ringed the room.

"But the rest are lies. The people gossiping about me have been at it so long they forgot that there was no secret to what happened to my daughter." Speaking the words 'my daughter' filled her with a rush of emotion, and she had to pause for a moment to let it subside. "The car crash that nearly killed me did kill my baby. She died on the side of the road in the hands of a firefighter at twenty weeks old." Her voice trailed off in a whisper.

She could almost feel the reaction in the room, but she had to steel herself against it or she'd break down. Keeping her eyes on Greg, whose expression was compassionate but not pitying, she went on. "It's incredibly painful to speak about this, but it's important you understand the truth because it did influence how I intervened with Brittany and Jake. After my daughter died, my fiancé ended our engagement and started the rumors that I'd been unfaithful to cover his own affair."

Greg's eyebrows lifted, but otherwise he didn't react.

"I was dismissed from my teaching position and vilified in my church. It was . . ." Katherine shook her head. "I helped Brittany and Jake because I know the difference between being held accountable for your actions and being judged and even hated for them. I'm not talking about righteous judgement; I'm talking about the human kind; the kind that leads others to hate someone for their sin. It's the kind I experienced and what I wanted to spare them."

"Then you're admitting you lied on their behalf." Stephanie wasn't going to let it go.

"I did no such thing."

"But you did. You knew the real reason that Brittany was taken out of school by her mother from the beginning. You should have informed me. I was on Elaine's computer, and I read the email she sent with the home school paperwork, and she told Erin—"

"Wait, you were on Elaine's computer?" Pete asked.

"It's school property," Stephanie snapped.

"You logged into Elaine's workstation and accessed an email."

"I'm not sure what you're getting at." Stephanie's eyes narrowed. "I'm the director. I have access to all her emails on the server."

"But you said you were on her computer, at her desk."

"And again, it's school property, so I'm failing to see what your point is."

"My point is that Elaine's blog was hacked. Since most everyone knows she writes the Lowdown, it could have been any of us. They'd only need her login and password."

"Are you accusing me of something?"

"Evidence might be circumstantial, but I'm betting if I know Elaine, we can go to that desk right now and find her login and password on a sticky note or inside a drawer or—"

"On her desk under her keyboard," Mindy interrupted in a frustrated mutter. "She keeps them on a pink sticky note, like nobody's gonna see." Mindy was louder this time and sounding exasperated. "I told her she'd get hacked if she didn't hide them."

"Mindy, you know I wouldn't—"

It appeared Mindy had changed her mind about a few things. "I really don't know, not anymore." She looked away, her lips pressed together.

"Did you do this?" Greg leaned forward.

Stephanie seemed to sag in place, as if losing Mindy's support was too much to take. "You wouldn't listen when I told you she was trying to get rid of me." Her voice took on an almost pleading tone.

Greg shook his head. "She wasn't. I was."

Katherine's mouth dropped open.

"Your contract is up this year, and after the mismanagement

we've already had to suffer, there was no way I was going to sign off on renewing it. I insisted we hire Dr. Grant so I could present that mismanagement in black and white. I have to say I'm shocked at how much worse it was than I had expected. Your ego is out of control. The fact that you'd attack students to get your way shows how far past what is reasonable or right you have been willing to go."

Stephanie looked like she was about to be sick.

"These are harsh words and I apologize. Had you not forced this confrontation, you would have had more measured ones, offered in private." Greg turned from her and addressed the rest of the board. "This is an unusual circumstance, and it requires action. I'd ask all non-board members to leave, with the exception of the director." Quickly and silently, they filed out.

After a few minutes, Stephanie came blowing through the door.

Greg appeared in the portal. "How about the rest of you join us again?"

They all settled back in their chairs.

Greg spoke. "The board has terminated Mrs. Campbell."

Katherine nodded, expecting to hear that.

Dan Connors held up his hand, and after he was acknowledged said, "Can I suggest that we pray? There's a lot that has been said, and some ragged emotions right now." He received an enthusiastic and virtually unanimous response. Dan's prayer was simple, but it was powerful, and the one thing that stuck in Katherine's mind was, "Forgive us, Father. We so desperately don't deserve it, but our broken hearts need it beyond all things. Help us forgive those who have hurt us in turn."

"You know what I'm going to ask." Greg had followed Katherine back down to her office after the drama was over. "Just until the end of school. How about that?"

"It may not be a popular decision. Some people may consider me compromised."

Greg gave her an assessing look. "Then they would be fools. You're the best person possible to step in and fix this mess." He sat back and waited while she weighed the pros and cons.

Truth was, she didn't want to leave Sweet River yet. This would give her more time with Mac without forcing a commitment she didn't feel ready for or even capable of. "Okay, Greg; until June."

After he left, she sat trying to process what had happened. It seemed impossible. She'd never witnessed a meeting like that. She closed her eyes and prayed for Stephanie. "Forgive her," she whispered aloud, feeling that with the depth of her soul she had already forgiven the woman. Stephanie was bitter, blinded by her love of status, and lost, so very lost.

Katherine's eyes shot open as that word banged around in her brain. That's what it was like when you were drowning in your sin; you were lost. Had Tom been like that? So blind that anything was possible, even rejecting a broken and ragged woman he had promised to love? Was he, even now, still lost?

Pulling up a blank sheet of paper, she took a pen and wrote.

Dear Tom,

You may wonder why I'm writing you after all this time, and I'm not sure I'll ever send this. I need to say these things because I've let what happened to us poison my life. The truth is that for many years I have hated you, and I need to ask your forgiveness for that. But, I also know that in order to finally be free from the bitterness, I need to forgive you as well. I'm not sure if you fully understand what you did to me, so I want to get it out. I don't say these things to hurt you. I want to be free so these are the things you need to know.

In leaving me, you taught me not to trust. In cheating on me, you taught me that men lie. In lying about me to cover your affair, you taught me to doubt my fellow Christians. In allowing those lies to spread unchecked, you taught me that the church was no place of refuge, only a place to be judged. In refusing to acknowledge the death of our baby girl, you taught me that my life and hers were worthless. After the car accident you left me broken, and then you let the church that should have known the truth—that should have been a place of healing—break the pieces that were left.

For years I held on to those lessons and let them poison my heart, and as a result, I was lost. God found me and has been faithfully overwriting those lessons with His truth. I know now that I've sinned, holding onto my anger, thinking that because I was the one wronged, I didn't need to forgive you; that being hurt meant that I was blameless, and it was okay to hate in return. I am as much a sinner, as guilty. God has forgiven me of all my sins; how can I withhold my forgiveness from you? You have it, Tom.

I was reminded that your debt to me is paid by Christ who has paid the debt for all of us. You may never ask for my forgiveness, but it doesn't matter. The account between us is settled. You are forgiven.

God bless you,
Katherine

CHAPTER TWENTY-TWO

KATHERINE HEARD A KNOCK ON HER door and took a peek beyond the curtain to see exactly who she suspected. Normally the sight of Mac would make her giddy; instead, her stomach twisted into a knot. The blog came down a short time after it was posted and, so far, it seemed they'd caught it before it spread all over town. Greg had extracted a promise from everyone present, even Stephanie, to keep it confidential, but Mac might have heard something. It was smarter to tell him herself, before the rumors started flying. Bracing, she opened the door, but didn't even get out a 'hello' before he pulled her out onto the porch and into his arms.

"What on earth--?"

Then his mouth was on hers, his arms tight around her, and her brain stalled. Catching back up, she slid her arms around his neck and held on for what was the sweetest kiss he'd ever given her. When he finally let her up for air she was almost dizzy.

"June?" A wide smile broke out on his lips.

Such a smile was a rare thing, so she took an extra moment to appreciate it.

So long, he gave her a little shake. "Pete said you'd signed on for the rest of the year. I have you until June." And there was a deep sound of satisfaction in those words.

"Yes, you crazy man, I'm here until June."

He kissed her again, a slow and leisurely sort of kiss, like he had all the time in the world, and they weren't standing in the freezing cold on her front porch.

"I don't suppose you'll come inside?" she asked when he was done.

"I'd like to, but I've got to feed the animals. Jake's confined to quarters, so I've lost my ranch hand. Which reminds me, Pete said you'd fill me in on all the details. Apparently that was quite the board meeting. What happened?"

Katherine slowly pulled out of his arms. "That's not a conversation for my front porch."

"Is it a conversation for a barn? You can fill me in while I work."

Mac's barn was huge. He said it was the only thing left upright on the property when he bought it. Built somewhere around 1900, he'd decided to fix it rather than raze it. Along one wall were a half-dozen horse stalls where both Misery and Agony were housed. As Mac began to work, Katherine stroked Misery's sleek neck and tried to find a good place to start. "So, you heard about the brouhaha with that blog post and Stephanie?"

"Not the details, but Pete said she was forced to resign, and that's why you're here until June. Also heard Jake is confined to quarters because the truth finally came out about him and Brittany. Can't say that's a bad thing; it would have been better if he'd had the chance to do that himself, though. Maybe he shouldn't have followed my advice."

"Did he talk to you?" Katherine turned towards Mac in surprise.

"Not about the meeting, but yes, he told me he got Brittany pregnant."

"Huh. He never said he talked to you." She paused. "You never said."

"Wasn't my place to share, but I told him that he should wait to take any action until Brittany said she was ready. This is all harder on her than it is on him."

Katherine felt a nudge, and it wasn't Misery pestering her to keep petting him. God was telling her that now was the time. "You're right about that," she began. "One of the reasons I was so keen to help Brittany is that . . ." *you can do this,* she told herself. "I was once in her shoes."

Mac put down the bag of feed he'd been lugging and stared at her.

"It's why that meeting was called. Stephanie did some digging into my past. She heard rumors and then added those to the blog post she put up about Brittany and Jake."

Mac's expression was impossible to read, and Katherine wondered if he was angry she hadn't shared. "You need to know that until a week ago, I hadn't shared this information with anyone outside my family and Heather. I buried it deep and hoped it would never surface. Pete sort of . . . I guess he could tell I had a story to tell."

"You talked to Pete?" Mac didn't seem angry or resentful; instead it seemed like he was relieved it was Pete.

"He really ought to hang out a shingle, 'Pete the Mountaintop Counselor' or something."

Mac barked out a laugh. "You're not kidding. The day I met him he started on me. I was clearing brush when he drove up and introduced himself. He stood there and watched me wrestle a bunch of vines, telling me how life could be like a patch of bittersweet; a tangled mess of trouble with its season of beauty or something like that. I'm probably quoting him wrong. At the time I thought he was a nut-job, but after getting to know him I realized he can't help himself. Wounded birds, lame animals, broken humans; he likes to rescue God's creatures."

"Broken humans?"

"I was not in good shape back then."

"Cindy." Katherine guessed.

Mac nodded his head.

"Pete set you straight?"

"God set me straight. Pete pointed the way."

"He's good at that."

"So, I'm glad you talked to him." Mac gave her a long, searching look. "Is it something you can talk to me about?" His tone was careful, his expression kind.

As anxious as she was about sharing any of the details, she couldn't help but feel a rush of warmth at his question. "Thank you for asking; considering all you've shared with me, you have every right to demand I be as open."

"Hold that thought." Mac finished feeding the horses and then took her hand and guided her over to a stack of hay bales. Sitting down, he pulled her down beside him. "I want you to tell me what you're comfortable telling me. Don't worry about evening the scales. You said you were once in Brittany's shoes and, yes, I'm pretty curious about why, but only if you're ready."

"Ready or not, it all went out in that blog. Elaine took it down pretty quick, but there's no telling how many people saw it."

"Well, I didn't, and if someone tries to say something to me, I'll tell them to shut it." He reached out and took her hand, holding it tight. "I only want to know what you want to tell me."

Katherine closed her eyes for a moment and took a steadying breath. The smell of hay, horses, and old wood was strangely comforting. Between that and Mac's strong hand around hers, she felt safe, supported. "It was over ten years ago. I was engaged, and I got pregnant."

Mac's expression didn't change.

Katherine's eyes dropped to their linked hands, not wanting to watch him react to what she said next. "We were in a car accident. When I lost the baby, and the doctors said there would be no more, my fiancé called off the wedding. Knowing he needed a good excuse for abandoning me when I was still in the hospital, he made up a lie about not being the father. That rumor spread far and wide, and in the end I was fired from my teaching job."

Mac's hand tightened around hers.

"There's more." She felt too shaky to get into any detail. "But can we . . . It's hard to—"

"Kate." His voice was low and soft as he pulled her into his arms.

She felt her eyes start to sting. She curled into him, hiding her face against his chest.

"I'm so sorry," he said it softly. "That's what you meant."

She raised her head and gave him a puzzled look. "When we were at the Moose, I asked you if you'd planned on going into administration all along, and you said you were aiming for wife and mother."

"Right." She felt a tightness in her chest. "I gave up on that dream. I can't have children, Mac." Bracing, she waited to see the change, the disappointment in his eyes, the withdrawal, but instead he pulled her closer and kissed her forehead.

"I'm so sorry for that, too. But it doesn't change anything for me."

She looked up at his face and saw the sincerity there.

"It kills me that you wanted to be a mom and that was taken from you, but it would never change how I feel about you."

"Are you sure, because a lot of men—"

"Aren't me," he interrupted. "I never thought I'd have the chance to be a father after Cindy died, so instead I've tried to be the kind of man who can step up wherever needed; like the guys who were there for me after my dad died."

"And you're awesome at it." She put her arms around him and held on tight.

"Hardly." There was a smile in his voice.

Katherine slowly let him go and sat back. "Thank you for being patient with me."

He reached out and cupped her cheek with his hand. "You're welcome." For a long moment he held her like that before dropping a light kiss on her lips. "Dinner? Tomorrow night? We can celebrate the extension of your contract to June."

"Oh, I can't." She felt a swell of disappointment. "I promised

Pete I'd meet him at Maria's. It's our usual night. He never misses the Thursday night special."

"What's that?"

"New England Boiled Dinner."

"Seriously?"

"Unfortunately, yes. How about Friday?"

"It's a date. I'll swap with Cruz and work his shift tomorrow." He stood up and pulled her to her feet. "C'mon, let me drive you home."

"It's a five-minute walk."

"Be kind to an old man; I'm beat."

"I can walk home by myself, Captain Control Freak."

"You can, but you shouldn't have to." And the way he said it made her feel warm again.

"Okay. You win."

"How is it?" Pete asked, and the expression of distaste on his face was more than Katherine could take.

She laughed out loud, dropping her fork onto her plate. They were at Maria's, and Pete had ordered the special while she decided to try the moussaka. Normally she wouldn't eat lamb, but Maria kept pushing it, so she thought she'd order it once and shut her up. Turned out it was incredibly good, so Katherine had to pretend it was made with something other than baby sheep in order to enjoy it.

"You should see your expression, Pete. You'd think this very nice dish is about to grow fangs and launch itself at you."

"It might. Sounds like a character out of the Lion King."

"It tastes great. Anyway, stop insulting my food and let me tell you my news."

"Okay, you were saying that you got some test scores back."

"Yes, the ones the kids took right before Christmas. We were expecting a modest improvement over last year, but what we got was crazy-good. So good I actually screamed, right there in my office. The state is thrilled, the parents will be thrilled, and I'm hoping the board will be thrilled."

"You betcha. Greg already thinks you walk on water. Mindy is finally coming around, but don't expect too much there. Stephanie was her pick, after all."

"Seriously?" Katherine asked. "Is that why she 'forgot' that I was supposed to have that rental downtown and gave it to Erin instead?"

"I suspect so. But in the end, aren't you kinda glad she did?"

Katherine tried not to smile.

Pete didn't miss the lift of her lips. "You can't help it. Exactly like him." He took a sip of his coffee. "I knew I was right."

Katherine rolled her eyes. "I heard Brittany and Jake set the date. An April wedding."

"Yup." He set down his mug. "I was glad Erin agreed."

"She told me she's still not happy, but that it seemed for the best." As the waitress approached and left the check, Katherine grabbed it.

"No, you're not paying."

"Yes I am. Don't be silly." She hopped up off her stool and made it to the register before Pete could wrestle her for the check. She'd let him leave the tip. While she waited for a waitress to be free and ring them out, Pete got a call on his cell. It must have been short since he hung up after a few seconds. "What's up?"

"Nothing. Got a few of those today. Hang-ups. Somebody's probably hoping to get my voicemail instead. Sometimes people like to leave messages when reporting something. They don't want me asking them any questions. Hey, I'm gonna go start the Jeep so you don't freeze on the way home." He gave the check a hard stare.

"You're not getting it out of my hands, old man," she said with a smile.

He shook his head and muttered something about 'women's lib' before pushing through the doors and heading outside. A waitress finally came to the register and Katherine paid the check. On her way out she looked for Pete, catching sight of him off to the left instead of next to his Jeep. Then she saw him half-stumble.

"Hey!" she shouted as she saw a man come out of the shadows, hanging onto Pete's jacket, spinning him around and punching him in the face. Pete staggered back, but kept on his feet, catching hold of the man and blocking his next swing. "Hey!" she screamed as her feet came unstuck from the steps, and she started running. The guy on Pete was young, probably not even twenty, and he was fighting like crazy, landing every blow he could. Katherine didn't stop to think. She jumped into the fray and grabbed his thick, flannel coat, pulling as hard as she could.

The man aimed a swing at her, but she was already falling back with the momentum of her pull.

"Stay back!" Pete shouted at her, so she grabbed her phone out of her coat pocket and called 911, her fingers shaking so badly she almost couldn't punch the number. The man aimed another punch at Pete, and this one landed right on his temple. Pete went down.

"Leave him alone! I've called the cops." she screamed at Pete's attacker.

The man turned like he was going to come for her. His face was twisted into a kind of rage she'd never seen. He wasn't right. Maybe he was high or insane, but he definitely wasn't caring that she'd called the cops. Behind him, she heard a distinct sound of a gun being cocked.

"Hands in the air, Sawyer. Get on your knees. Now!" It was Pete. He was still on his knees, but he'd drawn his gun and had it leveled on the man in front of her. "Now!" he shouted again, but the man turned and lunged for Pete.

A deafening crack split the air, and Katherine squeezed her eyes shut, crouching, not sure if the shot might go wide and hit her.

When she opened her eyes, Pete was lying on his back, but the man he'd called Sawyer was holding his belly and screaming. Someone came out of the restaurant and shouted. Sawyer took one last look at Katherine and stumbled away.

Mac was beat. It had been a day full of frustration, irritation, and boredom in equal doses. The last call had been a doozy, and he parked his cruiser outside the station, thinking it was time for a few days off. He had one more report to write up and then a phone call to Katherine and bed. He pulled open the door to the station and was hit by a wall of sound. Not the usual noises from dispatch and various conversations; this was almost chaos.

"Mac!" Annie was standing at her station, headset on, fear etched into her face. "Multiple calls coming in from Maria's. Shots fired. At least one hurt."

Mac spun on his heel and ran out of the station. He was back in his cruiser, lights on, speeding up Main Street before he could even process what she'd said. Knowing Pete and Katherine were at Maria's for dinner, it was impossible not to feel the panic. He couldn't think straight, so he prayed instead, asking God to take his emotions, his panic and fear, and turn them into resolve.

"Pete!" Katherine shouted, but he didn't respond. His eyes were open, but barely. The cut on his forehead from his last fight with the Sawyers had opened up again. The blood was streaming down. She searched her pockets for her pack of tissues and finding them, folded them into a wad and held them against his head. Maybe he had gotten woozy from the hit? Katherine held his face still while she leaned her cheek down to his lips. He wasn't breathing.

"Oh no, no, no, no," she chanted as she felt along his neck for his pulse. She tried at his wrist, but she was shaking so hard she couldn't get a read on it. At his neck she felt nothing. "CPR, we need to do CPR," she said to the patrons and waitresses that had gathered behind her. No one stepped forward so she started chest compressions, hoping that years of first aid and CPR training would kick in. She'd never thought she'd actually use any of it. "Are they sending help?"

"They said they'd come as fast as they can," someone answered.

"Yah, but that could be a while. Heard there was a big wreck up on the highway. They might not be able to send—"

"What about the fire station?"

"They're at the wreck." Another voice chimed in.

Katherine could feel panic taking over, and she prayed silently for God to save him, this man she loved like a father, this man who had cared for her, protected her, loved her.

"Please, please, please," she muttered as she counted out compressions. The tears spilled out of her eyes and streamed down her cheeks. Leaning over, she blew a breath into his mouth and checked for a pulse before beginning the compressions again.

Mac pulled into the parking lot in front of Maria's to find what looked like half the town crowded around. He started barking orders and they parted, revealing the crumpled form of Pete with Kate kneeling beside him. She lifted up her face as he approached, and the look in her eyes was enough to drive him to his knees. "Mac, help me."

He looked down at Pete and hit his knees, desperately feeling for a pulse. "C'mon." Under his fingers he thought he felt a flutter, but he couldn't be sure. He took over the CPR from Katherine and waited for the EMTs, working the scene like the thousand before it, but this time with a desperate urgency. The deputies arrived moments later, corralling the crowd, taking statements, two of them peeling off after Sawyer. Then the paramedics arrived and he got up, pulling Katherine up and out of the way with him.

Mac issued orders, called the state police for assistance, called the wardens, although that proved pretty unnecessary. They'd already heard it on the radio and got there about a second after his call. All of them clustered around the paramedics, hovering, praying.

Mac had seen death too many times not to recognize it hovering over his friend. He prayed for a miracle as he searched the crowd for Katherine. He found her a few yards behind him, looking gutted, completely alone in a crowd of people, her face ashen. Mac went to her and took her in his arms, holding her tight.

"I tried to—"

"I know. I heard you giving Walter your statement. I know what you tried to do. You were so brave it scares me. Sawyer could have killed you." He pushed that idea right out of his head. "You did all you could. Pete's…" What could he say? Chances were, Pete was not going to be okay, and he wasn't about to give her false hope. "You're freezing. Get inside and warm up. I'll stay with him until they're done."

"I'm going to the hospital with him."

"Uh, no you aren't."

"But Mac—"

"Honey, right now they need all the space they can get to save his life."

It looked like she was going to fight him on it, but then her shoulders sagged and she nodded. As she started to climb the stairs to Maria's, she stumbled, like her strength was gone. Mac helped her up the stairs and through the door. He got her through the door and into a booth. "Maria. She needs tea." Maria nodded and immediately headed back into the kitchen. Then he turned to the packed restaurant and said, "I'd like anyone who witnessed what happened tonight to stay a little longer. Even if you've already spoken to a deputy. Just to be sure, okay?" He got a bunch of nods and then headed back outside.

Fatigue was setting in. Katherine was tired, and her eyelids fluttered closed. Maria brought her tea and tried to talk to her, but gave up when Katherine couldn't respond. *Shock. That's probably what this is,* she told herself. Closing her eyes, she tried to pray, tried to find some bit of her that wasn't internally screaming or weeping or numb. That's how Mac found her when he came back fifteen minutes later. She heard his low voice first and then his hands gripped her shoulders and sat her upright from where she'd leaned on the table, her head on her crossed arms.

"They've taken Pete." He looked to the side like he was gathering his courage. "They got his heart started, but I'm not going to lie to you. It isn't looking good."

She tried to get up, but he gently pushed her back down.

"You need to sit tight and get your legs under you again. You're exhausted, probably in shock, and it's not going to do him any good if you—"

"I'm fine." She pushed up again, and he let her this time. Sliding out of the bench seat, she heard him sigh as she pushed past him and headed for the exit. Behind her, voices of a couple of people stopped him with questions. She was through the door and halfway to her car when he called her name.

She pivoted.

Mac was jogging after her, looking angry. "Katherine, wait!" he half-shouted as he caught up. "You're in no shape for this right now. I'll give you a lift home, and you can get some rest. I promise I'll keep you updated and call you as soon as we know something. Then I'll take you to him myself."

"I'm not waiting at the cabin for word, Mac. And for the last time, I'm fine." She turned her back on him, heading for her car again.

Mac reached for her arm, but she yanked it out of his grasp. He lunged for her again, this time taking hold of her and spinning her to face him. "What are you trying to prove? That you're stronger than anyone else? That you don't feel as hurt as anyone else? That you're in control? Because any of that might be true on any other day, but not today. You need to go home, Kate. I swear to you that I will call you the second I hear anything. Then we can go together in the morning when you're stronger."

"You don't get to decide for me if I'm okay."

"Yes I do." His voice was firm, like there was no question, and she saw that he meant what he said.

"Why do you think you have a say in what I do?" she shouted.

"Because you're mine!" he shouted back. "And I care what happens to you. You and I are still working this stuff out, but we're together now. I'm responsible for you, for your safety, and I take that seriously."

"Responsible? No you're not." She was totally floored by the entire turn of the conversation. "Just because we're . . . whatever we are, doesn't make me yours."

"Yes, it does." He said it with conviction, and the eyes on hers spoke volumes she was not ready for.

"Mac, you need to stand down. I get that you feel . . ." She stopped and shook her head. One wrong word here and she'd hurt the person who needed it the least right now. He didn't deserve this. She was still reeling from what happened and scared for Pete. Whatever she said here would be spoken out of that; not from her heart, but from her fear.

Mac stood back, scrubbing a hand over his face. "Kate, can't you trust me?"

She heard in his voice that he was asking about more than just this moment.

"Haven't I shown you that I'll do what's best for you? Haven't I shown you that I'm not like him . . . whoever it was who hurt you so bad?"

"I can't do this, Mac, not now. Please let me go before we say something we can't take back." She tried to walk away.

Mac reached out and held her again. "I'm not going to say anything I want to take back. Katherine, you need . . ."

"I know what I need right now, Mac, and it's not you. Please leave me alone!" She twisted out of his grasp, turned her back on him, and walked away. Behind her she heard him exhale, like she'd punched him in the gut, and she knew that even though she hadn't meant to, she'd cut him to the quick.

CHAPTER TWENTY-THREE

KATHERINE LEANED HER HEAD BACK AGAINST the wall of the waiting room, trying to ignore the smell of cleaning fluid, bad coffee, and the fear that always seemed to permeate such places. The room was packed with people so she chose to stand in the hallway. It gave her some distance from Pete's colleagues discussing various 'outcomes' with the detachment of people well-used to tragedy. Katherine wondered what they must see every day and how they could take it. How could Mac take it?

Her stomach pitched when she thought of Mac. Once again she'd pushed him away. He didn't deserve it, but she couldn't seem to get the words out to tell him why. When something hurt her, she'd rather run off on her own and lick her wounds than lean on anyone. She realized she was doing it now, separating herself from Pete's friends. They were as anxious as she was and had offered comfort the moment she walked in. Katherine felt too broken, too raw to accept it so instead, she chose to be alone yet again.

Someone new arrived—another warden from the look of his uniform. His face was pale as he approached the group. "How is he?"

"Traumatic brain injury." One of Mac's deputies answered. "Heart's okay, they got him ventilated, and sedated right now. Running tests. Pete's daughters are here. They're all in the clergy room with the pastor from Pete's church and Mac."

Katherine had spotted the girls arriving and was glad when

Dan whisked them away into the room the hospital set aside for clergy. They looked shocked and afraid. Mac would help them too. Between them, Dan and Mac were about the steadiest guys she knew. Except for Pete. Her stomach pitched again as she remembered him sprawled on the ground and the blood on his face.

Listening to the crowd of wardens, policemen, and others begin to discuss similar cases and comparing Pete's odds was too much. Closing her eyes she let the cool of the cement wall sink into her, calming her frantic heart. Again she prayed the only prayer she could think of 'Please let him live.' Pete had swiftly and almost effortlessly become a second father to her. Watching her dad walk away from her family had been hard, and it had taken a long time to heal. The idea that she'd lose Pete was so painful she couldn't let herself even consider it. She had spent so long closed off from people that she didn't know how to take a hit like this. Instead, she made herself go numb, cutting off any thought that led to anywhere that wasn't the next update. Opening her eyes, she stared at the ward's doors and waited for them to open.

After another hour ticked slowly by, and the room thinned out as everyone began to realize it would be a long wait. Katherine gave in to her body's fatigue and decided to find a chair. She picked one across from the clergy room that was big enough for her to pull up her feet and fold herself into a ball. She closed her eyes and prayed for Pete and for his girls. Then she prayed for his friends, for Dan ministering to everyone, and finally for Mac. When she exhausted those prayers she prayed for forgiveness for herself, opening her heart to God and asking him to heal it.

Mac searched the waiting room until he found her, curled up in a chair and fast asleep. She looked so vulnerable, but he knew she'd be back behind that armor when she woke up. As he stood over her, he brushed her hair aside and gently cupped her cheek. "Kate."

Her eyes flew open and in them he read remorse, fear, relief, hope all bundled together. "Pete?" She blinked up at him.

"Medically induced coma. Doctor says it's the best way to reduce the swelling on his brain. The good news is that the rest of his body is operating as it should. It's going to be a few days though, maybe longer before we hear anything."

"Can I see him?" When Mac didn't immediately answer, she unfolded herself from the chair, stood, and took hold of his arms. "Please. I can't get that image of him on the ground out of my head. I'll never sleep tonight if I don't see he's safe and sound . . . for now."

"Okay, I'll see what I can do." Mac kissed her forehead before walking away, a wash of mixed emotions rushing through him. He was still angry with her for not listening to him, still reeling over the assault on Pete, still anxious for Pete's daughters. They'd sat in that room with Dan beside them, dry-eyed but clinging to each other. Having lost their mother too early and facing losing their father too, it was a wonder they held it together at all. He knew that from experience.

Walking up to the nurse's station, he caught the doctor going over charts and wheedled a five-minute visit for Katherine. When he pushed back through the doors to the waiting room, she was right there, waiting. He almost wanted to smile. Instead, he took her hand and led her to Pete's room. "The best I can do is five minutes."

"It's enough." Her voice was quiet and a bit rough.

"His room is here." Mac stopped her outside the shut door. "You need to brace because—"

"It's okay." She opened the door and stepped inside. Mac caught it on the close and followed her in while suppressing the desire to pull her out into the hall. He wanted to make it clear that he didn't like being interrupted, and that he understood she was a strong, independent sort of person, but that even he had flinched at the sight of his friend in a coma. He knew she wouldn't listen, or at least right now she couldn't listen. It wasn't the assault on Pete, or at least not that alone, that seemed to be affecting her.

He wondered about those details of her past she hadn't shared. He could only imagine the wounds she had suffered, and he reminded himself for what had to be the tenth time that he had to go slow and careful if he wanted this to work. Katherine wasn't any fainting flower, but she could be a morning glory at night, twisting into herself and locking the world out. Locking him out. He wished he knew the triggers that he was in danger of tripping. He was getting tired of blindly running into them.

Katherine stood at Pete's bed side, and Mac watched as her stoic expression cracked. She dropped her face in her hands, her shoulders shaking. Without a word, he came around the side of the bed and took her into his arms. Pete's face was wan and slack. His body seemed deflated somehow, connected to tubes and surrounded by machines. Truth be told, he looked dead. There was nothing of his vital energy in that bed. He was on the edge between this world and the next, and Mac guessed Katherine could see it too.

"Mac." She said his name like a plea, and he knew she wanted him to say something to make it better.

"He's in the best hands. There's nothing you or I can do here. We have to put our faith and trust in God's Providence. I wish I could tell you he was going to be okay." He felt her nod against his chest and held her a little tighter. "Right now the best thing we can do is support his girls and pray."

Katherine lifted her head. "Are they okay?"

"No. But the church has put them up at the motel down the street, and the hospitality committee's making sure they're fed and shuttled wherever they need to go."

"Oh good." Her voice was clogged with tears, but she seemed calmer. "Those women do works of wonder."

"Right, they welcomed you, didn't they?"

She only nodded. Mac shifted her in his arms so she was tucked to him as he led her out.

Katherine parked Henry and climbed the stairs to her front porch with legs that seemed full of lead. It was almost dawn, and she was facing a full day's work, not really sure how she was going to handle it. Next week was February break, so whether or not she felt like handling it, she had to go in today. There was too much to do to call in sick. Besides, so many of the kids knew and loved Pete. They'd need support and if unable to ask for it, were far more likely to seek it by acting out. She'd probably have a parade of students in her office from first bell to last.

Mac had gone right from the hospital to his office. The hunt was on for Sawyer, and Mac was in charge. He warned her he'd be out of touch for a while. They hadn't talked much after he led her out of Pete's room. They'd run into Dan with Pete's daughters. When Dan introduced her, Ally, the oldest, tried to thank her for helping to save her dad, but burst into tears instead. Katherine immediately hugged her only to find the other two circling them with their arms as well. Then Katherine had lost it, and they stood in a knot and cried in the corridor. They must have been a sight, but no one said a thing.

When Katherine was finally inside the cabin and divested of coat, boots, and purse, she sat down in her rocker. It would be smarter to get up and go to bed or at least the couch but sitting in the rocker, the gift from Mac, it was almost like he was there, holding her. Pulling a quilt over her, she set her phone alarm for two hours and fell into a shaky kind of sleep. Her brain kept her on edge with one nightmare after another until the alarm rang. She got up again, knowing she'd regret it later, but determined to do what she could. It's what Pete would do for her if their positions were reversed. She changed clothes quickly, grabbed a granola bar, and headed out.

The day was heavy with emotion. The students were as unsettled as she'd predicted. It was as if the whole building felt off somehow. The teachers and staff sensed it too. Everyone was quieter than usual—somber. Even Elaine wasn't her usual self, and there was little that ever got to her. Pete wasn't on campus daily, but he was the kind of person whose spirit was so substantial that his presence was felt even when he wasn't there. Today he was absent, and they all felt it.

Katherine called Dan to get contact information for Pete's daughters, and they met up at Maria's where she found out they used to work there as teenagers. She listened while they told old stories and played 'remember when' while trying not to cry. Beth reached across the table at one point and took Katherine's hand. "Thank you." She squeezed it and then let go. "I think this is exactly what we needed. We're driving ourselves crazy sitting at the hospital."

"Well, tomorrow is Senior Saturday at church, and we throw a mean luncheon. I'll be bussing tables, but you could always come by and see a few friendly faces." Katherine thought they could probably use as much time off hospital property as possible.

"We'll let you know. I'm kind of hoping we might have news by then." Lori glanced at her sisters who looked less hopeful. "They keep telling us it's too soon."

"Because it is." Ally said it gently, but Lori still winced. "Monday is the earliest they'd consider backing off on the meds and letting him come out of the coma. It's far more likely it will be even later in the week. Don't get your hopes up, Lori."

Katherine wasn't sure if she should say anything or even what to say, but she forged ahead. "Well, for however long, I'm here, and I'd be happy to help in whatever way I can. Even if it's only getting you out of there for a meal. Please let me know if there is anything I can do."

"We will, count on it." Ally tried to smile and for all the sadness in it, there was a kind of bravery in the attempt that Katherine deeply admired. Pete's daughters were just like him hopeful, kind, and strong.

CHAPTER TWENTY-FOUR

KATHERINE WOKE UP ON THE FIRST day of February break and immediately regretted it. Every muscle in her body protested as she tried to move. Even opening her eyes hurt. The last few days had been hard on her emotions, and after spending all day Saturday volunteering with the seniors and most of the night with the boarding students playing games at their rec night, she was exhausted. When she was asked to ferry the seniors back to the nursing home after church and then take over the junior high youth group that night she was tempted to say no, but knew they were asking because Pete couldn't. She was already feeling the effects of her sleepless nights. Mac had warned her she was doing too much. Once again, he was right.

Checking her voicemail, she got the message from Mac that Pete's daughter Ally had been right as well. The doctors had decided that Pete needed to be kept under for at least a few more days. With no news on the horizon, Ally and Beth were headed back to Portland to try to get a few days' work in while Lori sat with Pete. Knowing Lori was in the capable hands of the ladies of Calvary Church, Katherine thought a drive down to Rhode Island to see Heather and maybe squeezing in a day at the Cape to see her mom if she could swing it was probably the best idea. No sense in spending the break wringing her hands over what could happen. If Mac were around it might be different.

Mac was gone. Sawyer was 'in the wind' and Mac was chasing

down every lead, determined to find him. She never had an idea where Mac was. She'd tried to catch him at the station, tried him at his house, and even left him a voicemail saying they should make time to talk, but he had no reply. Other than his one voicemail, he'd sent only two texts, one to say he would be out of communication for a while and one to remind her to take care of herself. It was radio silence otherwise. Part of her worried that it wasn't only the investigation keeping him away. Maybe he was still hurt over how she had yelled at him that night. Maybe he was thinking she was too much work, too difficult, too wounded. Sometimes she thought she was too. Another reason to go away for a bit and maybe get her head together.

She pulled out a suitcase and started filling it, trying to ignore the pounding in her head. By the time she was packed, with the cabin all shut down for the week, she felt horrible. It was not the normal 'I've got a cold' horrible, either. Dragging her suitcase outside, she stuffed it into the trunk, and that almost drove her to her knees.

It was a four-hour drive, so she stopped at the pharmacy on the way out and grabbed non-drowsy cold meds to make it down the mountain. She tried to reach Mac, but got his voicemail. She stopped one last time in town to fill up at the gas station, hoping he'd see her missed calls and return them before she left. He didn't.

As she sat in her idling car, she tried to understand what she was feeling. Confusion, fear, and longing mixed together, and she couldn't sort them out. She was worried about Pete. She missed Mac. In a corner of her mind she knew that what she needed right now was more of Mac, not less. She was a little afraid that even a few days away would end by breaking them up. In the weeks that they'd been slowly walking together towards something like love, she'd been checking for exits the entire way. He'd been the honest one and, now that he'd pulled back, their relationship felt tenuous at best.

She called him one last time and again voicemail picked up.

Fighting off a sob, she left a message. "Hi, it's Kate." She hated how wobbly her voice sounded. Taking a breath, she tried to calm down. "I didn't want to leave a message, but I can't get a hold of you." She paused again, trying not to burst into tears. Of course the one time she really needed him . . .

"It's all too much right now. I know we talked about spending time together soon, but . . . I'm kind of a mess." She had to stop as her voice warbled again. "And I think I'm coming down with something, which is probably why I'm sounding so stupid." Wanting to kick herself for being nearly incoherent, she took another breath and tried again. "Wherever you are, I hope it's going okay. I'm sorry I didn't tell you sooner that I'd be leaving for the week. But I need a break. I'll see you when I get back."

The drive was excruciating, and it started raining hard, making her head hurt worse. Maine rivaled Texas for sudden, brutal storms. As she navigated through a doozy, she tried to be grateful it wasn't snowing. The meds she'd taken to hold off her symptoms were not working. She was having trouble seeing through the rain, her head pounding, her body feeling weaker and weaker.

After an hour of it, she knew there was no way she could drive a mile further, much less make it to her destination. This wasn't a regular cold; this was something much worse, and she'd end up killing someone at this rate. Luckily, she was passing Portland and there were plenty of hotels. She pulled off the highway at a funny circular one by the mall and checked in. Heading upstairs, she flopped on the big hotel bed and called Heather.

"I'm sick as a dog, Heather." Katherine felt like she was going to pass out.

"You sound it. Who do you want me to call for you?"

"No one. You're the only person who was expecting me anywhere. I'm going to sleep this cold off, and I'll see you tomorrow, maybe the day after."

"Okay, call me when you wake up, though; I'm concerned

about you."

"Yes, Mom." And she hung up.

Katherine kicked off her shoes and undressed until she was in her t-shirt and undies, and crawled under the covers. She prayed that whatever was making her so ill would pass, then she prayed for Pete and his daughters, and finally for her broken, messed-up heart and the beautiful man she wanted to give it to, but was so afraid of. Nothing like a little delirium to make her emotions sort themselves out.

Hours, or it might have been days, later, she woke up when a slightly rough hand coasted over her forehead like it was trying to take her temperature. "Kate," a voice called, and she opened her eyes. A man was leaning over her. "You're burning up, honey, so I called the hotel doctor." Her head was in a very swimmy place and she couldn't quite make him out.

Oh! She knew who the voice belonged to.

He laid his hand on her forehead again, and she could hear him praying. *Good grief, how bad was she?* Her head felt . . . strange. Everything felt strange. And it all hurt. It was probably better not to be awake than to feel like this. She slipped into sleep, listening to the soft yet urgent words of his prayer.

Low voices woke her next, the room was lit up bright, the covers down at her waist. She wanted to pull them up again, but her arms had no strength. She felt so cold.

"Is that temperature okay? I mean it's higher than I've ever seen an adult go." It was that voice again, Captain Kyle Patrick MacAlister.

"Actually with influenza, fevers this high are pretty common. We need to get it under control, for sure. Once we're treating it, you'll see it drop down to something manageable. There's no need to worry, Mr. Grant."

Mr. Grant? That would not go over well. Katherine sort of snorted with laughter.

"Katherine, are you feeling a bit better?" the doctor asked, and she heard a low chuckle from her left.

"I think she's laughing because you called me Mr. Grant. Grant is Katherine's last name, not mine . . . for now anyway," he said, and she snorted again.

"Well, if she has a sense of humor, then that's a good sign." The man checked her vitals again. "Give the fever reducers as I've instructed. Her lungs are perfectly clear, which is great. Here's what to watch out for . . ." Their conversation got boring so Katherine stopped listening and seemed to float along for a bit before she felt the hand on her forehead again and heard the whispered prayers. She fell asleep, nuzzling into his touch.

Katherine woke up, and the room was dark. She was in a huge, king-size bed with a pile of pillows and soft, warm covers. Her head, however, oh dear heaven it hurt, and her body even worse. She had to have been hit by a truck, maybe twice.

"Kate," a low voice called to her.

She opened her eyes as wide as she could to see who it was. She raised her hand and touched the cheek of someone leaning over her, a rather stubbly cheek. "Kyle MacAlister," she said, and she could feel him smile.

"Yes, Katherine Grant. You are one ill woman, but I have to say, still as beautiful as the dawn over Martin's Meadow. You remember that meadow, don't you?"

"Yes, you yell at me for running through it."

"I do because you're gonna break an ankle. But I'm not yelling at you today. Not until you're better, and then I am going to yell, but only a little." His lips grazed her forehead. "You're never going to listen to a thing I tell you, are you?"

"I forget . . . what did I do wrong this time?"

"I told you to take it easy and rest. Instead you stayed up to all hours of the night with Pete's daughters, worked a double at the senior center, and managed to catch the flu."

"Oh no! You shouldn't be near me, then."

"I got the flu shot back in October, my love," he said, brushing his lips across her forehead again. "It's kept me healthy enough to rescue a poor maiden holed up in a roadside hotel, sick as a dog."

"Heather called you? The traitor."

"No, I tracked her down after I got your message. I wanted to be sure you got home alive. You sounded miserable. I wasn't sure you'd be able to make it. Thank God I did," he added softly.

"Thank you, Kyle MacAlister," she said.

"Why are you using my full name?" he asked and she could hear the smile in his voice.

"I like it. And I like Kyle better than Mac. Mac sounds like a truck. Kyle is nice. I don't know why you don't use it. I bet your mom called you Kyle. I'd call you Captain if you'd let me, but you won't. You're so bossy."

"Then call me Kyle," he said, but she was already drifting back to sleep.

The next time she woke, it was her mother's hand at her forehead, and her face smiling down.

"Mom?" she asked in confusion and looked around the room.

"Captain MacAlister called me to help take care of you."

"You drove for hours, through Boston, on the highway?" Katherine was astonished. Her mom didn't like to go to the corner for milk, let alone a road trip.

"You're my daughter. I'd cross the Sahara for you. But I have to be honest. He had me ferried up here when I confessed I hadn't driven in a while. A very nice young woman in a town car picked me up. It was quite relaxing watching the scenery go by."

"Where is he now?"

"Getting us lunch and checking into the room next door. Poor man has been sleeping on that chair in the corner. He had the hotel roll in a cot for me, though. That was thoughtful."

"That's him," she said quietly.

Her mom got up and came back with a thermometer, sticking it in Katherine's mouth and waiting for the beep. "Not bad. 101. Your fever's under control now. Mac said it was raging for a while, even when treated. I think you worried him, dear. Thank God the man called Heather and found you here. You truly might have . . ." Her mom trailed off and Katherine watched while she regained her control. "Don't be so stubborn next time, and take better care of yourself."

"Yes, ma'am." She sat up a little and groaned as every inch of her seemed to be in pain. "Can I take a shower?"

"Absolutely." Her mom eased her out of bed, got the shower going, and helped her take her clothes off. Nothing more humbling than having your mom help you undress and take a shower when you were thirty years old.

"I'm as weak as a baby deer," Katherine admitted while her mom pulled back the shower curtain. "But I think I've got this part."

"Good. I'm going to call housekeeping to see if they can change the bed now and bring us more towels." And her mother left.

Katherine reached out a hand to the shower wall to hold herself up. There was an old-lady grab-bar there, and she clung to it for dear life. The water felt amazingly good, as did the shampoo and soap. She washed away the sweat from her fever and probably the drool that was all over her face. *Yuck.* He had now seen her at her very worst. *Nice.*

When she emerged from the shower, her mom wrapped her up in a towel, then the hotel robe, and finally wrapped her hair in a towel, turban-style.

"I remember you used to do this when I was little. I thought it made me look like a grown up."

"Then you'd find my heels and prance around in your Minnie

Mouse bathrobe and a towel on your head like you were walking a runway."

"Hilarious. Can you grab me something to wear?"

"Of course, right here." And she pointed to a nightgown that had to be hers, since it wasn't one Katherine owned. "I had a peek through your luggage and all you have are those sweatpants things and t-shirts. That's not what you need when you're sick."

"But, Mom."

"You need easy on, easy off; that's a nightie." And over her head she slid the nightgown. She didn't complain once it was on. It was silky and soft, and the neckline made it look more like a 1930 starlet's dress than a nightie.

Her mom led her out of the steamy bathroom. The maids were finishing the bed, smoothing down the wrinkles in the coverlet, and arranging the throw pillows. They took one look at her and folded down the covers instead, murmuring concerned and soothing words in what sounded like Russian and letting her mom guide her back under the covers.

"Okay, I'll leave you to have a nice rest. Here's the book I found in your suitcase. Your Captain may be back in a few minutes for lunch. In the meantime, I'm going downstairs to see if I can get you an herbal tea. There's a mall right across the street, so I'll pop over there later and grab a few things. Get some rest now," she insisted, and then she left the room.

Katherine was feeling warm and comfortable, but not like resting. What she wanted to do was take her hair out of the towel and comb it out, but there was no way she could lift her arms over her head. She'd have to wait until her mom got back. Right then she heard the door open, and Mac appeared with what she assumed was lunch.

"Hey, you're up." He set down the bags of food. Coming closer, he gave her a hard stare before concluding, "You look like you feel a good deal better."

"Ah, diplomatically stated. I know I'm a wreck. The

housekeeping staff treated me like I had one foot in the grave."

"Don't," he said quietly, and she was shocked to see the pained expression on his face. "I can't laugh about it yet. Give me ten years or so."

"Was I that bad?"

"When I got here you were comatose . . ."

"I'm surprised the hotel staff let you in."

"Badge," he said simply.

"Right," she said, trying to sit up and failing. He looked around the room as if searching for something.

"Where's your mom?"

"She went to find herbal tea for me. What do you have for lunch?" Now that she was awake and showered, she was actually feeling hungry.

"Chicken broth and orzo. There's a restaurant across the way. When I told them what I needed they were happy to make it for me."

"That's it?" she asked, and his face grew stern.

"Woman, you have not had any food in two days. You need something with protein and carbs that's not going to challenge your system." He sat down on the bed with the little takeout container of soup and a spoon. "You keep this down and we can move on to solids later." He handed them to her with a napkin, and sat next to her with a container of his own.

"Aww, did you get soup, too? An act of solidarity?"

"While I was waiting for yours, I could smell the minestrone they were making. Had to have a cup," he said after a mouthful.

"This tastes like heaven," she said, because it did. It might have been basic as could be, but every nuance of flavor was shouting out to her disused taste buds. They ate in silence until Katherine waved her container at him. "That's all I can eat."

He looked in, seeing that she'd barely managed half, and gave her a frown. "We'll try again later. Maybe when your mom comes back with the tea. Do you want to lie down for a bit?"

"Yes, but this towel." She pointed at her head. "I've got to get it off my head and brush out my hair."

"I'll do it."

"Uh . . ."

But he ignored her hesitation, found a brush, and sat beside and slightly behind her. He unwound the towel and slowly began to brush through her hair. It felt so good she closed her eyes. His hands were strong, but gentle as they worked out the knots her long hair was prone to.

"You're good at this." She felt him pause and then start brushing again.

"I wish it was for a good reason. When Cindy was using . . ." She waited for him to go on. "Sometimes I'd find her with her friends, but more often than not, I'd find her in some dump, strung out and sick."

She felt a terrible stab of empathy. Of course he'd know when to call a doctor, what food she should eat. This must all be a stark reminder of how he tried to save Cindy and couldn't. And Katherine had put him through this; forcing him to relive it.

He finished combing her hair out by running his fingers through it, an intimate gesture that made her feel cherished. She felt the bed move as he got up and wondered what words would convey to him that she understood, that she appreciated what a sacrifice this all was. He'd dropped everything to take care of her. Looking up at him, she saw his face unguarded for once and it hit her: this was Kyle, the man he didn't share with very many people. It meant everything that he had let her in.

"Thank you." She grabbed his hand and held it. "For everything, Kyle." And she tried to make him understand, looking into the stormy ocean of his eyes. He stood there for a moment, and then sat on her bed, holding her hand in his.

"Kate, everything I do for you . . . it's not out of some noble instinct. I'm a nice guy, but I'm not that nice. Had you been anyone else, I would have called the EMTs when I found you, let your assistant know, and gone home. I'm here because I . . ."

"Hello!" Her mother's voice sang into the room.

Mac looked up to the ceiling like he was pleading for patience.

"Oh good, lunch has arrived. Smells wonderful," she said, poking into the remaining bag.

Mac got up from the bed and took the bag of food over to the small table in the corner of the room "Lauren, I got you a bowl of minestrone and rolls from the restaurant across the way. There're a few cookies under there, too."

"Hey—you didn't offer me any of the cookies," Katherine protested.

"Well, of course he didn't. Here, I found a coffee shop and got a tea to go, and bags so we can make our own." Her mom handed her the cup. She got a few sips down and had to stop.

"I know I sound like a baby, but between showering and eating I'm exhausted. I'm going to take a nap." Her mother helped her lie down and settled the blankets around her. It didn't take long for her to drift off again.

Mac sat at the table while Lauren finished her lunch. She was like her daughter and not. She had Kate's coloring, but was tall and thin, with refined features. She appeared delicate, while Kate with her large eyes and full lips was more . . . hardy? That was a stupid word for it, but Kate had a kind of old-fashioned beauty; softness with strength behind it.

He glanced at the bed. She didn't look strong now. Her eyes were shadowed, even in sleep, her cheeks hollow and pale. That first night while waiting for the doctor, he thought for sure he would be standing at her grave exactly as he had Cindy's. Her breathing had been so shallow, her body so hot, and the craziest things tumbled from her mouth. He'd prayed over her with his whole heart.

"You're in love with her, aren't you?" Lauren said, startling him out of his skin. "I'm sorry, but right now it's written all over your face."

"I . . ." He was at a loss for words, but he wanted Lauren to know, and he wanted her blessing. "I'm going to ask her to marry me." He pulled the ring he'd asked Erin to make out of his pocket: Three strands of silver in an open weave, with tiny gems embedded where they intersected. He handed it to Lauren. She gasped and held it in her hand as if it was the most precious thing she'd ever seen. "It looks custom."

"Erin Sullivan, a silver artist and a mutual friend of ours. I told her what I wanted, and she did the rest."

"Oh, I approve, and I know Katie will, as well. This is exactly her taste. She'd never want a big rock. These little gemstones, they look like tiny flowers."

"I thought she'd like that."

"She'll love it." She handed it back to him with a sigh. "Do you have an elaborate plan for asking her?"

"No. I might do it the next time she's delirious, though–that might be the only way I get a yes."

Lauren laughed out loud at this, and then seemed to remember Kate was sleeping and lowered her voice. "Oh my; she is hard-headed, isn't she?"

He looked at the sleeping Kate again and wondered for the thousandth time how this would all work out. He had to get back on the trail of the bail jumper or he was going to lose him. Lauren said as soon as Kate was well enough she'd be taking her down to the Cape. He wanted Kate with him, or at least in Sweet River where he could get to her, but he knew that was selfish. He had to find the balance between what he wanted and what she needed.

Lauren was still watching his face. "You know about her past?"

"The man who abandoned her, yes."

"It was so much more than that. Losing her daughter was . . ." Lauren trailed off before adding. "Do you know she was conscious that whole time?"

Mac shook his head, too overcome with sympathy to speak.

"She never speaks of her losses, but they shout from her actions."

Mac could see that, too.

"If you want my blessing, you have it, but you'll have to be patient, so incredibly patient with her. Can you do it?"

Mac looked over at Katherine lying in the bed, and answered from his heart. "God willing, I can."

CHAPTER TWENTY-FIVE

EARLY THE NEXT DAY, MAC CAME into her room and sat at the edge of her bed. Her mom was downstairs at breakfast, so they had a few minutes alone. "I have some cautious good news." She immediately tried to sit up and he guided her back down. "Rest. Doctor's orders and mine, or I won't tell you my good news."

"Okay, I'll behave."

"They eased Pete out of the coma, and he's conscious."

She gasped and tried to sit up again.

"Uh-uh." He settled her back down again. "Conscious, but not speaking. They're not sure what they're dealing with yet, and they have to be patient—so do you—for a few days while they watch closely for improvement."

"Oh, but that's good news either way."

"It is. Depending on how fast he recovers he could be moved to a rehab facility in a week."

"Wow, so fast?"

"Ally's picked out a facility in Portland."

She fought off a rush of disappointment. Portland was a long drive, probably only something she'd be able to swing on the weekends. "That makes sense, but I hate that it will be so far away."

"Speaking of which, by the time you come home, I'll be in Augusta. The job there is gonna be at least a week, maybe longer."

The disappointment that had rushed in now stayed and pooled around her. Right now she didn't want him to go home, much less up to Augusta.

He squeezed her hand. "But when I get back we'll talk."

"Uh-oh." Her disappointment morphed into anxiety in record time. "That never means anything good." She was hoping he'd make a joke and say it was nothing, but he didn't.

"Sometimes it does." He traced her forehead with a single finger, brushing her hair aside to drop a kiss there. "A week or two and I'll be home, okay?"

"Okay," she said, but she didn't feel okay. She wanted to grab hold of him and make him stay.

A day later, Katherine called the school to ask for a few extra days to recover. She was finally well enough to drive down to the Cape with her mom. It was a bit white-knuckled since her mom did most of the driving, but they made it in one piece. Her sisters and Heather came up later in the week, and she spent the rest of her time off visiting and recuperating before driving back to Sweet River on her own.

On her first day back, despite having been on a recent vacation themselves, the kids were all nutty. She had a grumpy student in her office pretty much every other hour, all day, every day. There seemed to be twice as much work as there should be and half as many people to do it. Going home to a cold cabin every night and a dinner she had to fix for herself was rough. She'd been avoiding eating at Maria's, due to memories of Pete's assault and avoiding the Moose, due to longing for the still-absent Mac. Things did not improve the second week, and Katherine knew by this time she was pretty grumpy herself.

She was worried about Pete . . . that was part of it. He'd recovered enough to be moved to the facility in Portland, but his speech was terribly slow and his mobility drastically limited. They'd asked for no visitors for the first few weeks so he wouldn't be taxed. What made it harder was Mac's continued absence due to the hunt for Sawyer. Calls from him were infrequent at best. When he did call they tended to argue. She knew full well that she picked each of those fights. Needing him, missing him, made her vulnerable, and she lashed out. Knowing it and preventing herself from acting like a big jerk were two different things, though. She kept praying that God would heal whatever part of her needed it, so that it would stop. She had apologized for it so many times now; she wondered why he didn't give up on her.

The final week of March began with a typically horrible Monday. She made it home that night and didn't have the energy to bother with dinner. She flopped onto the couch, wondering if she could talk the pizza guy into delivering this far when there was a familiar knock. She hopped up and dashed to the door. As tired and cranky as she was, she drew strength from knowing he was finally home. Maybe he'd come inside, and they could order that pizza, and he'd stoke the stove so it would be warm. Maybe he'd stay and they could sit by the fire.

She pulled open the door and saw he was in uniform, but for once he didn't look tired. He looked elated. "You got him," she said, knowing that could only be the reason for him looking so pleased.

"Watched them book him an hour ago. It's done, and I know it probably doesn't make anyone feel any better, but—"

"Of course it does. It's closure. It's what we all needed."

"Yah, it is and I'm glad to be off the road for a bit," he said, not stepping inside. "I wanted to stop by and let you know."

"You're going?" Her shoulders slumped, and she felt the telltale sting of tears start.

"What's wrong?"

"It's nothing." She shrugged. "It's everything. I'm sick of the cold, the grumpy students, this stupid cabin."

"What's it done now?" he asked with a twitch of his lips.

Katherine was not in the mood to laugh. "It's freezing. I don't understand why, since I keep that stove going day and night."

"I'll check it out." he said patiently.

"And the hot water ran out on me again this morning."

"It will if you wash your clothes in warm water and then take a shower right afterwards."

"In the civilized world that's not a problem. And I like hot showers and clean clothes. This is the cabin time forgot and I'm strung-out, missing Pete, and so tired." And to her horror, she started to cry.

Mac was through the door with it shut behind him before she could blink. He crossed the room to hold her in his arms while she all-out sobbed like a big baby. "Come on," he said softly. "Sit down. I'll fix the stove." Mac took her over to the couch, and she flopped down, her head in her hands. With his usual skill he had the fire roaring in about a minute.

"That's revolting," she said.

He gave her a puzzled look.

"How quickly you can do that. I've watched you a dozen times; I still can't do it that fast."

"Call me anytime, Kate, and I'll take care of it."

"I don't like having to depend on you."

"Ah, the familiar refrain," he said with a sigh, and she made a face at him before sitting back and tucking her feet up. Katherine expected him to go, but instead he sat down, reached over, picked her up, and deposited her on his lap.

"Hey, this is against the rules."

"Necessary exception."

"Because I cried on you?" *Humiliating*.

"No, because your day was bad enough to make you break that iron resolve of yours to never be vulnerable. Since right now it's clear everything I say is the wrong thing, I'm simply going to hold you."

She laid her head on his shoulder and tried not to melt right into him, but it was nearly impossible. He stroked her hair and whispered a prayer over her, asking God to fill her with strength and banish her stress. It felt so good to let go and let him take care of her.

After a few minutes of quiet bliss, he spoke to her gently. "I'd like to have that conversation now, the one I said we'd be having when I left you in Portland."

"Maybe later? I can't take anything heavy today, Kyle." She was finally warm and comfortable, nestled against him.

"Okay," he said, with not a small amount of exasperation in his voice. "I'll leave it be tonight. There's something you need to know, though."

She lifted her head to face him.

"I haven't been patient when it comes to you. I've always been confident in my feelings for you, and I've pushed you to catch up to where I am. You were right to slow me down, to make me wait. But I feel like we're past that now, and I want to finally be able to tell you that I love you. So much," he added in a whisper.

Katherine froze. She had no idea what to do with that.

"I know you're not there yet. I'm not expecting you to say it back. But I need to tell you that. Been trying for weeks," he said with a laugh. "Considering all you've been through, it's no surprise you locked your heart down." He shifted her on his lap so that she was cuddled against him again and spoke his next words with her head tucked close to him.

"Having a man you loved betray you must have left you with wounds I can't understand. I'm sure you still have feelings about what he put you through."

"All I can do is pray he finds his way," she said. "For me, that's all done now."

"You found a way to forgive him?"

"I found my way back to God. He took care of the rest."

Mac sighed, and she felt his breath brush past her ear, making her shiver. He pulled her closer. "I'm content to leave things as they are tonight, but I want to have that conversation sooner rather than later, honey."

Katherine woke with a start to find she had fallen asleep in her clothes on the couch. The quilt from her bed was covering her. She pawed through her foggy memory. Mac had come over and turned her world upside down by saying he loved her and wanted to have a 'conversation' that she was pretty sure she wasn't ready for. He'd shown her what kind of man he was again by holding her when he knew that's what she needed and agreeing to wait to talk.

She got ready for work, thinking about what a good man he was and how she wished she could accept his love. She'd never met anyone like him, and she loved being with him, even if it was sitting watching the fire burn low. As soon as she got to work, the activity of the day distracted her from thoughts of Mac. Between helping to proctor the state's standardized testing, dealing with two fifth-graders posting evil comments about each other on Facebook accounts neither one of them should even have, and taking a call from a disgruntled parent ticked off about their eighth-grader's C in art, she was done. She'd forgotten what the daily grind of being the principal was like.

The rest of the week went about the same, but that weekend she shut off her phone and spent the entire Saturday with Kyle. It was a golden day. The weather was perfect, and they took the Mustang and drove all the way to the coast. They had dinner at a tiny restaurant perched on a bluff overlooking the ocean and sat on the beach to watch the sunset. They drove back in the dark, talking of nothing and everything. It was the best date ever.

On Monday, Mac brought her lunch at work.

"Better start to the week?" he asked, walking into the office and handing her what looked like a take-out bag from Greta's Gourmet, a sandwich shop that had just opened for the season and that she'd already been to twice. Of course Mac would have noticed that.

"You have no idea," she answered and poked her head into the bag. "Better and better: I see a cookie."

"I know what a sweet tooth you have and came armed." He pulled a chair over in front of her desk and sat across from her to share lunch. "I have good news and bad news," he said once they had finished their sandwiches.

"Good news first."

"I managed to get reservations for Friday night at the Lincoln House."

"Ooh, I've heard about that place. It's supposed to be excellent. And I get to dress up, right?"

"Yep. I'll pick you up at six if that works."

She nodded.

"Now the bad news. I've got another training session. Only a week this time."

She felt a pit open up in her stomach, despite having almost inhaled her lunch. "I hate it when you're gone," she said without thinking.

"Kate, maybe it's time we had that conversation, the one you keep trying to avoid."

"Not sure I'm up for it today," she muttered.

"Are you ever?"

"Well. No," she admitted, and she tried to smile like this was all lighthearted repartee.

Mac wasn't having it. "Okay, not today, but will you answer a question for me?"

She raised a brow.

"You know how I feel, what I want."

Right. Love, marriage, forever . . . which required submission, dependency, and vulnerability. Pretty much everything that scared her to death.

"I know you're not there today, but is there gonna come a time that you are?"

"That's not a fair question."

"Yes, it is. You're letting me put myself out there while you stay safe." Standing, he gathered the remains of his lunch. "You've kept me back while trying to hold me close, letting me in only so far and then freezing me out. I'm trying to be patient, but there's a limit," he finished in a far softer voice.

"Kyle, when we first started dating, I told you I was working some stuff out. If you want to walk away . . ." she whispered back, a heavy weight in her chest.

"And leave you? No. I'm going to stick around, and we'll see if I've got whatever magic word is required to open your heart." He slowly leaned down and kissed her, his lips lingering for a moment then moving to her ear to whisper a prayer that her day would go well, that her work would be blessed.

Touched once again by his kindness, she closed her eyes and soaked in the words. She looked up in time to see both hope and the tension at war in his eyes before he shut it all down, gave her a wink, and headed out.

"What is wrong with me?" she asked the empty room when he had gone. The empty room didn't have the answer.

CHAPTER TWENTY-SIX

FRIDAY NIGHT, KATHERINE SAT IN A corner table at the Lincoln House restaurant with Mac, soaking in the ambiance of flickering candlelight and fine china. She'd worn her very best little black dress and heels since the snow had mostly melted. They'd come in her BMW, looking like a far cooler couple than they really were.

"You look fantastic tonight," Mac said from across the table. "Have I mentioned that yet?"

"Um, maybe, once or twice," she said, smiling. "You look pretty amazing yourself. I love the suit." And she did. It was charcoal gray, and he'd worn a black dress shirt underneath it with no tie; formal, yet not. More from his New York wardrobe, probably.

"All for you," he said with a smile. "Hey, I was thinking on Saturday we could ride. Misery and Agony miss you."

"Aw, I'd love to, but it will have to be late. I'm helping Brittany with her dress." Katherine had the idea while she was down on the Cape with her mom. She had never thrown out her wedding dress since it was made for her by her cousin Cora, and even if she didn't think she'd ever wear it again, she wasn't about to toss it. She'd gotten it out of storage and brought it back with her. Brittany had taken one look at the dress and squealed with happiness, so with a week to go before the wedding it was time for alterations. Katherine wasn't a seamstress, but she could take in a dress with no problem.

"You're making her dress?" Mac asked in confusion.

"No, I'm giving her mine."

"Your dress." His voice was flat.

"The one I never wore. I still had it. My cousin made it for me, and I never had the heart to sell it, so it's been stuffed in a box, waiting. I pulled it out of storage and offered it to Brit, and she loved it. Match made in heaven." She smiled.

Mac didn't seem pleased.

She kicked herself for having mentioned it, and changed the subject. Mac didn't snap back out of it, though. Something was off, but she let him have his thoughts, not sure what might be going through his head.

By the time they were driving home, she decided that letting him have his thoughts was a completely stupid idea. The night had gone from wonderful to a long, awkward silence. He seemed totally preoccupied. Finally, she decided she couldn't take it anymore. "What's up?"

"Huh?" he asked, like he'd been deep in thought.

"At dinner you kinda drifted away on me, and right now you're still pretty distant. What's wrong?" She looked away from the road for a moment.

His face was pensive. "June first is coming up."

"In two months or so, yes."

"In two months you're headed home." He said it with no emotion, simply stating a plain fact.

"Right, we have months."

"You hate it when I'm away, but in two months you're leaving for good."

She hadn't really thought of it that way. She'd been trying not to think about it at all. "But…That's a ways away."

"Still gonna get here, Kate, and we're still not having that conversation."

"Mac, I—"

"No." Now his voice was full of feeling. "You call me Kyle. You're the only one who does."

"Kyle," she said softly. "Stop borrowing trouble. We have time."

His eyes searched her face for a long moment before he nodded and went back to looking out the window.

Katherine felt a seed of apprehension sow itself in her gut. Mac's determination to stick with it and unlock her heart might be at an end. What he didn't seem to realize is that he already had her heart.

Trust was what she needed, not love. Love she had in buckets full, not that she'd tell him that. She loved the way she could eke a smile out of him when he was in a stony mood. She loved the way he cared for the people he served, for the kids he worked with, for his unending patience with the little old ladies who liked to tell him off for almost everything. She loved the way he kissed her, held her, prayed for her when she had a lousy day. She even loved the way he bossed her around, because she knew he was trying to keep her safe.

But there was no way to know if his love was the real thing— she'd thought Tom's love was real, and the consequences of that mistake nearly killed her. Mac would never think to cheat or to lie to her, she knew that, but he could leave her. He could decide one day that she wasn't what he wanted, and there was no way she'd survive a second betrayal, not with him doing it.

"I love you, Kate." He was still looking out the window, his voice low and gloomy. "That isn't going to change if you leave. But we have to be realistic. I don't have the kind of career that makes a long-distance relationship possible. Neither do you, although I guess you could come back once in a while. I've thought this through, and I'm out of ideas."

"We'll work it out." They had to work it out. No way was she ready for this to end. Mac didn't answer and he didn't try again. She dropped him off at his house, he gave her a sweet kiss goodnight, and that was it.

CHAPTER TWENTY-SEVEN

"I LOVE IT!" BRITTANY STROKED THE blue satin ribbon at the raised waistline of Katherine's wedding gown. It was now made perfect for Brittany, whose eyes began to fill with tears. Katherine looked in the full-length mirror to see why. Erin. She stood behind her daughter, tears running down her face. Brittany turned around and flung herself into her mother's arms.

"This is not the time I wanted it," Erin choked out, "but this *is* what I wanted for you."

"I'm sorry, Mom." Brittany buried her face in her mom's shoulder.

Katherine had to take a deep breath to avoid bawling with them. That was the thing. The wedding had a bittersweet taste. Yes, it was a happy occasion and babies were blessings, but no one could kid themselves and say these two teenagers weren't about to have a rocky start. *Rocks.* That reminded her. "Brittany," she asked softly. "Did you tell your mom the news?"

"What? Oh, no! I totally forgot."

Jake had been over earlier and filled Katherine in on how God had provided. Now Katherine got to watch as Brittany's face lit up while she laid it out for her mom. "Jake got that job with Stone & Field, even though they know he's in trouble at school. And this is even better. The owner offered us a plot of land, real cheap. Jake's had his eye on it for a while. He says it's already got a foundation poured. We can go to the bank after he's worked steady for a few months and get a loan to build a house."

"A house?" Erin looked shocked.

"Yes, a house. Jake's gonna pay the owner a down payment on the land and then part of his paycheck every week while we wait to build up credit for the bank loan. We'll have a house in a year, he thinks, because we only need a loan for the materials. He's gonna do the rest. It will just be a two-bedroom ranch, but we can add on and—"

"A house." Erin pressed her lips together and looked up at the ceiling.

"He's gonna take care of us, Mom, exactly like he said. He's . . . he's a good guy. I know you don't think so, but he really is."

Erin pulled her daughter into a hug again and this time Katherine didn't fight the tears. This was good. It was healing. Erin probably would need another ten years before she'd like the boy, but Jake would win her over because he loved her daughter, already loved the child they had created, and he intended to do right by them.

Brittany had decided that graduating from high school was enough for now. College was a dream she'd have to put off. When Katherine had pressed it she'd said, "Actions have consequences. These are mine." It was sweet of her to echo Jake's noble statement, but Katherine planned to write her a letter of recommendation anyway. Just in case.

"We can't stand here crying. Brit, pull yourself together." Erin was joking, since they were both still a mess.

Katherine handed out tissues and then helped Brittany out of the dress. She carefully put it back on its hanger and hung that from a hook in one of the ceiling rafters. Tomorrow she'd steam it, and that weekend Brittany would wear it.

Erin and her daughter left, leaving the cabin far quieter and a good deal less cheerful. Mac had called that morning to say the weather was too rainy for a ride and that he might stop by tonight. "'Might' being the operative word. So she'd encouraged Erin and

Brittany to stay longer than they probably should have, simply because she didn't want to face more hours of angst.

Things were so unsettled. Ever since that gloomy drive home it was like there was a shadow hanging over them. She wanted to talk him into giving the long-distance thing a try. She loved him, she really did, but marriage was something else. It meant tying herself to someone who could hurt her if he wanted to, could tear her up, not that she thought he would. But what if something went wrong, what if he got bored? *He wouldn't,* her heart pounded out the words.

She was cleaning up when she heard his knock. Katherine let him in, immediately spotting his troubled expression. The seed of apprehension in her gut bloomed out in full.

"I'm dropping by like I said I would. There's something I need to . . ." He trailed off, staring up at the wedding dress. He stepped closer and took a long look at it. "This was yours."

"It was." She watched him, alarmed at his almost bleak demeanor. "Brittany's happy with the alterations. I added the blue ribbon so I could lift the waistline easier. It fits her perfectly."

"It would have looked stunning on you." His voice was low and a bit thick. "I'm surprised you were able to give it away."

"Well, it's not like I'm ever going to wear it."

"No, you won't. Will you?" There was such a wistfulness in his tone that she whipped her head around to look at his face, almost giving herself a crick in the neck. He was staring up at the dress, like he'd lost something worth more than life itself. He looked . . . bereft.

Katherine felt like she was standing at the edge of a cliff and her heart was telling her to go ahead and jump, it would be fine because he'd be there. He wanted forever. She moved towards him and started to speak, but he beat her to it.

"I got a job offer." He met her eyes, but she couldn't read him.

"Really?"

"Not only a promotion; a whole other division. I was gonna

turn it down because it means more travel. A lot more, but . . ." He looked back at the dress again and closed his eyes.

Katherine felt the apprehension in her gut turn to dread.

"I can't do it, Katherine."

"Do what?" Her voice was barely more than a whisper.

"I thought I could handle it. That these last few weeks would be precious to me—later—when you'd be gone, but it's torture."

"Kyle, what are you saying?"

He turned to her, and his face said it all for him.

"You're giving up, aren't you? After saying you wouldn't, after swearing you'd hang in there." She was almost shouting at him. "We can work this out. I can come up and visit. If you're here or on the road, it won't matter."

"Visit?" There was a mountain of disdain in that word.

"I said that wrong." She moved towards him, taking his face in her hands. "I don't want this to end. It doesn't have to. I can come up, and we can spend time together."

"And then you leave again? A weekend here and there and then it's done, right? 'Cause no one can maintain a relationship like that. You know it."

"People do it all the time."

"No, people try to do it all the time, and they fail. I'd rather we make the cut clean than drag it out over a year, so it rips us apart slowly." He took her hands away from his face, but didn't let go.

He didn't want to let go, she knew it. He didn't want to do this. "Please, Kyle, let's at least try."

"I can't do it." The pain in his voice was almost more than she could take. "Knowing you're gonna walk away is killing me, and I know I can't change your mind. If it's gotta end . . ."

"It doesn't have—" He stopped her mouth with a kiss and in it was every ounce of feeling it seemed he had. She wrapped her arms around his neck and answered with every feeling of her own. *Don't go. I love you. I'll make you stay with me.* She felt a tear hit her cheek as he tore himself away. It wasn't hers.

"God bless you, Kate. God protect you and keep you," he whispered the prayer against her lips.

Her eyes flew open as she felt him leave. He was at the door when she heard, "I love you. I always will."

Before her muddled mind could register what had happened, he was gone.

"Hey, calling back to let you know that I'll take that job after all." Mac was standing on his back deck, overlooking the side of the mountain. He'd bought the property just for this view. It made him feel settled, grounded. In the months after Cindy died he'd been like a nomad, wandering to whatever pleased him, whatever deadened the pain. Buying this property, building this house, it had grounded him, given him roots. Now he was ripping them up again. "You need me to start Monday?"

"Yah, buddy, if you can." Mike Waller sounded pretty surprised. It would stand to reason, considering how many times Mac had turned him down. But Mac needed out of Sweet River, out of the county, away from Katherine. This job was his ticket.

"I can. I've got a kid coming by to take care of the animals, and he's about to graduate from school so he can sublet the house as well. I assigned Markham and Fisk to this area, so the station is covered."

"Great! Then get your butt to Bangor on Monday, nine sharp, and I'll buy you a cup of coffee so we can go over the details. You're going to love this job, Mac. It's almost zero paperwork."

"Well, that's something to look forward to." Mac wasn't looking forward to anything other than escaping the pain that was consuming him. Maybe time would be kind, and before long it wouldn't feel like he'd ripped his own arm off.

CHAPTER TWENTY-EIGHT

"GET OFF THE FLOOR, KATHERINE." ERIN stood right inside the door, hands on her hips. She looked seriously unhappy, but it didn't matter. Nothing mattered anymore. Erin huffed out an impatient sigh. "I knew it was bad when Elaine said you'd called in, but this is ridiculous. We're all worried. Heather called me three times this week alone. You shouldn't be doing this to your friends."

Katherine didn't have anything to say to that. If she felt like she could get up and make a call to reassure someone, she'd try to call herself.

The first week after Mac left was miserable. She'd dragged herself through each day, pretending everything was fine, only to cry herself to sleep at night. Brittany's wedding had been a bright spot, but the rest of March was rainy, cold, and bleak; a perfect fit for her mood. April wasn't any better. When May finally came she thought she'd be okay, that the end of school stuff would pull her through, but every day it was the same. Her heart hurt; it ached, and there was nothing she could do.

In a weak moment she'd called him, desperate to hear his voice. He'd sent her call to voicemail. She'd hung up on it. Resolving never to call him again, she deleted his contact info from her phone to resist the temptation. Turned out that was a mistake. She'd have been prepared today if she knew that number on her voicemail was his. Instead she'd been blindsided by the iciness in his voice as he left his dismissive message:

"Give the key to Jake when you leave. He can shut down the cabin. Take your stuff when you go, and he'll handle the rest. Thanks."

She'd been standing when she listened to it and collapsed to the floor when it was done. Mac was done, and he was making that crystal clear. It hurt so much she couldn't bring herself to get back up. This was ridiculous and dramatic, but she couldn't help it. The idea that Mac had cut her from his life and that he'd never be anything to her again was beyond devastating. The feeling needed a bigger word.

"Tell everyone I'm sorry, but for today at least, I can't function. Catch me tomorrow."

Erin rolled her eyes heavenward and then got down on the floor with her. "I wish I could do the Pete thing, where I say the right words to fix your hurt or kick your butt, whichever it is you need."

A few days ago Katherine would have laughed at this, but now nothing mattered.

"But I can't. I wish I could do the Heather thing, so you'd know what to do with all that you're feeling. But I'm all you've got right now." She reached out and stroked Katherine's hair.

It felt nice, but it didn't matter.

"I want to tell you something, and I'm not sure if it will hurt more or help, and not being a wise old man or a lifelong friend, I honestly don't know, so brace."

Katherine braced.

"He had me make you a ring."

A strangled sort of sob came from her mouth before she could stop it. *A ring.* He had a ring. It was more evidence that she'd been so afraid of the pain of losing him that she drove him away. All that fear was a self-fulfilling prophesy. She'd taken the love of a good man and thrown it away. Even worse, she'd sabotaged her own happiness by failing to do the one thing that might have made a difference–she'd never once asked God what His will was. She'd only followed her own path, a broken trail.

"Oh man . . ." Erin got up on her knees and pulled a sobbing Katherine up to sit. "I'm sorry! I guess I shouldn't have told you, but don't you see? It's not too late. If you love him, then track him down and tell him."

"It's too late."

"No, it's not."

"Erin, you didn't see his face that night, you didn't hear the message he left me today. He's done. He cut me out of his heart. He gave up on me."

Erin sighed.

Katherine crawled up onto the couch. "It's better this way. I'll be able to get used to not having him, before I go home where I'm not going to have him for the rest of my life."

"Do you even hear yourself?" Erin asked, looking down at her. "Katherine, this isn't like you at all. How can you give up like this? You're a fighter, so fight for him."

"I can't. He's done. I told you. Listen to the message yourself." She handed off her phone, since she'd still been holding it when she fell to the floor and started crying her eyes out an hour ago.

Erin listened to the message and Katherine watched while her face grew troubled. "Okay, this is not good, but it's not impossible."

"Any other day, your optimism, the fact that you came out here to check on me, it would be such a gift, but today everything—"

"Okay, it looks bad right now." Erin sat on the couch with her and pulled the blanket off the back. "Take today to rest. You're a mess. When was the last time you ate?"

"Yesterday, lunch . . . I think."

"See, that's part of the problem. You're not the kind of woman who doesn't eat. It's messing with your head."

"Nice, Erin."

"You know what I mean." She waved a hand dismissively and then headed to the kitchen. Katherine could hear various cabinets opening, and Erin returned with a bar of chocolate and a glass of milk. Katherine raised an eyebrow. "Milk is to fill your stomach, chocolate is to soothe your soul. It works, trust me. Would be better if we had ice cream, but this will do."

Katherine wanted to cry again, but she didn't. Instead, she reached out and grabbed Erin's hand. "You're not Pete and you're not Heather, but you are a good friend, Erin Sullivan."

Now it looked like Erin was going to cry.

Katherine ate her chocolate and drank her milk. "How's Brittany?"

"She had her checkup yesterday and," a smile broke out and lit her face, "it's a girl."

"Oh, that's great."

"Yah, because girls are way harder, and now I get to say 'I told you so' about a thousand times. Actually, I'm glad it's a girl because Brit's cousin had a girl two years ago and that means loads of hand-me-downs. She's already brought over a bag of baby clothes. The crib and stuff I have in storage, so we'll drag that out soon."

"Are they still living with you?"

"No, they're subletting for the summer, from Mac actually," Erin said with a wince.

"Oh, right. That new job and, of course, even on his days off he doesn't want to be here. Probably doesn't even want to drive past and see . . ." That hurt so much, Katherine couldn't finish the thought. But it was likely true. He didn't want to be reminded of the woman who let him go. She didn't burst into tears again, although she wanted to. Instead, she bit off a hunk of chocolate and decided that today she'd be broken, but Erin was right. Tomorrow she had to pull herself together.

"I want to say something again, but I'm afraid you'll freak."

"I've resolved to let today be the day for that, so knock yourself out."

"That first day, I think he knew he could fall in love with you, and he worked hard to stop himself because he knew what today was going to feel like, for both of you. I don't know why he changed his mind, but he did, and that love isn't going to simply fade away. He's not that kind of man."

"You're right. He isn't the kind of man to let love fade. That's why he had to kill it."

"Don't hang up, okay?" Erin's voice shook Mac out of the sleep he'd barely fallen into.

Mac groaned and sat up in his hotel bed, the tenth bed he'd seen in the last two months. Taking the job had seemed a great idea when he wanted to escape even the faintest reminder of Kate, but this hotel to hotel business was not getting any easier. He didn't know how she managed to do it year after year. "I'm thinking you're gonna say something I don't want to hear." The fact that Erin was calling him so late at night was not a good sign.

"You missed the wedding, you big loser."

"I got your pictures, though. They look very happy."

"They are. One of these days I'll stop wanting to shoot him."

Mac laughed. It had been a while since he'd done it, and the sound was strange to him.

"Did you see *all* the pictures I sent?"

He had, especially the ones with Katherine in a light blue dress, her hair up, those pieces of it falling around her face. He'd deleted it. "Yup. Listen, Erin, I appreciate what you're trying to do, but—"

"She doesn't sleep."

"What?"

"Not really, not enough. I think she gets maybe three hours a night."

Mac felt like she'd punched him in the gut. "She doesn't eat unless someone reminds her. She does the interviews for the new director, and then she goes back to the cabin, and she doesn't come out again until she has to do another one."

Mac closed his eyes and tried not to feel anything. "I'm sorry to hear that."

"I bet you still have that ring in your pocket."

He did. That's how much a sap he was. He couldn't get rid of it, couldn't even stick it in a drawer and forget it. He kept it in his pocket, his fingers tangling with it when he went for his keys or for change, a constant reminder of what he'd lost.

"She loves you, Mac. What she's going through is hard to watch because it's like grief. It's like you died and she's mourning you. But you're not dead, Mac. You're stubborn."

"She's leaving, Erin."

"I think she'd stay if you asked."

"I asked."

"Not if you ask her now, but it's got to be you coming to her. She won't come looking for you. She thinks you gave up, that you're done with her. She said you cut her out of your heart."

Mac almost laughed; if only it was that easy. Katherine was still very much in there, burrowed in; he'd never get her out.

"If you'd come back, you'd see it yourself."

"I'm not hanging up on you, but I am going to end this call."

"Mac, wait, one more thing."

He wasn't sure he could take one more. "You're not going to want to hear this, but as your friend and hers, I have to say this."

"Then get it over with."

"You broke her."

Mac drew in a breath, taking those words like a hit to the chest. "You made her fall in love with you when you knew she was fragile. She was frozen over, but you got her to melt for you. She let you in, and you broke her when you left."

"Erin . . ." He had no defense against the truth of her words.

"You broke her. Now, come pick up the pieces." And she hung up on him.

You broke her. Those words chased around in his head until morning.

CHAPTER TWENTY-NINE

KATHERINE DIDN'T KNOW WHY THEY WERE bothering with this candidate. He was terrible. He was about as bad as the last two put together, but with the salary they were offering they couldn't expect top-notch. *Still, this guy . . .* "Thanks for your time. We'll be in touch when we make our decision."

He nodded, smiled for the board, and then left.

Katherine didn't bother to hide her sigh. She looked over at the board members who'd taken time off from work for this interview, and she shook her head. Most of them got up, looking glum, but Greg stayed behind so the two of them could go over the few remaining candidates, ones they hadn't even bothered to call because their qualifications were so scanty.

"What if . . ." Greg began, and Katherine knew exactly what he was going to say.

"You're not serious."

"You'd have the whole summer off. No need to break in a new director if you were the new director. Don't forget that it means time off around the holidays, too. Not a bad way to spend a year. Or two."

"Greg, you know I never said I'd—"

"We need you, Katherine. This was a hard year, I know . . . for you, too. Maybe we can all help each other." Greg's face was full of hope, but also compassion. In the time she'd been working with him and the other board members to find a new director, she'd learned that Greg was a total grandpa. He wanted everybody happy, and he'd knock himself out to make that happen. He was generous and gregarious, but he was also deeply intelligent and wise. He didn't have Pete's same sage-like quality, but he wasn't shy about sharing the wisdom of his years. "This is a good place to drop a few roots."

"I'd need better housing." Did that really come out of her mouth?

"You know that farmhouse up the way from the town hall? White, blue shutters, barn and garage?"

"I think so."

"Happens to be vacant. I know the owner, being that it's me. Would that be adequate?"

She was discovering that Greg was also Maine's version of her friend Helena, the DC kingmaker. He was no fool, dangling that house in front of her. He also hadn't missed that she'd been so lost in her gloomy grief over Mac that she'd failed to make any alternate plans. He'd probably asked Heather and learned that she had nothing scheduled, nothing even in the pipeline. Was this maybe God's will for her?

"The house has Wi-Fi, cable, and a walk-in-closet. Not to mention a laundry room, butler's pantry, and there's this little room off the back with two big windows and plenty of space for artsy stuff, or sewing, or whatever." He rattled the details like he knew what was on her wish list. "Y'know, in case that might make the offer more tempting."

"Only a year?"

"How about two?"

"How about one?"

"Okay fine, one." She realized she'd been expertly maneuvered into saying yes to a year as director, without even taking time to think it over. It was almost laughable.

"Well, now that we have that settled, I'll call the board and give them the good news. You go ahead and pack up the cabin. You can move into the house this weekend." That did make her laugh. "Now that is a sound I like hearing, Katherine." His voice was soft and kind. "I'll see you tomorrow, and I'll bring the keys." She gave him a smile as he left the conference room.

What had she done? Pulling out her phone, she made a call. "You are never going to guess what is about to hit the inbox."

Heather chuckled. "Something interesting?"

"A new contract."

"You tricky thing. What have you done?"

"I've lost my mind."

Heather didn't immediately respond. Her end of the call remained silent. Katherine heard her friend take a deep breath. "You've signed on there, haven't you?"

"For a year." She braced for the likely scolding.

"I am so, so glad." There were tears in Heather's voice.

Katherine couldn't remember the last time she'd heard them. "Honey…"

"I have been praying so hard that you'd stay."

"But he's gone."

"Who, Captain Cut and Run? No, it's not about him. It's about who you became up there."

"Broken, but in the right way?"

"Yes," she whispered. "And I was so afraid him leaving you would ruin it all. I should have had more faith." She sighed. "And maybe a teeny tiny part of me hopes that if you're still up there, that pinhead will get his act together and come crawling back."

"Heather!"

"Sorry, I know you love him, but it could still happen, and I'd still be a bit ticked at him. It will pass."

"I know him, and he's not coming back."

"Well . . . Are you staying in his cabin?"

"No, let me tell you all about the house I'm apparently getting."

Two days later she was sitting in her office, signing the contract for another year, and suddenly an almost overwhelming flood of guilt and grief washed over her. Here she was, staying after all, and he was gone. She should have had a little faith. Mixed in with the guilt was anger. She was angry with him for giving up, angry with God for not clueing her in before it was too late, and angry with herself for being so fearful. She dropped the pen, closed her eyes, and called out to God for peace.

As she searched for the words, her heart cried out, and God responded. There was no sense of completion or even contentment, but she felt the anger, guilt, and even grief slide away as a new thought filled her head. She was home. Sweet River had somehow become home. Despite Mac leaving, this was home. The place and its people had woven their way into her heart. Erin, her new and slightly caustic friend; Elaine, her nosey, but loveable admin; Brit and Jake; the church . . . had all become part of a new home; one that wasn't about shared history, but about love. In a way, Mac was still part of it. Everything that reminded her of him might be painful right now, but eventually it would be bittersweet, and she'd take that.

She still ran through Martin's Meadow every afternoon she could, even though the trail was crowded with memories of Mac. She still took the turn that led past his land, because losing those places and the happy memories that they held wasn't worth the illusion of peace that avoiding them would bring. Living in a place that shared happiness and grief on every street corner was far better than living in emptiness.

Mac stood at the check-in counter of the Holiday Inn Express and wanted nothing more than his bed. He'd driven from his last job out east to what the rest of Maine called "Massachusetts North," the section of southeast coast that was populated by Mass expats and tourists. His back was aching, and he knew he should probably find the exercise room and work out instead of crashing, but he was too tired. Sleep had been elusive since Erin's call. It only got worse when Jake called to say Katherine had turned in her keys early. Knowing she was gone was supposed to make it easier, but somehow it was ten times harder.

He took a shower in his room and hit the sack, but he couldn't shut his thoughts down. It was Kate. Getting up, he took his gear and went downstairs to the workout room. An hour on the treadmill did wonders for his body and not a blessed thing for his head. He sat up and watched TV for a while, hoping it might help, but a cable news show he half expected to see her on wasn't the best choice. It was boring enough, though, that he finally started to feel tired. He laid down again, waiting for sleep to finally overtake him.

An hour later he was awake, and he knew. This was a mistake. This job wasn't the cure. Nothing was the cure but Katherine. He'd blown it. Huge. He'd run like a little kid, and he'd broken her in the process. God forgive him. He swung out of bed, grabbed his cell, and made the call. "Mike, when you get this call me. Need to talk about the job."

Almost immediately he felt a kind of lightness in his chest, like he'd been carrying a burden and hadn't known it. Amazing how that worked. He'd been fighting this feeling for weeks, and now that he'd finally given in, he felt fifty pounds lighter. At forty-two he still forgot at times that it was easier to live in God's will than outside it.

He needed to go home and regroup, get his head on straight by hitting his knees a bit more. God had been trying to get through to him, but he hadn't been listening. He was too busy feeling sorry for himself. A ride through Martin's Meadow might help. The horses probably needed a good workout. Jake and Brittany had the house, but he could find a place to rent. *Wait.* A plan began to form in his head. He'd start by gutting that cabin.

He made another call. "Mac, something up?" Jake answered, sounding freaked. He looked at the clock beside the bed and cringed.

"Sorry, kid, forgot what time it was. Nothing's wrong. I wanted to know if you've started at Stone yet and if not, can you do a demo job for me."

"I can always do a demo job for you, boss. Just say what and where."

"The cabin, and now would be good. I'm coming home in a week. Take it down to the studs. Tear out the loft and storage room, too. I'm gonna do the rest."

"Uh . . . okay. I can get the demo done in a week. You need me to get materials in for you?"

"No, I'm gonna make calls tomorrow, see if I can work a miracle. Can you get going on the permits for me? Town hall's open tomorrow."

"Sure. Can I ask why you're bothering, though? To tell you the truth, it would be cheaper to doze that thing and start over."

"There's history in that cabin."

"Yah, I guess there is. Okay, Mac. Consider it done."

Mac switched his phone off and fell back against the pillows. Maybe now he could finally sleep. He closed his eyes and said a prayer for her for the first time in two months. He prayed that God would hold her in His hands until Mac could do it himself.

Katherine sat in the breakfast nook of her new house, looking at the river in the distance. The windows on this side faced the backyard, which wasn't terribly big, but it was at the top of a hill so the view was something else. The house was everything Greg had promised, and Katherine let herself spend two whole days at junk shops and thrift stores finding the perfect furnishings. Since she didn't have anyone to cart the stuff for her, she'd done the unthinkable and sold Henry to buy an SUV. She'd almost cried, but it was bought by one of the seniors who was off to Bowdoin in the fall. It was easier handing Henry off to what was basically a younger version of herself.

Her Yukon was everything a woman in the mountains of Maine would need: good in the snow, could take a hit from a moose, haul wood, furniture, groceries, and a bunch of passengers. She'd already installed a baby seat, anticipating carting Brittany and Jake's baby around. Jake had announced the name at the baby shower – Katherine –Erin—and then rolled his eyes as his wife, his mother-in-law, and Katherine all cried.

They were happy tears, though. Katherine had had enough of the other kind. Most days were fine. She could bury her feelings and function, but she'd get surprised now and then, and the loss was so sharp it left her breathless. Like the day Jake gave her the news that Mac had ordered him to demolish the interior of the cabin. He hadn't meant to drop that bomb on her, but it fell all the same. It was like Mac was erasing all evidence she'd existed, sweeping her away. She'd found herself up in her new bedroom, with a real bed and an eight-foot ceiling, sitting in the rocking chair she'd brought from the cabin, bawling her eyes out.

But that had been weeks ago, and the sting had started to fade. She was content, if not happy. The life she was beginning to build was a good one. Her heart might not be ready to accept it, but eventually, the ache would go. Running helped, so that afternoon she headed out on the familiar trail, smiling as she passed Pete's land, saying a prayer for his recovery. His speech was almost fully restored and according to Ally, he was walking with a near-normal gait. In a few weeks he'd be moving back to his cabin. Sadly, it was already handicapped accessible since his wife had lost her mobility before she died. The girls planned to hire Pete a home health aide until they were sure he could handle his basic living needs. Katherine was looking forward to spending real time with him. In a way it felt like maybe things would begin to seem normal again if at least Pete was back.

Running Martin's Meadow was another way to return to normal. It was a beautiful spot, and today, with the afternoon sun painting the world golden, it was perfect. The meadow was a sea of green with the occasional drop of color from a wildflower. In the distance the pine trees swayed a bit in the wind, and she could catch the smell of their needles, drawn out by the heat. Summer in Sweet River was still slow in coming, but every day it seemed to get warmer. She was looking forward to starting a container garden in the front, since she'd missed her chance to put out tomatoes or strawberries. With her mind on which planters would look best on her new front steps, she missed that the wide, flat track she was on had changed into the rough trail of the lower meadow.

Her foot twisted as she hit a rut left by an ATV, and she pitched forward. Before she could stop herself, her momentum flung her face-first into the dirt. Stunned and winded, she lay there for a second before slowly picking herself up, doing a bodily inventory. Her knees and shins were skinned, as were the palms of her hands. Tomorrow she'd be one big ache, considering the force with which she slammed into the hard-packed dirt. Stepping gingerly, she tested out the ankle. "Agh!" Her shout of pain scared a flock of birds in the distance. They flew up and out of sight.

From where she was on the trail, there was no calling for help. There was nothing to do but hobble out, ankle or no ankle. Going slowly, she made her way up the trail, but after a few minutes she had to take a break. She sat down on the side, trying to stay away from the high grass that was probably crawling with ticks. As she rested, the world grew quiet around her, and she prayed for the strength to hobble back out. In the distance she could hear a noise that didn't match the rustle of the grass or the chirping birds. It was a rhythmic jingle and clop. There was only one thing that made a sound like that.

Her eyes flew open, and she surged to her feet, wincing when she put too much weight on her ankle in her hurry. The horse and rider coming into view might be Jake, exercising Misery. He'd already started his new job now that school was over, but construction guys got out early. If it was him, she could hitch a ride, and even if it wasn't, the rider could get help.

She stood in the middle of the trail as they rode closer, one hand shading her eyes. The sun was now fully in the west behind the rider. She heard a man's voice directing the horse to slow. They were stopped near enough that she finally got a good look at her rescuer. In her surprise, she stepped back and put her full weight on her ankle. With a shout of pain, she went down hard for the second time.

CHAPTER THIRTY

"Here, let me help you," a deep voice said.

Looking up at its owner, she felt her stomach twist into a knot. "Kyle." That one word took all the air out of her lungs. She stared up at him like he was a ghost, an apparition of her imagination summoned by the pain in her ankle. His hands were there, slipping off her shoe. "Ouch." She winced.

"Still not listening to me, are you?" His voice in her ears was everything sweet and wonderful in the world, mixed with ragged, jarring pain. The world had tilted right off its axis. He didn't belong here. He was supposed to be on the road someplace. She tried to sit up and brush him away. The last thing she needed was one of his lectures topped off by his pity. He must be home for a visit, riding his horses and seeing to his property. What rotten luck to meet him here.

"Nothing to say to me?" he asked, his voice softer. "I figured you'd at least tell me off for making you fall."

"You didn't make me fall, the pain in my ankle . . ." she trailed off, hoping he hadn't heard the emotion in her voice. He needed to go away now. Seeing him was too much. She wanted to throw her arms around him and beg him to try again. She wanted to tell him she was staying, and that he'd been a fool to walk away.

Instead he scooped her up into his arms and stood.

"What are you doing?"

"Taking you someplace where I can help you with that ankle."

"No. No thank you. I'm fine. I'm going to walk back to my—"

But Mac ignored her and hoisted her up into the saddle. He swung up behind her and took the reins.

This was the last place Katherine wanted to be, crushed up against the man who'd broken her heart, his arms around her as he guided Misery back onto the trail. She could feel the heat of him against her back, his breath on her cheek. It was torture. Was he feeling this? Was he feeling anything? "Can you take me back to the road? I left my car there."

"Not gonna do that."

"Why?" she asked, trying to turn in the saddle.

He squeezed her with his arms and her heart skipped a beat. "Sit still."

"I will not. Let me get down--"

"You're gonna spook Misery, and he'll land us both in the pricker-bushes. Sit still."

He had a point. Misery didn't seem jazzed about carrying them both, even if he did like her. They rode in silence for a minute before she noticed where they were going. This was the way back to the cabin. She wasn't sure her heart could take that. And besides, he'd gutted the place. He couldn't have redone it by now. "I see where we're headed and I would really rather—"

"Kate, please."

There was something about the way he said her name that made her belly flutter. Her head was trying to keep up and failing. What was going on?

His arms tightened and then his lips were next to her ear. "Here we are," he whispered.

She couldn't suppress the shiver that ran through her. It was the good kind of shiver, one that she was pretty sure he felt. The cabin was hidden by a row of pine trees. When they cleared them, her jaw dropped.

The entire exterior of the cabin had been re-shingled. Not only that, but the windows were larger, and the door had been replaced with a big oak one, solid all the way through. The front porch had been scrapped and instead there was a short, wide staircase, more like a series of small decks stacked on each other.

Mac dismounted and held his hands out so Katherine could do the same. But she was having trouble taking it all in. Apparently he wasn't going to wait. He reached up and pulled her off Misery, but didn't set her on her feet. Instead he reached down and swung her up in his arms. "Kyle!" she shouted as he started carrying her up the steps to the cabin.

"I missed hearing you call me that." He shifted her to open the door and let them in.

Katherine blinked, completely in shock. The cabin was transformed. She didn't recognize anything other than the hearth. Every other inch of it had been altered. It was now all one big room. At the back he'd blown out the wall and extended it to the end of the deck, enclosing that whole side in huge windows. The walls, ceiling, and floor were still pine boards, but he'd sanded and stained them, and they shone. The kitchen was in the corner, with granite countertops and high-end appliances. There was a rustic, but elegant table, and two chairs opposite it. In front of the hearth, two leather chairs and an ottoman were positioned on a large rug.

Across the room where the storage closet used to be stood a floor-to-ceiling frosted glass enclosure she could tell housed a bathroom, and opposite it sat a huge soaking tub. The loft was gone, and in the center of the entire cabin stood a four-poster bed piled with pillows and covered with soft-looking blankets and a puffy down comforter. This wasn't a hunting cabin anymore, it was a honeymoon cabin. The nicest she'd ever seen. She took this all in as he placed her carefully on the bed and went to the kitchen. She could hear him getting ice, and he returned with it in a towel as well as a first aid kit. Of course he'd already have a first aid kit there.

"What . . ." she trailed off as he carefully removed her sock and examined her ankle.

His hands were soft and careful as he placed the ice and

adjusted her foot. Then he gave the same careful attention to the road rash on her hands, and then on her knees. "I'm thinking July," his voice broke the silence. "We should probably have it at your beach house on the Cape if it's available, since all your people are down that way, and I don't have any people that aren't here in Sweet River. I want to come up here after, and I'm thinking with all we're facing ahead and all we've been through, we deserve to take a month to ourselves. Then we can figure out where you're off to next. I'd like it if you'd pick another long job. That way I can find something temporary wherever you go, and we can rent a place instead of doing the hotel thing. Hated that. If not, maybe we could use the beach house as home base, and you fly or drive home when you can. I've got a friend who runs a private security firm on the Cape, and I'm pretty sure I can find work with him."

"What?"

Mac looked up from her ankle, and she could see it there; he hadn't killed it. He might have buried it, or ignored it, but he hadn't managed to kill it. He loved her. She fell back against the pillows, completely overwhelmed.

She was so pale. And too thin. He'd done that. He'd broken her. Even now he wasn't sure if he could fix things. He didn't even know why she was here, running that stupid trail, but he wasn't going to miss this moment. It was a gift from God, and he was taking it.

"It was a few weeks ago that it finally dawned on me." He shook his head. "I was working what should have been my dream job, but I was miserable and feeling sorry for myself. Sitting in that hotel room, it hit me. I'd blown it. I'd made the biggest mistake of my life." He sat on the bed by her hip and reached down to stroke the hair off her forehead. "I quit. Now I go where you go. If that's the only way this works, I'll do it."

"What?" She looked stunned.

He couldn't decide if that was a good thing or not. "I love you, Katherine Grant. Until a few weeks ago it was a pretty selfish love. I was digging in my heels, trying to turn the universe on a dime. And I let it go."

"But . . ."

"We'll work it out, just like you said."

"But . . ."

"I love you and I want to be with you, so I go where you go. I'll even learn to like living at the beach, but I'm taking my truck. Your BMW is nice, but it's—"

"I sold Henry," she blurted out.

"You sold your car?"

"Bought a Yukon."

"Now? Now when you're leaving, you buy an SUV?"

She smiled, and it was a beautiful thing. The words she said next were even better. "I'm not leaving. Guess who's the new director?"

He didn't bother to answer. Instead he pulled her into his arms. "Say that again."

"I'm not leaving."

Mac didn't know what to do with the gigantic ball of feeling in his chest. It was part joy, part relief, and all of it threatened to spill out. He closed his eyes and rested his forehead on hers. "You're not leaving," he whispered.

"No, Captain Obvious, I'm not leaving."

"I missed that, too."

"Only you would miss me being mean."

"It meant I got to you. I wanted you to react to me back then, I didn't care how. See . . . selfish." He still had his eyes closed, still resting his head against hers.

But she pulled back and gently kissed his forehead. "I love you, Kyle MacAlister."

He pulled her closer, entranced by those words. "You're not leaving," he repeated again and she snickered. "So that means you're marrying me."

"Don't I get a proposal?"

Mac let go of her long enough to dig the ring out of his pocket, find her finger, and slide it on.

"That's it?" she said before breaking out into a laugh that was music to his ears.

He set her back from him a bit and sighed, drinking in the sight of her. "I thought I'd lost you."

"I thought the same."

"I love you, Katherine Grant. I will until my dying day. Will you marry me?"

"Yes, absolutely yes."

Mac wrapped her in his arms.

She wriggled into what appeared to be a comfortable position, resting her cheek on his chest. "This is against your rules, buddy."

"You're wounded; necessary exception."

"Did you do this cabin for me?"

"You're all I thought of the entire time. I needed a place to stay until I found you, but I didn't want to waste the opportunity to turn it into something you'd love. I worked like a madman, figuring I could get it done in three weeks if I really pushed it. Jake is sick of the sight of me. I commandeered him. Told him to keep it quiet, too. I didn't want anyone interrupting me. Today was the first day I've been out. I've done nothing but eat, sleep, and work on this cabin. It almost killed me, but I can charge a small fortune for it now so . . . there's that."

"Oh man, I just realized, you quit your job for me. Now what?"

"No, don't blame yourself for that. I quit because it was a huge mistake. I hated it. I took that job to escape you and got the punishment I deserved. Didn't have a complete night of sleep the whole three months I was gone."

"But can you get your old job back? What will this mean for

your career?"

"I'll make some calls, but it doesn't matter, Kate. I'll find something. What matters is that we're together." She leaned up and kissed the underside of his jaw. His voice was low when he asked, "So, how about that July wedding?"

"That gives me about two weeks to put together a wedding. That's insane."

"Shoulda kept that dress."

She twisted so she could frown at him. "That's what did it, what took you away from me, isn't it?"

"No, it was my lack of faith. Seeing that dress, knowing you never planned to wear it, that you were likely never going to take a shot to be with me, that killed me. But I had already made the decision before I walked in that night. I should have put my trust in God's timing and stopped trying to control everything. I actually thought I was doing the right thing."

"I felt the same way, the lack of faith thing, I mean. But my own heart was in my way. It's hard for me to trust. For years I let what happened to me poison my soul, and it made me bitter. If you hadn't stuck it out . . ." She shook her head. "I could be nice and loving with people I thought were safe like Heather or my mom and eventually Pete, but I was a fraud to anyone else. I showed them this pretty version of me and hid what I had become so deep, even I didn't see it. If they dared to try to get past my façade, I'd bring out my thorns so they wouldn't touch me." She laid her hand against his cheek. "You fought those thorns and it's like . . . you freed me."

"Kate." He was moved by what she said, but it had been more God than him.

"You deserve a medal."

"No, I don't. I deserve y—"

She laid her fingertips over his lips. "I had this epiphany when you left. I finally understood what I had been doing, why I treated you the way I did. I was so afraid it was too late for us."

"It wasn't."

"I finally learned to trust God and believe the rest would fall into place."

"And it did. Beautifully."

"By the way, how did you know I was running that trail today?"

"I didn't."

"That was a God thing."

"Yes it was." He looked down at her in wonder. "I can't believe you're really here."

"Right here, not going anywhere. Especially since I can't walk."

He rolled his eyes and then he kissed her.

EPILOGUE

MAC WALKED THE SHORELINE, WAITING FOR the last of the guests to make their way home. Katherine was taking forever in saying goodbye to her sisters, and he wanted to give her time, but he also wanted the house empty so he could finally be with his bride. Alone.

He looked up to the house and fist-pumped in the air as his wife crossed the deck and started down the stairs. She was still in her wedding dress, one that had surprised him. It wasn't anything elaborate, but a simple ivory dress with lace all over it that kind of shimmered. She'd looked like a queen. At the ceremony he'd openly gaped at her when she walked slowly towards him, holding hands with her mom and smiling like something was funny. Then Pete poked one of his canes into Mac's foot so he'd pick his chin up off the sand.

Mac smiled as she slowly approached him again. They'd had the ceremony at sunset, but now it was fully night. The few lights reflected off her dress, making her look like some sort of fairy in the dark. As she approached, he pulled her into his arms. "Finally," he muttered into her hair.

She laughed. "You are not the soul of patience, Kyle MacAlister."

"Yes, I am. I waited a whole month for you to put together a wedding."

"And you were such a big help."

"If it'd been up to me we would have had you, me, and a minister, but as you can see, I'm flexible."

She leaned up on her tip toes and brushed his lips with hers. "You are not, but I love you anyway." Her expression grew serious. "I'll love you for the rest of my life, Kyle. Even if you are a stubborn, stubborn man."

He pulled her closer and kissed her quiet, unable to respond. Tonight their life together started, and he prayed for them both, for God to bless their marriage.

An explosion sounded offshore, and he pivoted on the spot, half-throwing her behind him. Katherine laughed as the lights bloomed in the sky. "Fireworks. The house across the way gets a little rowdy in the summer. I bet it's them. Were you expecting incoming missiles?"

"Sweetheart, with you I have to be prepared for anything." Then he pulled her close again, and they stood in each other's arms as the fireworks from across the bay lit the night.

A Sneak Peek at Book Two

The Redemption Road

CHAPTER ONE

ERIN SULLIVAN HUNG UP THE PHONE and resisted the temptation to kick something. Instead she closed her eyes and took a deep breath. She could smell the mint tea the guidance counselor stocked in the staff pantry, the leather of the lounge chairs, and the coffee pot left half-full on the beverage bar. The down-side of being the athletics' director was that her office in the gym was far from soundproof, definitely not private enough to make a call to a parent about their two sons who were about to be thrown off the basketball team for failing to attend practice yet again.

To make that call she'd picked the teacher's lounge, right in the administrative office, since it had a door that closed, and would be empty as a tomb at four in the afternoon. Slowly exhaling, she realized her calming breath hadn't done its job. She said a quick prayer, hoping the knot of angst she felt in her stomach would disappear once her heart was emptied out and her head was clear.

She heard a soft knock and then the door creaked open.

"How'd it go?"

She didn't have to open her eyes to know who it was. Katherine MacAlister was both her boss and her friend, and Erin had briefed her on her struggles with the Murphy boys. Katherine knew how difficult calling a parent could be and that a call to Claire Murphy would be that and more. The Murphys were a legacy family, three generations had been students here. They were also donors. That was a boon for the school, but Claire tended to see it as a reason to receive special treatment. Erin didn't believe in giving anyone special treatment, and now two weeks into the basketball season Claire's twin boys were in trouble.

"Awesome." Erin turned to Katherine with a wink. "Claire apologized for telling her boys that practice didn't matter and that it was okay if she didn't take them. She's resolved to make sure they're at every one from now on, and she's taking me to lunch tomorrow to celebrate what a fantastic job I'm doing."

"And without the sarcasm?" Katherine raised an eyebrow.

"About how you'd imagine." She ticked off Claire's excuses on her fingers. "It's not her fault for the boys missing practice because she refused to drive them. Practices don't matter anyway. We always schedule them at an inconvenient time for her. She ended with a zinger though." Erin tried to imitate Claire's smooth diction. "I assume that a woman like you would understand." Erin mimed slamming a phone receiver down. "Dial tone."

"A woman like you?"

"A single mom. She said something about how her husband works so much she might as well be single, but then she laughed."

"Could be it's a car issue?" Katherine shrugged. "I'm trying to assume the best of Claire, but maybe it's too late in the day for soul calisthenics."

"Soul calisthenics?" Erin had to laugh. Katherine had a gift with odd turns of phrase. "I love that." She sighed. "But I think I need soul boot camp after today."

"The Murphy boys are a challenge."

"To be honest, I don't really mind them. They're like most boys; they've got more energy than activities to occupy it. They're not bad kids, but they need more structure. That reminds me, I've been meaning to ask you if we can add a morning PE elective. It would be before first bell, but after breakfast for the boarding students."

"What do you have in mind?"

"Something active, but peaceful. Nothing to get their heart-rates up, something to get their muscles stretched and their brains focused. We could start with the kids who seem to need it, and then open it up for others if it's a success."

"That's a great idea. I'll take a look at the schedule." Katherine began to leave then added "Do me a favor though—send me an official proposal, because this is something that I'll need okayed from the board. It's your bright idea, so I figure you can do the paperwork."

"Thanks, boss." Erin called as Katherine walked away with a wave over her shoulder.

Erin said goodnight to the admin staff as she headed back to the gym. The dance team was finishing up as she walked in. Tchaikovsky was playing on a set of small speakers propped up on the bleachers. The girls were all in a line, going one by one to do a series of steps that ended in a grande jeté. They spotted her and instantly begged her to join them. Although it had been years since she'd studied ballet seriously, her body hadn't forgotten much. Erin toed off her sneakers and joined the back of the line behind the smallest girl who gave her a thumbs up. The girl was tiny, but clearly talented as she executed her steps well and had perfectly flat legs on her grande jeté.

Erin's jeté wasn't as grande as she would have liked, but it was fun all the same. "How'd I do?" The girls all cheered as if she'd soared eight feet high with perfect legs. The teacher gave her a wink as she rounded up her students and the headed for the locker room.

Erin waited until they left and took a look around the gym to be sure it was empty. Seeing she was alone, she raised her arms and began to dance. She started slow and then moved into a series of chaînés. Her hair fanned out around her, and she could feel the wide smile form on her face as joy, there was no other word for it, filled her heart.

She didn't get the chance to dance very often. Her little house, while being perfectly lovely, didn't have a room large enough. Sometimes before or after school she'd try to get in a session, but she was almost always interrupted. A night like this, with no one scheduled for at least another hour, meant she could dance off the stress of that phone call in peace.

In her mind she still heard the music playing as she twirled and circled her way across the floor. When she missed a step and had to catch herself before landing on her backside, she actually laughed out loud, her mood so different from when she started. She tried the grande jeté again and nailed it. Clapping sounded from the doorway to the corridor, and she spun around to find Pastor Dan Connors leaning against the door frame like he'd been watching, a slight smile on his lips. Erin's breath caught, and a thousand butterflies took off in her stomach.

"I'm sorry I startled you. I was hoping to find you in your office."

Her stupid heart kicked up its rhythm, and if she wasn't wrong, the heat on her cheeks meant she was blushing. Dan was in his usual suit, but he'd taken off the jacket and loosened his tie. His hair was a bit rumpled too. For some crazy reason it only made him more attractive in her eyes. He looked more approachable, not that she ever would.

"I'm afraid I'm not going to be at the meeting tonight. I meant to email you days ago, and it slipped my mind. It's been a hectic week. I figured I could tell you in person." He looked tired, like life had taken too much out of him today. If not for her screaming crush on him, she might be able to ask him what was wrong and see if talking about it would help. Not that she'd ever talked with the man. He'd been the pastor of her church for almost four years, and she hung on his every syllable, but never said more than 'Hello' and 'Goodbye' to him.

"So . . . if that's okay with you."

Erin's tongue was still frozen in place. It was always like this when she ran into Dan unexpectedly. Or, truthfully, whenever she was near Dan at all. She had a full-body reaction to the man. Her brain froze, her tongue tied, her heart fluttered, and her stomach became a butterfly air show. No one else did this to her. She'd been around more attractive men and hadn't suffered from paralysis. It was something about Dan.

Finally, she pulled her synapses together. "Sure."

"Okay." He stood in the doorway for what seemed like an unusually long time before he waved and then left.

Erin grabbed the stuff she had dropped earlier and all but ran back to her office. Of all the people she could be hung up on, she had to pick Dr. Dan Connors. It wasn't that he was taken, he was definitely single, but he was so far out of her league she'd never stand a chance. If only her heart would realize that before it was too late.

Dan headed for the parking lot, his mind in a whirl. He needed a minute, maybe ten, to shake off what he was feeling. The image of Erin Sullivan twirling across the floor, her hair in a fan of gold around her, a smile like he had never seen on her face, was burned into his brain. As soon as she'd spotted him she turned into her usual deer in the headlights. Her shyness meant he'd never gotten to know her despite her membership in the church and his volunteer coaching at the school. It was almost as if she was intentional in her avoidance, but that made no sense. He'd never got the impression she disliked him.

"Any chance of a lift?"

Dan looked up to find Pete Coleman slowly making his way out of the school toward him.

"Of course." Dan shook his head to clear it as Pete opened the passenger door.

"You sure it's no trouble? You seemed deep in thought." Pete gave him a quizzical look.

Dan knew many things about Pete and paramount among them was his sage-like ability to look into your soul. Dan didn't want anyone looking into his soul today. It was a swirling mess.

"I've got an hour before my next meeting, plenty of time to drive up to your place." He opened his door and climbed in. Starting up, he pulled out of the parking lot and headed out of town and up the mountain where Pete lived. "How are you doing?"

"Oh, can't complain or well, I guess I could." Pete settled his cane next to his leg. "Therapy is harder than I thought it would be, not being able to drive is a pain, having my daughters fuss over me is getting old, but . . ." He took a deep breath and let it out. "But that right there—breathing in and out, walking on my own? Beats the alternative." Pete chuckled.

Dan was glad to hear it since the struggle back from brain injuries like the one Pete had didn't always go well. Dan would know. He'd seen that struggle fail and lived with the outcome.

Pete spoke, and it was like he'd been reading Dan's mind. "I saw you at Brookings Rehab the other day. Figured you were vising your mom. How's she doing?"

The lead weight that always seemed to be in his gut got heavier. He knew the question was a kind one, but he'd rather no one ever ask it again. Every visit with his mom produced the same mix of guilt, anger, and sadness, and there was no way he'd burden anyone with that. Today was no different. Calling it a visit was a stretch. His mom lay in her bed or sat in her wheelchair and stared into space. If it was a good day she might say a few random sentences or make eye contact once or twice.

"She's about the same."

"And how are you?"

How was he? Useless. That was the honest answer to Pete's question. Only a miracle would change his mother's condition, and despite the thousands of prayers sent up, God had said no.

"I'm about the same too, I guess."

"Not overdoing it?" Pete was squinting at him again.

"Nope. I've always said that one of the advantages of staying single is that I can devote my whole self to God. I like being busy."

"Hmm. Saw you signed up to coach basketball again. Were you up at the school to meet with Erin?"

Dan's stomach did a strange flip. "Uh, sort of." The image of Erin dancing popped into his head again only to be replaced by her expression of surprise and fear when she'd spotted him standing there. "I'm surprised she chose teaching as her vocation. It must be a challenge with her shyness."

Pete looked at him like he had two heads and both were spinning. "Shy?"

"Yeah, she's super shy. She doesn't say a word to me unless she has to. When I'm coaching she's officially the boss, but she's said more to me in an email than she ever has in real life."

Pete gave him an odd look, shook his head, and muttered "Sometimes it's the bright ones . . ." But he didn't bother to explain. "Your best bet is to talk to Erin. See if you can make her more comfortable around you. Put a little effort in."

"Uh. Okay." Although that seemed counterintuitive, he'd give it a go. Maybe she'd get over it and they could be friends.

As the minutes ate up the miles out to Pete's house Dan thought about Erin Sullivan. It made sense that she was a dancer since she always moved with a fluid kind of grace. It was beautiful the way her hair moved with her. He imagined it was soft and silky. Immediately, he shook the thought off. Nothing good could come of contemplating the beauty of someone so unsuitable for the kind of life he wanted.

He wasn't sure how much longer he'd stay in Sweet River. He'd come home to help his mom, and she was far beyond his help now. His heart yearned to return to India. Sometimes he'd dream he was back at the mission, in the heat and the spicy air, and then he'd wake up and feel the spike of disappointment again. A woman like Erin would wilt and suffer in a place like West Bengal. In the years he'd been home, he hadn't met anyone he thought was prepared for the harsh realities of the climate, the living conditions, or the work. He wasn't going to make a wife miserable for his own comfort.

He'd been alone so long it felt natural, or at least it did until he'd seen her smile, her sparkling blue eyes, and felt that hit of longing. Something he hadn't felt in a long time, if ever. Pete had to be nuts suggesting he talk to her. It was best he left her as alone as she wanted to be. What would be the point if he ended up going on a mission anyway?

But later that night, long after he'd dropped off Pete and sat through his meetings, after he'd heated his dinner and ate it watching a Celtics game, he couldn't get her out of his head.

ABOUT THE AUTHOR

The working title of this book was *Bittersweet* because during an early scene that was cut, I had Katherine making a wreath out of the vine, and leaving it as a peace offering for Mac at his house. I thought it was a great metaphor for the story itself since Katherine arrives in Sweet River with a bitter heart.

If you're not familiar with bittersweet, it's a vine that grows wild here in New England (and other places I imagine) along the sides of the road, meadows, and woods. It's not an especially pretty or useful plant early in the season, but in the autumn it's something else. The unremarkable blooms of summer end up these strange little fruits, a red berry inside a yellow-orange coat. Late fall the coat around the berry opens, almost like flower petals. The effect is lovely, and in my neighborhood, you can see folks pulled over at the side of the road, risking a late season case of poison ivy by wading into the bracken to harvest the vines.

Like that vine, true beauty can come out of bitterness if we're willing to let God work in our hearts. Holding onto the pain inflicted on us will keep the hurt 'evergreen' so to speak. When we fail to forgive those that wrong us, we invite bitterness in and it sets up shop, poisoning our happiness, stealing our trust in others, and building a wall between us and God.

Brokenness, the good kind, is what begins to break down the bitterness, but what kills it off is forgiveness. Being broken in the right way allows us to embrace our own need for forgiveness and extend it to those who have sinned against us. Whether it's the deep wounds Katherine experienced or the mild, everyday sort of scratches of life, forgiveness heals.

The title became *The Broken Trail* in part due to a conversation Pete Coleman has with Katherine where he warns her that love isn't a smooth path, it's a rough trail. Pete was the favorite character of many of my early readers, and they were dismayed when he died in the early version of the book. After my publisher pleaded for him to live, I rewrote those scenes. It was a sweet moment writing him into the epilogue, since I love Pete too. His character is based on a combination of my dad's southern story-telling and generosity of spirit, and the strength and steadfast kindness of the Maine natives I've known. It usually takes a while for a New Englander to warm up to you, but once they do, you have a friend for life.

I hope you enjoyed the book, and if you've never been to the woods of Maine, take time off and make your way up. Equally beautiful are its rocky coasts 'Downeast' and its sandy shores in the south. I'll be on those shores this summer with my family. There's nothing like a Maine beach vacation. It's days at the ocean, firefly nights in the woods, and books, board games, and cookouts at the cabin. Nothing beats it. Thanks for reading!

Connect with Christa:
Website: www.christamacdonald.com
Facebook: www.facebook.com/groups/1538432676468229
Twitter: @cricketmacd

BOOK CLUB DISCUSSION QUESTIONS

1. When she first arrives in Sweet River, Katherine struggles with her bitterness as it infects her relationship with Mac. Have you had a bitter season? What helped you overcome it?

2. In order to heal and open her heart to Mac, Katherine first had to forgive a man who will never ask for her forgiveness or admit he hurt her. Is there someone in your life who needs, but doesn't deserve, your forgiveness? In what way do you think you might be able to achieve that?

3. Both Katherine and Mac struggle with placing their faith in God rather than their own strength. Are there times in your life you realize you're relying on yourself rather than God's Providence?

4. Gossip can be as innocuous as the Sweet River Lowdown or as poisonous as the rumors Katherine faced after the death of her daughter. Have you experienced gossip like that in your life? What do you do to avoid it?

5. Pete was a calming, steadying influence in Katherine's life, while occasionally being an irritant in Mac's. Have you had someone who spoke truth into your life? Did it affect you like it did Katherine or more like Mac? Why?

CPSIA information can be obtained
at www.ICGtesting.com
Printed in the USA
LVOW01s1541271016
510551LV00010B/817/P